THE PERILS OF
SKIRTING CONVENTION

"I've only put my skirts up because
I was compelled to climb into that tree, you know,"
young Lynden, flushed with embarrassment,
explained in an anxious voice as she tugged uselessly
at the knotted cloth. It occured to her that
this handsome aristocrat was seeing more of her
slim legs than any male since Dr. Brother had
slapped her into the world seventeen years ago.
"The situation is plain to the humblest intelligence,"
Lord Melbrook assured her with
his tantalizingly impassive smile.
He returned his attention to the stubborn knot
in her sash for which she had beseeched his aid.
"Don't worry, I'll have this off in a minute."
It was this unfortunate speech that assailed the maid's
startled ears as she opened the chamber door.
In one shocked second she dropped her ewer with
a large crash, gave a scream that would curdle milk,
and altered Lynden's reputation forever.

Also by LAURA LONDON

THE WINDFLOWER
A HEART TOO PROUD
BAD BARON'S DAUGHTER
THE GYPSY HEIRESS
LOVE'S A STAGE

MOONLIGHT MIST

Laura London

A DELL BOOK

Published by
Dell Publishing Co., Inc.
1 Dag Hammarskjold Plaza
New York, New York 10017

Dell® TM 681510, Dell Publishing Co., Inc.

ISBN: 0-440-15464-4

Printed in the United States of America
One Previous Edition
New Edition
First printing—October 1985

To George and Kathleen Blakslee
With Love and Thanks

CHAPTER ONE

The high-chimneyed, brickwork manor house had been built much earlier in the reign of poor mad King George III, but never before in its prosperous, if not particularly distinguished career had it been honored with so notable a guest as now stood before its threshold. The house looked smug today, as smug as a house could in late February after a winter's battering. It condescended more than usual to the small neighboring cottages; its pseudo-Gothic swirls and furbelows glared with pomposity, accented by a spiky frieze of blue crystal icicles that lined the eaves like over-abundant jewelry on the bosom of a pretentious matron.

It is a common reflection that a dog will absorb its owner's personality. The same might be said for a house. And all the self-satisfied respectability of this house was reflected in the demeanor of its master, Mr. Monroe Downpatrick, who stood by his handsome wife, Eleanor, at the top of the front steps, beaming in obsequious welcome as a tall impeccably dressed gentleman descended gracefully from an elegant bay stallion. The stallion's satiny coat shimmered as the animal turned and pranced away, led by a waiting groom. An attractive blaze on its forehead shone like white marble in the late sun.

The expression of the tall gentleman himself was bland, even distant, as he turned to face his hosts, but as he responded politely to their greetings it was impossible to tell whether he found the effusive warmth of his reception distasteful or whether it was merely his habit to appear noncommittal.

It was the opinion of at least one of the three young women watching the scene from behind a well-trimmed yew hedge that the tall gentleman's sentiments fell into the former category.

"Depend upon it," this young lady remarked in a censorious tone, "he despises them! Ugh! Did you ever see Uncle Monroe toady so? Only consider how Aunt Eleanor will lord it over her acquaintances about Lord Melbrooke there having been a guest, when in fact he is only spending one night here to break his journey to his home in the Lake District." These words were accompanied by a sweeping movement of the hand to indicate the tall visitor being subjected to her uncle's handshake. "And I daresay he wouldn't have stopped here at all, despite Aunt Eleanor's flagrantly fawning letters, if Downpatrick Hall had been as much as one mile out of the way! As for Lord Melbrooke himself— why, he's not at all what I was led to expect! I must say, Lorraine, I was never before so taken in!" The speaker, Miss Lynden Downpatrick, had been kneeling on the frozen grass, peeking beneath a low-hanging evergreen branch, but as she spoke, she rose to her feet, brushing bits of twig from the front of her French blue velvet winter cloak.

Miss Lynden was a diminutive lady of seventeen summers with heavily lashed brown eyes that had the oddly enticing ability to change shape with her passing moods, becoming wide and almost round with wonder one minute and then narrowing with amusement into slanting, sparkling gems. Her hair was inky black and curled in wild, lustrous exuberance beneath the rabbit lining of her cloak's hood, as though the hair had absorbed the liveliness that was so much a part of the lady's character. Add to this a pair of shallow mischievous dimples and it was easy to see why Miss Lynden's fond Papa, unhappily now deceased, had called her his "elf." Papa's elder brother and Miss Lynden's current guardian, Monroe Downpatrick, had continued his brother's habit of describing Lynden in supernatural terms though, unfortunately, in his less fond eyes she was "the imp" and sometimes, when he was more than usually enraged with her, "that little witch."

"Well, Lynnie," said the young lady who had been addressed as Lorraine, "Lord Melbrooke has received as many blessings as one human being can. He's wealthy, titled, connected by birth with the first families in England, and he's . . ."

"He's handsome as sin!" chirruped the third member of the trio, a heavyset, round-faced girl whose mobcap and the white apron showing beneath her woolen overcoat proclaimed her status as a chambermaid.

This remark drew a smile from Lorraine. "Yes, Peg, and handsome, too," she said. Lorraine was near to Lynden in coloring. It was easy to place them as sisters; they were, in fact, twins, having arrived into the world within minutes of each other, Lorraine in the lead. It was the last time in Lorraine's life that she would lead, however, for Lynden was clearly the captain of the pair, the chief instigator of mischief, the more willful.

Lorraine was five inches taller than her twin, with a straight, willowy figure and black hair that lay in wide, well-ordered waves; her eyes were the same warm brown tones of her sister's, but their message was more consistent and sweetly serene, though without insipidity. She continued: "But what I had planned to say was that Lord Melbrooke is one of the nation's most renowned young poets. Imagine, the gentleman that His Highness himself labeled the Bard of the Lakeland, knocking on our front door!"

Lynden sniffed and rubbed the cold tip of her nose with one mittened hand. "As for knocking on our front door, why, he never got the chance, what with Aunt Eleanor and Uncle Monroe practically falling over each other to meet him! Besides, it is his being a poet that makes his . . . well, his gentlemanly appearance so disappointing. They call them the romantic poets, don't they? Lord Melbrooke doesn't look in the least romantic! Where's his brooding expression? The disordered shock of tumbling curls? Why isn't he wearing a cape that he whips from side to side as he walks and carrying a silver-tipped cane? Romantic poets, indeed! If you want my opinion, I think the public is being gulled by a lot of cagey publishing firms! And no one, Peg," she ended, emphatically, "who ties his cravat with such painstaking neatness could have such a wicked reputation with women as you've led us to believe."

Peg had known the twins since childhood; the three girls were much the same age and had shared many childish adventures, but her loyalty to the twins did not prevent Peg from bridling slightly at this aspersion of her credibility.

"A lot you know about wicked reputations," said Peg, with spirit. "I've heard tales of Lord Melbrooke from Mademoiselle Ambrose, Lady Eleanor's lady's maid herself, who's been with Lady Eleanor these seven years and more, long before she came to marry your Uncle Monroe two years ago. And Mademoiselle Ambrose has lived in London for years, which is more than you've ever done!"

"Much I care," retorted Lynden, bending over to pick an apple-green kite from the ground where she had laid it some few minutes earlier. "From what I hear of London, it's a smelly place full of disagreeable, snobbish people. And as for Mademoiselle Ambrose's tales, if the one you're talking about is how Aunt Eleanor tried to set up a flirtation with Lord Melbrooke before she married Uncle Monroe, why, I've heard that already, and let me tell you, it does nothing to romanticize Lord Melbrooke's reputation. Quite the opposite! Because the way I recall the story, Lord Melbrooke barely even noticed her existence and Aunt was

12

mad as fire. That's hardly the meat of which scandal stew is made!"

"There are other stories," said Peg darkly, trying to look mysterious and world-weary. "Stories repeated around the wide kitchen fireplace in the servant's hall late in the night, when the young ladies of the house are tucked snug in their feather beds."

"Of all the bouncers!" exclaimed Lynden. "As though you ever stay up late at night when you know very well that you get up at the crack of dawn every morning so you can flirt with Farmer Judd's son when he brings the milk! And the only people who have feather beds in this house are Mama and Aunt Eleanor. Besides, I'd like to know how anyone could tell a tale around the fire with Cook there, because she never lets anyone steal in a word edgewise."

"Cook wasn't there at the time," said Peg, undeterred. "And Mademoiselle Ambrose gave us lots of tales about Lord Melbrooke and his seducing ways."

"Well, I, for one, don't believe he's ever seduced anyone," said Lynden, pulling a soft pastel scarf from the capacious pocket of her cloak. "If the way Aunt and Uncle slaver over My Lord is any indication of the way other people behave toward him, I don't imagine he would ever learn to be seductive because it must be easy enough to get all the women he wants as it is." She pulled another silk scarf from her pocket and began to knot it to the first.

Lorraine had been watching Lynden's actions with a puzzled frown, then suddenly she gasped and said, "Lynnie, aren't those Aunt Eleanor's zephyr scarves? What in the world are you doing with them?"

"Knotting them together to make a kite tail." Lynden gave one scarf a yank, to see if it would hold, before drawing a third scarf from her pocket and connecting it to its hapless fellows. "I had the idea when I saw Aunt Eleanor riding yesterday with her pink scarf caught up by the wind behind her. It looked elegant and put me right in the mood to fly kites today!"

"Kite tails, indeed!" cried Peg. "Lady Eleanor will have *your* tail if she finds out you've made off wi' her scarves. She's straightway forbid you to touch her clothes again. And don't say she won't find out neither, because that's what you said when you took her cashmere shawl to make bedding when the barn cat had kits. Well, she found out, didn't she? And pret' near screamed the roof down, too! Not to mention that she boxed your ears red, and locked you in the school room for a day wi' only bread 'n water to sustain ya."

"Lynnie, Peg's right," said Lorraine, worry filling her soft brown eyes. "There'll be the most awful row if it's discovered and you know how Aunt Eleanor can be."

Lynden had finished knotting a fourth scarf to the train and held her finished product aloft to test it in the breeze. "There!" she said. "It looks grand! Don't worry, you two. The shawl was a much different matter because it absorbed the dirt so and no matter how we tried we couldn't get the stains out. The scarves will fly high in the air; how could they get dirty? And I'll have them off this evening and back into Aunt Eleanor's drawers before she's any the wiser."

From around the corner of the brick house came the dull clank of a heavy brass bell.

Peg groaned. "That'll be the housekeeper signaling me in to help ready the guest rooms." Looking over her shoulder at Lynden, she cast a final pleading glance, entreating her to see sense, and then fetched up the folds of her skirt in one hand and hurried around the corner of the building toward the kitchens.

Lynden secured the end of the scarf tail to the kite and grinned at her sister. "So. You've lost your ally, Rainey. Will you come kite flying with me like a sport or will you keep on scolding?" She felt in her pocket for a moment before bringing her hand out empty and saying, in an exasperated tone, "Botheration! I've forgotten the string."

Lorraine sighed, drew a bobbin of thin cord from her pocket, and handed it to her sister, whose face brightened with delight.

"You remembered it, Rainey! Don't I always say you're the best of sisters? Come on, you know it won't do the least good to argue with me and it will waste time when we could be aloft in the meadow. Race you!" she said, and went running down the lane without waiting for an answer.

Downpatrick Hall sat on the edge of a small Yorkshire village, cradled at the foot of a steeply wooded limestone hill. A row of picturesque cottages clustered near the Hall and a short tree-lined lane led to a red sandstone church. Lorraine chased her twin down the lane, following the brightly colored scarves of the kite tail as they whipped in the frigid wind. Her ears and nose grew numb from the stiff February breeze, and she tried to shout, calling on Lynden to slow down, but her words were blown back at her and left behind. She could only run harder, her mittened hands reaching up beneath her hood to cover her ears lest they freeze solid and crack off in the cold.

Lorraine saw her sister's hood blow back from her head, leaving her tangled brown curls dancing and streaming in the wind as she passed the tidy, half-timbered cottage of Mr. Helm, the apothecary-dentist-barber. The varnished oak door opened and Mrs. Helm, grimacing from the chill wind, waved a cloth and hailed Lynden.

"Ho there, Miss Ruckus! Where are you going like the Fiend From Someplace Else is after you? And no covering on your head! Come in the parlor this minute and get yourself warmed up."

Lynden halted midpace with a curtsy and a dance step, and then went over to Mrs. Helm, a plump lady in an old-fashioned lace cap. Lynden laughingly held up the apple-green kite for her inspection.

"Thank you, ma'am, but we're off to sail our kite," announced Lynden, as Lorraine ran up behind her, out of breath. "Would you like to come?" asked Lynden with a mischievous sparkle.

"Ho! Kiting at my age? And in February, too! I'm not such a dandy young hoyden as you, Miss, nor never was, neither! And look at your poor sister! You run that gal ragged! If you're in a rush, let me give you a bit of warm plum cake I've just had out from the oven. You can eat it on the run." She disappeared into the cottage and returned, bearing two warm pieces of cake which sent out streamlets of steam that rushed away in the breeze. She shook her head sadly as the girls ate the cakes, Lynden munching with one hand, and holding on to the kite with the other. "Look at the appetites they've got. Don't they feed you girls at the Hall?"

"They do," said Lynden between bites. "But they've hardly the time today, what with the company they've got. Lord Melbrooke is staying tonight, but of course you know that already, as well as Mrs. Gilray and that horrid friend of Aunt's, Lady Marchpane. She's been here for three days already and"—here she paused to take another bite—"and I wish she'd go. Every time she passes one of us in the hall, she quizzes us on our Latin. Ugh! It's fine for Rainey, but I got by with as little studying as possible, and when she nabs me, I'm at a loss."

"It is too bad," agreed Lorraine, brushing a crumb from her collar. "Aunt Eleanor doesn't like Lady Marchpane much, either, but she is such a gossip, and Aunt Eleanor likes, of course, to have someone spread the news back in London that Lord Melbrooke is staying."

Mrs. Helm clucked in disapproval. "I never did hold with your Step-aunt Eleanor making you girls fill your wee heads with that foreign tongue that nobody speaks no more. Not to mention those doings of the ancient gods which don't bear repeating in modest company! But if kite flying you be at, then kite flying ye'd better do. It's the kind of strengthy wind that bears moving about in! Just take care that kite don't carry you to France!"

The twins blew around the corner of the red sandstone church like two crisp brown leaves. A gust set the old church bell in motion to send random peals ringing over the hills. Lorraine stopped to rest, leaning on the ancient Saxon cross, then followed her sister to the meadow behind the church. There was abundant space for kite-flying in the meadow and adjacent fallow field, but the gusty wind did the work for them. Lynden, to Lorraine's excited exclamations, was hard put to let the string out rapidly enough; and after a heart-stopping violent dive toward the hard-frozen, stubbly ground, the kite receded into the cold gray sky, its green paper flapping as if in protest and the bright pink tail dancing beneath, trying to escape.

"Let out all the string, Lynden, I want to see it go!" shouted Lorraine.

"I'm doing it as fast as I can," answered Lynden, laughing. "It wants to fly away!" The kite string whipped from the dowel in her hand with a pleasant hum. "It's singing to us, Rainey," she giggled. The kite grew small in the gray vault above their heads, where it danced and swirled like a green and pink pinwheel. "It's pulling so hard," said Lynden. "Isn't it beautiful, like a comet?" Suddenly there was a strong blast of air; the kite string went rigid in her hand, then lax, and far above them the kite began a slow, forlorn descent, blowing away from them as it dropped, flapping loudly. The girls watched in openmouthed disappointment.

"What bad luck!" cried Lynden. "Our comet's a falling star."

"Lynnie, we'll have to chase it. Remember Aunt Eleanor's scarves in the tail!" said Lorraine, a hand covering her brow as she bent back to watch the kite's erratic path. "Look, the wind's shifted and the kite's blowing toward the Hall!"

They ran after it, watching with dismay. As they ran, the kite floated and dipped lower to the ground. Their dismay turned to jubilation as the kite string caught on the spire of the church bell tower, causing the kite to lag in the breeze and come gently to rest, hanging upside down and undamaged against the red sandstone blocks.

The girls ran, puffing from the exercise, and had almost reached the church when another gust came and the kite took flight again, heading high above them down the tree-lined lane and toward the Hall.

"Lynden, I believe it will catch in the tree behind the house! Look, there it goes!" Lorraine pointed as the kite, after a swooping dive, came to rest in the crown of the lofty Scots pine which towered from the rear over Downpatrick Hall. The kite hung limp in the crown, a small apple-green splash of color against the blue-gray boughs.

"I think I can get to it from the attic," exclaimed Lynden.

The girls entered the house through the side door, mounted the servant's stairway, and clambered up three flights of wooden steps. The attic was nearly as cold as outside and smelled of old magazines and camphor. The sisters' footsteps reverberated as they crossed the floor, moving between shipping trunks, a mahogany writing chair piled with age-yellowed landscape paintings, and a tailor's dummy. A dim, sea-blue light slipped in through the octagonal stained-glass window at the rear wall. Lynden slid back a small bolt and pushed open the window.

"I see it," she said excitedly, "not four feet away. It's a peach; I'll only have to step out on that limb and grab it!" She tugged off her mittens, tossing them on the hardwood attic floor; and then pulled at the frogs binding her cloak, and it joined the mittens. When she sat down on the cloak and began pulling off her boots, Lorraine ventured a protest.

"You'll be cold, Lyn," Lorraine said. "And the bark will scratch your feet."

"I'll only be out there for a minute," replied Lynden, pulling off the other boot. "I can't climb a tree with boots on. You've got to feel the way the branches take your weight." She whipped off her bedraggled sash, held up her skirts to knee-length, and commanded Lorraine to tie the sash around her waist to secure them.

"Give it an extra knot, Lorraine. I don't want my skirt to fall and trip me up." Lynden, ready for the expedition, leaned out the window with one hand on the side sill and stretched out her other hand to lean on the trunk of the Scots pine. It felt cold and scaly against her palm. The crisp tang of pine surrounded her as she gave her full weight to the trunk, carefully bringing her feet to rest on the branch beneath her. The pine needles encompassed her like a stinging gray-green cloud, pricking her cold-numbed skin through her gown. The kite was resting against the deeply fissured black bark, its tail of scarves entwined around the branch above.

Letting go with one hand, Lynden leaned out to snatch it and missed. She tried again and missed again. Carefully repositioning her feet, she tested her balance, and, holding out one steadying hand, she made a quick successful snatch for the kite. Elated with victory, she pulled herself upright and felt for the branch she had been holding on to, but the sudden motion was too great for equilibrium and Lynden heard her sister's quick cry of alarm as she fell backward.

Clutching the kite, Lynden grabbed for a purchase but managed only a lacerating handful of gummy resin and stripped needles. The thick stratified branches acted as a yielding, but prickly, cushion, which handed her down, rapidly but gently, until she was brought to a stop at the junction of three thick, piny branches. The tree swayed and bobbed from the shock as she found a handhold, lying on her back and reaching out. A heavy, scaly gray cone bounced after her, hitting her sharply in the forehead and landing saucily in her lap.

"Rainey?" called Lynden in a voice that shook slightly. "I'm alive. Barely. I've got the kite, so stay where you are. I think I'll be able to get in through one of these rooms."

Lorraine's relieved reply was muffled by the soft squeak of an opening window.

Lord Melbrooke had been in his room, preparing rather unenthusiastically for dinner, when he heard an unlikely crash outside his window. He debated with himself for a moment, and then decided it warranted investigation. Clad in his dressing gown, he strolled to the window, flipped the bolt, and raised the pane. His interested gaze fell upon the shapeliest pair of legs he had seen since attaining manhood. He leaned his elbows on the sill, erasing a smile as his gaze traveled to the indignant face of the owner of the legs.

"You needn't grin at me in that odious fashion," said Lynden crossly. "I'm not always to be found like this, you know."

"Are you not?" he replied. "It seems a pity."

"Well, it may seem a pity to you, though I think that a very odd opinion, but it is not," she snapped, "to me." She wiggled to a sitting position. "You are the poet, aren't you? It's difficult to see with the light in back of you."

"Well," he said cautiously, "I am *a* poet. Have we been introduced?"

"No," Lynden replied. "And we're not likely to be because I'm probably going to die of pneumonia from being up a tree in the cold."

"Now that would *really* be a pity," said Lord Melbrooke. "Which emboldens me to ask if there might perhaps be some way I could assist you?"

"Yes! I wish you would pull me out of this tree! But the needles may rub on your clothes and perhaps resin will get on the sleeves and you may not like it, because I've heard that London poets are excessively foppish!"

"Well," he said in a chastened voice. "I will try to be, er, unfoppish for a moment and lift you in. Do you think it would inconvenience you to lean forward a little more?" He leaned out as she leaned toward him, and, placing his hands firmly on her sides, he plucked her from the tree branch and swung her effortlessly in through the window and set her on her feet.

The poet was housed in the best guest room that Downpatrick Hall could offer, appointed with Indian carpets and rosewood furniture from fine London warehouses. Inside the well-lit room, Lynden had her first opportunity for a close view of her rescuer. He was, as Peg had said, handsome as sin. His body was long and fluid. Because she was short, his tallness made him seem high above her; she had to bend back her head to meet his eyes. The soft lamplight shone full on his wheat-colored hair, setting off sharp amber sparks where it curled loosely against his wide forehead and temples. Below blond eyebrows were gray eyes—sensual, cool, and as sheer and subtle as lake mist. They were eyes that might have been intimidating if one failed to notice the softening humor shaped into his mouth. This afternoon when she had seen him from a distance, the self-confidence of Lord Melbrooke's carriage had led Lynden to place his age over thirty. Close at hand, she could see that he was still in his late twenties. His attractive face contained a well-controlled sensitivity—friendly enough, but not terribly accessible.

Lord Melbrooke met her inquisitive glance with an appraising one of his own, and his lips bent in a slow smile, setting Lynden's heart beating at something more than its usual pace.

He turned to shut the window and spoke. "I know that you might find this a little unconventional, but if you would allow me to introduce myself, I would tell you that I'm Lord Melbrooke, but I'm always pleased when my friends call me Justin."

"If you want to introduce yourself as Lord Melbrooke, that suits me all right, because I knew it was your name anyway," allowed Lynden handsomely. "But you needn't think that I'm so unversed with social usage as to call you Justin, because I know it's not the thing to call gentlemen by their first names unless they are relatives or close family friends."

"A fair recitation," said Lord Melbrooke, much impressed. The gray eyes twinkled. "Did your governess have you memorize many of these indispensable homilies?"

Lynden dimpled responsively. "She did, but I'm afraid it hasn't done much good. Uncle Monroe says I'm incorrigible! I have a sister—in fact, a twin—but I am the naughtier twin," she announced.

His lips quirked at one corner. "But how delightful. Forgive me if I seem vulgarly inquisitive, but you did say Uncle Monroe?"

"Oh, yes. I am Lynden Downpatrick. My sister, Lorraine, Mama, and I have lived here at the Hall since before Papa died and Uncle Monroe became our guardian."

"I see," he said, looking thoughtful. "Will I see you at dinner?"

"No, because we're not allowed to dine in company, not being out yet. Perhaps we'll be introduced into society this spring."

"Indeed?" he said, polite but unencouraging. "Perhaps we'll be able to meet, then, under more conventional circumstances."

"Maybe," Lynden said doubtfully. "But I'm not sure the thing will come off. You see, Mama ought to be our chaperone but her habits are sickly. Mama says she's prone to a weakness of the heart, but Uncle Monroe says she has a weakness of the brain. And Aunt Eleanor says that she wouldn't chaperone us to secure her soul a place in Heaven, because I'm too ill-behaved and my sister, Lorraine, is too pretty. You see . . ."

"Yes," interrupted Lord Melbrooke. "I can see you have a great many trials. And I wouldn't want to add to them in any way. Which is why I feel compelled to point out that your guardian might frown upon our meeting tête-à-tête."

"If you want me to go, then you should say so, instead of engaging in a lot of odiously tactful hinting," said Lynden with dignity. She turned quickly and would have marched from the room when she happened to glimpse herself in the long free-standing dressing mirror. She stopped, blushed, set her kite down in front of her, and began to fumble frantically with the tightly knotted sash that still held her skirts knee-length. The knot held firm. Lynden turned sheepishly toward Lord Melbrooke, her eyes wide with an unconscious appeal.

"Aunt will boil me in cabbage soup if she sees me like this . . . do you think that you might be able to unknot me?"

Lord Melbrooke walked to Lynden's side, took her shoulders and gently turned her to face away from him. She felt the sash press slightly against her waist as his fingers probed the knot. In one hot, uncomfortable flash, it occurred to Lynden that Lord Melbrooke had been privileged to view more of her slim legs than any male since Dr. Brother had slapped her into the world seventeen years ago. She blushed furiously and twisted her head to observe Lord Melbrooke's impassive countenance.

"I've only put my skirts up because I was compelled to climb into that tree, you know," she explained in an anxious voice.

Melbrooke gave her a brief, reassuring smile before returning his attention to the knot. "The situation is plain to the humblest intelligence. Perhaps you could manage not to wiggle quite so much? Thank you. How did you come to be, er, compelled to enter the tree? A matter concerning that very handsome kite you are carrying, I apprehend?"

"Oh, yes," said Lynden, brightening at his praise of her kite. "It broke loose from its cord and flew over the village, coming to rest in the old pine tree outside the window. I stepped onto the top branches from the attic window but lost my balance and took a tumble."

"Which accounts for the scratches on your cheeks and legs," commented Lord Melbrooke, pulling methodically at the knot.

"Yes," said Lynden cheerfully. "I suppose I should have thanked you for bringing me in the window. I'm not usually so rag-mannered but, you see, I was cross from the fall." A thought occurred to her. "When I think of it, perhaps you were embarrassed to be encountered in your dressing gown. Is it what they call a banian? Aunt Eleanor's lady's maid says banians are worn by all the fashionable gentlemen but if anyone mentions them to me I am to pretend that I don't know what they are or no one will believe I am a maiden."

Lord Melbrooke gave a swift choke of laughter which he discreetly turned into a cough. "Yes, this is a banian. And I wasn't embarrassed to have you encounter me in it because it covers me shoulder to foot and I perceive myself to be most modestly clad."

Lynden giggled. "How much of you is covered is quite beside the point because ladies in ball gowns wear far less. It is the type of garment that you're wearing that counts. Now, a banian is boudoir clothing which makes it unacceptable. But perhaps you have different standards because Peg says you are a great rake."

"A gross exaggeration, I assure you."

"Well, I think so," agreed Lynden, twisting again to face Lord Melbrooke and presenting him with a roguishly dimpled smile. "It seems to me that you could hardly be a very successful rake if you have this much trouble unknotting a lady's sash!"

The chattering and footfalls of ladies passing in the hall created a commotion that prevented either Lynden or Lord Melbrooke from hearing the light triple rap on the door.

"I'm sorry it's taking so long," said Lord Melbrooke. "When you want your skirts up, you don't take any half measures, do you? But don't worry, I'll have this off in a minute."

Peg, having knocked on the door and gotten no response, lifted the ewer of Lord Melbrooke's hot shaving water that she had set down, elbowed down the door handle, and shoved open the door with her hip. Immediately her startled ears were assailed by Lord Melbrooke's last unfortunate speech. For one horrified second Peg took in the apple-green kite lying unheeded by the bed, Lord Melbrooke in his bedroom dress, Lynden's half-bare legs. To Peg's shocked mind it looked as though Lord Melbrooke was attempting to embrace her dear mistress and Lynden, who had turned to see who had come in the door, was herself attempting to struggle out of his arms. Peg dropped the steaming ewer and gave a scream that would curdle milk. There was a loud crash and a flash flood of water spread out across the Indian carpets. Peg flew at Lord Melbrooke, shouting that no London rake was going to pull up the skirts of her Miss Lynden, be he poet or no!

Lord Melbrooke stared at Peg with interested surprise. Lynden gasped and took an involuntary step backward, tripping and falling across the bed.

Lady Eleanor Downpatrick, with her guest, Lady Marchpane, were the ladies passing in the hallway, and at Peg's frantic shouts, they rushed to the doorway to see Lynden lying across the big guest bed, her skirts traveled up to her knees, her hair disheveled, and her face brightly flushed. Lord Melbrooke was holding at arm's length an outraged Peg, who was attempting to attack him with a jagged piece of porcelain from the broken ewer. At the entrance of the ladies, Peg flung herself prostrate in the puddle, embracing Lady Eleanor's knees and sobbed, "Oh, My Lady . . . I came in the room with Lord Melbrooke's shaving water and found him trying to pull Miss Lynden's skirts up!"

Lord Melbrooke turned to Lynden, who lay paralyzed on the bed. "We might," he said slowly, "find this a little difficult to explain."

CHAPTER TWO

Lady Eleanor Downpatrick was the only child of an earl whose family tree was considerably more impressive than his list of disposable assets. The earl was a hard, self-consequential man. He placed the greatest value on aristocratic bloodlines, with wealth running a poor second. He presented his daughter to the ton in due form, announcing to the greater circle of his acquaintance that he would give his daughter in marriage only to a man who could match her in degree, promptly narrowing the field of suitors to earls or better. Eleanor was a handsome girl and several minor pretenders to her hand appeared over the years, only to be sent away disappointed by Papa. Eleanor was not two years short of thirty when it was borne in upon the earl that his daughter was well nigh in danger of becoming an ape-leader and that the servants had begun to call her an old maid. There was no high-degreed paragon in sight. Perhaps the lady's attractions were not so great as her father had thought, either because of her shrewish disposition or her tiny dowry.

When Mr. Monroe Downpatrick, a wealthy, childless widower, had appeared to claim the lady's hand, the earl brought himself to overlook Mr. Downpatrick's lack of noble birth and handed his daughter over with a sigh of relief.

What Papa, the earl, hadn't known was that his daughter had earlier made her own attempt at husband-hunting. A survey of the personable, well-born young men of the beau monde had shown Lady Eleanor one young gentleman she felt worthy to be taken as a husband. Lord Melbrooke was the lucky man she chose. She found nothing to deter her in the fact that he was already one of the most sought-after young men in the ton. Her confidence was so complete that she thought she had only to give him a genteel hint of her preference to seal the match between them. Lord Melbrooke had been impervious to genteel hints. Lady Eleanor, a good deal more than half in love with him, lowered herself to beguile him with an open flirtation. He politely avoided her. Finally, she so far forgot herself as to pursue him in a manner as immodest as it was unsuccessful. She had been kindly, but firmly, rejected. It was the greatest humiliation of her life, and when Mr. Downpatrick presented himself, she, too, had heaved a sigh of relief.

When Lady Eleanor came to the door of her best guest chamber to discover that her ill-behaved and uncomfortably pretty stepniece had been apparently more successful than she with the love-of-her-life, who had so shamed her years before, her first and by far most intense emotion was a fiercely burning jealousy, followed quickly by a white-hot desire for revenge on both parties. During the time that Peg clung weeping to her knees, Lady Eleanor engaged in a series of rapid mental calculations. "We might find this a little difficult to explain," Lord Melbrooke had said; and Lady Eleanor answered him, tittering angrily: "Not at all, dear Justin. Every allowance must be made for a betrothed couple. Peg, stand up at once! You forget yourself!"

The gossipy Lady Marchpane gave a breathy cry, her inquisitiveness soon to be gratified. Surprise banishing her tears, Peg leaped to her feet to stare at Lynden, who jumped from the bed, looking suspicious and confused. Only Lord Melbrooke remained as he was, his emotions cloaked beneath the disciplined impassivity of his features. Lynden brushed past Peg to

confront her aunt, meeting look for look Lady Eleanor's maliciously glittering eyes.

"Lord Melbrooke and I are not a betrothed couple!"
shouted Lynden. To her dismay, Lady Marchpane's
hand flew to her mouth, barely stifling a horrified gasp
of scandalized surprise. Peg burst into tears again.

"Dear little Lynden," purred Lady Eleanor. "Even
though your engagement hasn't been formally announced, surely there's no harm in letting such a close
friend as Lady Marchpane know, especially under the
circumstances. We wouldn't want her to have doubts of
your virtue, would we?"

Lynden was growing frightened and turned nervously
to Lord Melbrooke for support. "There aren't any
circumstances, are there, Lord Melbrooke? Tell Aunt
that it isn't so!"

Melbrooke glanced quickly at Lynden and then
looked at Lady Eleanor. "I'm sure, Eleanor, you'll
agree that there is no need for Miss Downpatrick to be
distressed. For now, could I prevail upon your good
nature long enough to dress?"

"How remiss of me," Eleanor replied, smiling
nastily. "Won't you join Monroe and me in the library
before dinner for a companionable chat?"

Melbrooke gave a cool, assenting bow.

Taking her stepniece's arm, Lady Eleanor led Lady
Marchpane and Peg out the door, closing it behind her.
Once in the hall, Eleanor turned to poor, tear-streaked
Peg and snapped, "Send another housemaid up to
clean the mess you've made and then retire to your
chamber. You're clearly in no state to carry on with
your duties this evening." Lady Eleanor then smiled
graciously at Lady Marchpane and excused herself,
saying she must escort her niece to her room, with a
murmured disclaimer that dear Lynden was "so highly
strung."

Lynden felt her aunt's fashionably long fingernail
dig into the soft flesh of her upper arm. Lynden's bed-

room was down a long corridor, around a corner, and up to a half landing. Lorraine was standing outside the room, and ran forward a few steps when she saw her sister and aunt coming up the stairs.

"Lynnie?" Lorraine said questioningly.

Lynden yanked her arm from Lady Eleanor's grasp. "Aunt Eleanor says that I'm engaged to Lord Melbrooke and I'm not!"

"You were not, but you are now, my little she-fox!" stated Lady Eleanor, her face set in a cold grimace. "Don't think that you can press yourself against a man without paying the piper!"

Lorraine gasped in horror.

"I wasn't pressing myself against him," said Lynden, white-faced. "I was only in his room because I had a fall from the old pine when I was climbing to get our kite."

"Ho," laughed Lady Eleanor. "Is that the marvelous explanation that's going to save your virtue? Don't forget, My Lady Marchpane observed you lying wantonly on Melbrooke's bed; we both know she's the biggest gossip in the British Isles and will spread that tidbit far and wide! You'd better think of a likelier tale than that, my girl!"

"It's not a tale, it's the truth," said Lynden hotly. "If you go back to his bedroom, you'll see the kite lying on the floor. I forgot to take it when we left. I had to get it out of the tree because I used your zephyr scarves as a tail for it and . . ."

She got no further as Lady Eleanor soundly boxed her ears. Lorraine thrust herself protectively in front of her twin and received a cuff for her pains. Eleanor threw open Lynden's bedroom door, sending it cracking against the wall.

"Horrid children! Get in there!" she shrieked, pointing to the room. She stormed in after them and grabbed Lynden by her shoulders, shaking her. "Wild, insolent little gypsy! I'll teach you to whore with the houseguests behind my back!"

Lynden swallowed. "I didn't do anything, Aunt Eleanor," she said, frightened by her aunt's rage. "Ask Lord Melbrooke, he'll tell you!"

"Don't depend on Justin to get you out of this. Seducing a young lady of quality in her guardian's own home will cause a scandal that even the Bard of the Lakeland will have trouble laughing off. And believe me, my dear, Justin's family hates scandal and he'll go to some length to avoid embarrassing them. He'll soon be convinced that it is easier for him to marry you than face the muck I could toss on him!" Eleanor sneered, pinching Lynden's ear with unpleasant strength. "Justin's family has been after him to marry and breed an heir for years, although I certainly won't pretend that they'll be pleased when he brings home an untidy little nobody like you. But he will contrive; it will be a small problem for him to stick you in one of his many houses and forget you while he goes about his rakings."

Lynden felt as though she was lost in a trackless swamp. She was beginning to realize that what had begun as a mildly exciting adventure was fast becoming the most serious scrape of her youthful career. Her aunt's spiteful reaction was anger, yes, but there was something more that Lynden, with her limited experience, could not quite comprehend. The atmosphere was charged with threatening nuances. She knew only that Lady Eleanor seemed serious in her plan to force her to marry Lord Melbrooke. Lynden was used to hearing that she brought trouble upon herself by her own rash behavior. She decided hopefully, naively, that the converse must be true. If she got into trouble by behaving impulsively, then she must be able to get out of that trouble by remaining calm. Trying to still the panic that was beginning to burn fitfully at the edges of her poise, Lynden summoned her strength, squared her shoulders, and faced her aunt.

"I haven't done anything wrong. At least, not if you discount taking your zephyr scarves. If you'll listen to me, I'll tell you everything that happened from the moment I entered Lord Melbrooke's bedroom and then you will see that there is no reason for him and me to marry." Lynden's voice was a bit unsteady, and she paused for a breath.

Lady Eleanor gave a short laugh. "I don't know if you are going to treat me with more of your convenient lies or regale me with the sordid details of your pre-marital adventure! I won't listen to either! You'll stay in here by yourself until you're summoned, Miss!" Lady Eleanor opened the door and beckoned imperiously to Lorraine. "Come along, Lorraine."

Lorraine stood still and said quietly, "I prefer to stay with Lynden."

Lady Eleanor raised her eyebrows derisively. "Then you shall." She turned and left, closing the door softly behind her, and the girls heard the lock turning.

The twins talked intensely and at length over the events just past, their voices rising and falling. It grew dark, and they had been left without a lamp, so they moved to the silver square of moonlight which fell through the window to lie in the center of the floor.

Peg came later bearing a snack of fruit purloined from the larder and a tinderbox to light the bedroom candles. She was subdued, apologetic, and quite as frightened as the twins.

"I followed Her Ladyship when she marched up to the school room with you," Peg told the twins. "I heard what you said to Lady Eleanor about you being innocent of wrong doin'. When Her Ladyship came into the hall again, I explains to her that it could be that I was mistaken in what I saw, because I'll tell you, Lynden, that I never heard you tell a lie, not in all my born days! But no sooner were th' words out of me mouth but that ol' witch starts to yell at me, saying that she knew I'd be full o' lies for you an' I'd better not repeat th' story again or I'd be outta a job!"

It was bad, the girls agreed. But Peg had worse tidings yet.

"Mademoiselle Ambrose says that Lady Eleanor is so vexed because her's fair sick with jealousy thinkin' Lord Melbrooke might prefer you to her. Loonier than a defeathered gander, is that aunt o' yours. She's out to get you, and him, Miss Lyn, and no mistake! There be some kind of argumentation goin' on right there in Mr. Downpatrick's library with your Mama in there, too, and her havin' spasms fit to beat the French. Oh, Miss Lynden, you ain't never gonna know how sorry I am for the trouble I've caused you!"

Lynden gave Peg a bracing pat on the shoulder and announced in an unconvincing voice that she was not afraid of Aunt Eleanor. It was another hour before an underfootman came to announce in a sympathetic voice that Mr. Downpatrick requested that Miss Lynden join him in the library.

Lynden had no pleasant memories of the library. It was the Bad Room, the Bogie Place of her childhood, where Uncle Monroe would lie in wait like a big brown spider in a web to lecture her on what he felt were the many defaults of her character. It was a place where every minor sin was amplified, where every childish mischief was a crime, and where she and Lorraine suffered from discipline conducted without love. Lorraine's hopeful counsel had been to "tell the truth and everything will be all right," but as Lynden neared the library, Lorraine's words became as elusive as silver-white milkweed puffs on a windy day. The library door was carved in Gothic bas-relief—a nightmare of distorted faces with bulging eyes, pointed and forked tongues, pendulous lips, and clawed feet. Uncle Monroe had purchased the door at auction in hopes that it would someday be "worth some money." Apprehensively, Lynden twisted the ball-and-claw door handle and entered the library.

Monroe Downpatrick was seated in his favorite leather armchair. His thick black eyebrows knitted under his creased bald pate, and his neat little mustache twitched. His pasty hands were crossed, resting on the barley-beer belly which even the most expensive tailor on Bond Street could not conceal.

Dressed for evening in a blue jacket, buff-colored waistcoat, and stiff white cravat, Lord Melbrooke had been seated near the fire but stood at Lynden's entrance. His demeanor was distant, his gray eyes cold and piercing like the blade of a newly hammered knife, the healthy, unlined skin drawn tightly over the high, sculptured cheekbones. His disciplined features revealed only a subtly weary distaste.

Lynden's mother, Mrs. Downpatrick, was curled in a chaise lounge in front of the fire, swathed, as was her habit, in a mound of draperies. The fringe of a lace cap peeked out beneath a wool bonnet, and a shawl covered both. Despite the warm wrapped brick that Peg had placed at her feet and the black nunlike robes she wore, Mrs. Downpatrick shivered irritably when Lynden's entrance caused a tiny draft to dart into the room.

In her forties, she was a pretty woman still, but with the melancholy self-absorption of a medieval madonna. There would be no help from that quarter—and Lynden did not even think of it. Her mother had never mothered her daughters. There was no room for parenthood in the sucking self-pity of her world. Directly after their birth, the twin's mother had thrust the girls into the care of a nurse and ejected her husband from her bedroom, vowing never again to allow herself to be subjected to the discomforts of pregnancy and the horrors of childbirth. For much of their young lives, Lynden and Lorraine had made attendance on her twice a week, on Monday and Friday mornings, for fifteen-minute periods during which they sang duets of "Before Jehovah's Awe-ful Throne," read Old Testament passages, and listened to a list of the many ways in which their births had ruined their mother's health. When the visit was over, the twins would leave, feeling like escaping prisoners.

Lady Eleanor wore a mauve silk evening gown. Mademoiselle Ambrose had braided her graying brown hair into a tight coronet circled tiaralike on the crown of her head, emphasizing her sharp classic features. She left her place behind Mr. Downpatrick and, with an air of smug triumph, led Lynden to Melbrooke.

"Lord Melbrooke has something to say to you, my dear," said Lady Eleanor.

Lord Melbrooke's demeanor was arctic. All trace of the drolly formal warmth that had charmed Lynden earlier had vanished; the gray eyes were chilly and unapproachable. He looked at her with what appeared to be dislike. Lynden's breath tightened miserably in her throat.

Simply and without preamble, Lord Melbrooke said, "May I have the honor of your hand in marriage?"

Lynden stared at him. I want to be sick, she thought. Then the sick feeling was doused by a cool rippling rage which seemed to tremble out from her to the corners of the room.

"No!" she said, her attempted shout stifled into a gasp. "I won't be intimidated into marriage with a stranger!" She stood on tiptoe and leaned her head back to look Melbrooke squarely in the eye. "You ought to have had more resolution!" she said furiously, "than to let *them* compel you into making me an offer."

Her mother spoke in a reedy but curiously potent voice. "Lynden! My nerves will not bear your uncontrolled tone! Such mannishness! I do not know what you can be thinking of in your precipitant refusal. Surely you know that you must marry the man you have sinned with."

"Sinned!" said Lynden, her eyes big with disbelief. "I don't know much about sin, but if what I was doing with Lord Melbrooke was sinning, then let me tell you that sin has been shockingly overrated by the poets!"

"Hold your tongue, Miss!" snapped Mr. Downpatrick. He had never liked either of the twins. Lynden was unpredictable and impertinent, and her sister, Lorraine, though more biddable in temperament, was bookish and more intelligent than he thought proper in a woman. They were a difficult pair and he would be glad to be rid of at least one of them. There would also be the convenience of not having to arrange a London season for Lynden. If she were married to Melbrooke, he would only have to pay for Lorraine's season. He glanced at his widowed sister-in-law. Damn her, how like her to abdicate responsibility for her daughter's behavior and leave *him* to put the chit in her place. Downpatrick transferred his gaze to Lord Melbrooke. He was not deceived by Melbrooke's noncommittal features. He knew the man was furious and probably thought them all a group of vulgar slyboots. He wondered if the chit's aberrant behavior would cause Melbrooke to cry off from the wedding. He almost wished that it would, thinking nervously that it would do no good to incur the enmity of a man of Lord Melbrooke's wealth and social importance. Downpatrick would have let the matter drop in a minute but for his eagerness to get rid of the girl and the likelihood that Eleanor would slice him to shreds if he failed to support her in the plan.

"Instead of screaming at us, Lynden," began Downpatrick, "you should be dropping to your knees and thanking Good Fortune that a man of Lord Melbrooke's station would condescend to marry so insignificant a chit as yourself. He is a far better man than you could otherwise have dreamed of . . ."

Melbrooke interrupted him mid-sentence. "Enough," he ordered frigidly, and turned to address Lynden. "Miss Downpatrick, I think you ought to know that your aunt has confided earlier in Lady Marchpane that you and I have an unannounced engagement of six months' standing, and that it has been her policy to allow us a liberal degree of privacy during that period. Do you understand what that means?"

"Yes," cried Lynden, scandalized by the deceit. "It means that Aunt is a cheat. And a liar!"

"Insolence!" Mr. Downpatrick broke in. "Your aunt was acting in your best interests. She was trying to smooth over an embarrassing situation. Ungrateful girl! Need I remind you of the obedience you owe me as your guardian?"

"I'm not going to obey a command that's wrong!" Lynden declared passionately. "I don't care what Aunt told Lady Marchpane! If people are so unjust and unimaginative as to believe that I did wrong with Lord Melbrooke, then it's no concern of mine."

Lord Melbrooke studied her face for a moment, and then wearily spoke. "My poor child, when you have been about the world a little more, then you will see that it is not kind to people who have violated appearances. It's a hard fact, but you cannot hope to make a marriage without an impeccable reputation. Unless we intend to strangle Lady Marchpane before she leaves the house"—he gave an enigmatic side glance to Lady Eleanor—"she will repeat tales that will destroy your reputation, unless you become my wife."

Tears of rage were tingling in Lynden's eyes, but she remained defiant. "I don't care."

"Inconsiderate girl!" whined her mother.

"Indeed she is," exclaimed Mr. Downpatrick. He took a step toward Lynden, his thick brows meeting in a low vee over the bridge of his nose, his round cheeks reddening. "You will listen to reason, my girl, because I'll have no wench branded a trollop living in my house! You'll marry Lord Melbrooke to preserve your chaste reputation or I'll have you out on the streets, aye, and your sister and mother as well! You've cost me a pretty penny over the years, you three, and on my Christianity! You try living on the pittance your father left you. You know what it costs me to keep your mother's nurse? Do you have any idea as to the expense of your tutoring, your dancing lessons, your gowns, your feeding? Mind you, miss, if you defy me now, I'll have no more of you!"

Lynden's mother suddenly began struggling for air, gasping and choking, clutching at her chest. Lady Eleanor ran to the door, calling the footman to summon the nurse, and then came back to wave the smelling salts under Mrs. Downpatrick's nose.

Lynden watched her mother's struggles, knowing somewhere deep within herself that it was all one foolish, prideless trick. Yet for seventeen years she had lived in a household that bent to the will of a selfish, querulous invalid. Seventeen years' habit was strong in Lynden and now, when it was most important to resist its force, Lynden found she could not. She passed one distracted hand over her eyes. "Very well, Mama. You win! You all win," she said in a small hoarse voice and ran blindly from the room.

CHAPTER THREE

Lynden reported the disastrous results of the library interview to Lorraine and Peg, her voice tight with frustration and shock. She was still in a state of stunned surprise, unable to truly believe the day's events had been real. Marriage? To Lord Melbrooke? He had not wanted to marry her and had only agreed to it to avoid an ugly scandal. How he must hate her.

Lynden's first impulse had been to run away. But where? To leave without Lorraine would be unthinkable. But how could she drag her gentle sister into a life that even optimistic Lynden realized might be filled with poverty and danger? She could not imagine Lorraine without her poetry books and her literary journals, or without access to the piano, which she played so beautifully. And, as Lorraine pointed out with a worried frown, they were minors under their uncle's guardianship; it was within his power to use legal means to compel their return.

"You're right, Rainey," said Lynden miserably. "We don't know anything about hiding from the law—there are probably a thousand skills to it that would never occur to us and they'd find us in a snap. Also, we haven't any money, so there'd be that, too." She had been sitting before the fire, her knees resting on her chin, looking across at Lorraine and Peg who were seated on the bed. "It's all so dismal. And the most humiliating point is this: I think Lord Melbrooke suspects that I am part of a plot to trap him into marriage." There was a cry of protest from her two listeners. Lynden shook her head affirmatively and continued: "Only consider how Melbrooke must view the circumstances. How *convenient* it was for me to have been in his bedroom when Peg came in with the shaving water and Guess Who was passing in the hallway. It wouldn't be the first time that matchmaking relations have used cheater's tricks to make a brilliant marriage for their charge, and Lord Melbrooke doesn't know me. What's to tell him that I wouldn't go along with the scheme? He was so cold to me in the library!"

Her head sank lower between her knees, muffling her voice. "I wish, oh, how I wish I would die of measles overnight and never have to face him again."

Whether from a lack of contagion or the unresponsive workings of Providence, Lynden arose the next morning unsmitten by disease and was summoned to the library again, shortly before noon.

As she entered the library, Monroe Downpatrick was seated behind his massive, leather-topped desk sprinkling blotting sand on a freshly inked document. Lynden looked beyond him to the bay window where Lord Melbrooke stood, a dark silhouette framed in the yellow glow of the morning sun. The sun's rays ricocheted cruelly from the long, marbled icicles along the piles of frozen snow on the window ledge to the transparent golden highlights in Lord Melbrooke's hair. He seemed like an exotic creature brought in from the winter to stand, cold and brittle, ensconced in a crystal bower. His riding attire fought romantic fancy, however: Lord Melbrooke was dressed in a pair of practical, if highly polished, Hessians, an elegantly tailored black riding jacket, and molded buckskin breeches. He scanned her with his cool gaze and murmured a good morning.

Monroe smiled with satisfaction as he carefully brushed the sand from his hands. "Well, Lynden, you're a lucky young woman."

Lynden rested her palms on the smooth leather of

the desk top, looking at him over the massive desk. "Does that mean the wedding is called off?"

Downpatrick's smile slowly faded into pouting displeasure. "No! Really, Lynden, I cannot fathom your lack of trust in our ability to arrange matters toward your best advantage. You must have more faith in the intentions of those who care about you."

Lynden tilted her head to one side, feeling the anger of humiliation seethe within her. "If you think it would be such a good match, Uncle Monroe, why don't *you* marry Lord Melbrooke?" she asked sweetly.

Lynden felt a small, futile prick of satisfaction as Downpatrick's skin gained a splotchy red flush. A gentle hand was laid on her shoulder. She turned and found herself looking up into Lord Melbrooke's opaque gray eyes. He shook his head almost imperceptibly, as though expressing in this one small movement the utter fruitlessness of her rebellion. Lynden stepped back, away from him, and Melbrooke let his hand drop to his side. He watched her closely a moment longer and then said drily, "Mr. Downpatrick has been discussing the . . . well, the marriage arrangements. He seems to feel that four days would be a sufficiently long engagement."

"Four days?" said Lynden, weakly, hardly able to believe even Uncle Monroe could have had the nerve to suggest so soon a date.

Downpatrick shifted uneasily, his embarrassment distracting him from his niece's earlier defiance. "Under the circumstances, it seems the most appropriate course," blustered her uncle. "Best get the thing over and done—the sooner it's over, the sooner talk will die down. We'll have a small affair—family, close neighbors—very cozy."

Lynden stared at her uncle, feeling the hard, panicked beat of her heart. Months, she had thought, surely it would take months to arrange the wedding. Months during which she could make plans, think of ways to avoid the marriage, to stop it from happening. Last night she had been angry and frustrated, but somehow it still had not seemed real that two people could be forced unwillingly into marriage. And especially if one of the partners was a man like Lord Melbrooke. But that was it. Of course. Her uncle wanted to be sure Lord Melbrooke had no time to get out of it. Surely there were legal formalities? Banns!

"But Uncle Monroe, there can't be a marriage in four days! Banns must be posted two weeks before a wedding," Lynden said, trying to steady her voice.

Downpatrick rubbed his palms together. "Not if one procures a special license. And there will be no trouble with that, what with His Lordship's brother being an archbishop." Lynden crossed her arms about her middle, feeling sick and trapped. "No, my dear," continued Downpatrick, his voice coyly insinuating, "there is no need for these maidenly tremors. Perhaps you are disappointed that you won't have a big, fancy wedding? Believe me, the elegance of your new life will more than compensate you for that. Lord Melbrooke and I have completed the marriage settlements. Your allowance will be most generous, in fact, luxurious. As Lord Melbrooke's wife, you will be mistress of five households. He has three lesser estates besides his principle estate in Buckinghamshire, as well as"—and here her uncle dropped his voice with reverent envy—"a hunting box in the Quorn." He cleared his throat. "I have, of course, explained to Lord Melbrooke how unprepared you are for such great rank, and he has generously promised that he will use you with the greatest patience. I hope," he finished, pessimistically, "that you will strive to be worthy of his toleration."

Melbrooke's eyes narrowed slightly at the corners and there was a subtle curve of disdain in his upper lip. "I'm not a schoolmaster, Downpatrick," he said abruptly, coldly, "nor a parson. I have neither the need nor the desire for Miss Downpatrick to be obliged to make herself *worthy* of me. And now, sir, if you will indulge me, I must take my leave if I am to make any distance today."

"Certainly, My Lord, indeed, yes!" said Downpatrick, bowing to Lord Melbrooke and then turning back toward his niece. "Lynden, Lord Melbrooke goes south to his seat in Buckinghamshire to order his affairs. He'll return for the wedding, bringing his carriage to convey you to London afterward where, Lord Melbrooke assures me, his mother will condescend to undertake your presentation into society."

Lynden closed her eyes, shutting out her uncle's face, the library with its punctilious leather trim, and Lord Melbrooke. They're going to do it, she thought. They are really going to do this to me.

She would be married coldly and without preamble to a man she knew only from rumor and the brief, innocent encounter in his bedroom. He had been kind then, but with the teasing charm that one might employ toward a clever child. Had it been only yesterday that she had pooh-poohed Melbrooke's rakish reputation? It had been one thing to do so from the childish security of the yew hedge. It was quite another to find herself suddenly and totally in his power.

They had nothing in common. Lynden was a country girl from the minor gentry with neither wealth nor age and experience to lend her cachet. Melbrooke was a titled aristocrat, a poet, a member of the intellectual elite of England. Surely he would forever resent Lynden as the "untidy little nobody" he had been forced to wed?

Lynden recalled her aunt's spiteful prophecy that Melbrooke would "stick" her in one of his houses (had he really *five* of them?) and forget her. She pictured herself alone in London, ignored or worse by her husband, despised by his sophisticated friends, and hated by his relatives who must see her as the encroaching adventuress who had tricked their Golden Poet into marriage. And did her uncle really think it would be any comfort for Lynden to be placed under the condescending thumb of her future mother-in-law, no matter how "kindly" she might be? Lynden opened her eyes and said, with a resolve born of desperation, "I don't want to go to London."

Her uncle's mustache bristled, the tiny, coarse hairs buzzing with angry energy. Lynden saw a startled light flash in Lord Melbrooke's smoky eyes. He raised a politely interested eyebrow.

"Where would you like to go?" asked Melbrooke calmly.

Suddenly Lynden found it hard to meet his gently exploring gaze. She looked at her uncle's desk, letting her gaze follow the line of brass-headed tacks that outlined its leather cover.

"I don't know," she said in a low voice. "But not London."

Monroe Downpatrick began a sputtering comment on his niece's perversity but was silenced by a sharp gesture from Melbrooke who said, "Very well, then would you rather come to my home in Buckinghamshire until the London season opens?" His voice was cool, formal, nonjudgmental. Lynden found it somehow soothing. She stretched her fingers toward the desk top, laying them against the cold metal heads of the upholstery tacks. Buckinghamshire. But how close that was to London.

"Would your friends come to Buckinghamshire to see us? And your mother?" she asked.

"More than likely. I think we must assume that my . . . acquaintance will evince no small amount of interest in meeting you, and I have a rather large acquaintance in that area. Yes, I think they would come."

"Then I don't want to go to Buckinghamshire," said Lynden defiantly. Her uncle muttered cholerically that Lord Melbrooke must be astonished by her effrontery, but when Lynden looked sidelong at Melbrooke, he did not seem astonished. In fact, to Lynden's surprise, he appeared to be amused. The gray eyes shone with the detached warmth that Lynden had seen on their first meeting.

"Would you like to go to China?" he asked civilly, as though it was really a possibility. "I doubt if even the most intrepid of my relations would pursue us there."

"I suppose you think I've been very rude, but I assure you I'm not." Lynden could not quite manage to meet Lord Melbrooke's eyes. She stared with dignity at a spot on the wall somewhere behind him and re-thought her last remark. "Well, I suppose I am but . . . do you think it would be so very bad if we waited, um, a while before I met your relatives?"

"Not at all," he returned quizzically. "I understand perfectly. With your experience, you must take a dim view of the whole Order of Relatives."

Lynden could not resist a quick triumphant glance at her uncle's flushing countenance. There was some gratitude in her expression as she looked back to Lord Melbrooke. "Were you not on your way north to the Lake District? Lorraine says that every year you go there for peace and seclusion and stay until April. Could I not come with you? I—I know that you will be writing at your poetry . . . but I would stay out of your way! I could be so quiet that you might not even notice I was there."

Melbrooke looked down thoughtfully into the plead-ing intensity of Lynden's warm brown eyes. "Yes," he said slowly, "I'm sure you wouldn't be in the way, my dear, but, frankly, the Lake country is not at its most congenial in the winter months. The climate is still uncertain in March. The landscape is mountainous and my home there is perhaps more isolated than you are used to. There are few close neighbors. The house it-self is small and old fashioned. You see, I'm afraid you might be unhappy. The living would not be ele-gant."

"Oh, but, well, I don't care so much for elegance.

A small, old-fashioned house sounds quite . . . snug. And I don't mind a bit about the weather because I'm very fond of the out-of-doors and go for walks even on the *coldest* days!" But with Lorraine, she thought fearfully. If only I could have Lorraine with me, I could face it all. The thought hit Lynden with merciless speed. They'll separate us, they mean to separate us. She felt a sharp, acid pressure behind her eyelids and she flinched as one bright, sudden tear traced a swift course down her white cheek. She caught it with the back of her hand as it reached the corner of her mouth.

"You're crying," murmured Lord Melbrooke. His voice, though gentle, carried no less dispassionate calm than he might have employed in commenting on an unspectacular period of weather. "If you told me why, I would help you, if it were possible."

"Well, it is," said Lynden, desolately folding her hands before her, looking at her pale knuckles. "But you won't like it, I know."

"If I don't like it, I'll tell you. That need not deter you from mentioning it."

Lynden quickly raised her gaze to Melbrooke's, finding this attitude more than a little unexpected in a male. A flicker of hope brightened her eyes.

Melbrooke saw it and smiled slightly, encouragingly. "Yes. Don't let the fear that I will give you a negative answer keep you from asking. I'm sure I won't mind—then you'll know and feel relieved."

"I want my sister Lorraine to come with us," said Lynden, rushing her fences. From the corner of her eye, she could see her uncle wince. Even Lynden, whose notions of propriety were hazy, knew how unconventional was her request. She was sure that her uncle was wondering how his brother could ever have fathered a female so abandoned as to demand the presence of her sister on her honeymoon. But Lord Melbrooke, it seemed, did not share this opinion. In

46

fact, he seemed to regard Lynden's anxiously voiced idea as the veriest commonplace.

"Why, of course, my dear. If you were triplets you would all be welcome. If it will make you happy to have your sister come, then, naturally, invite her. There will be little enough company for you as it is. My friends understand that I go north to work, so we have few guests—only occasional visits from neighboring landowners."

She had been closely watching the well-formed curve of Melbrooke's lips and studying the intense grayness of his eyes as she waited for his answer. A small, choked sob of relief escaped her at his words, and her palm interrupted the silver path of another tear as it made its way down her cheek.

"That's very magnanimous of you, I think," Lynden said grudgingly. "Because there's no reason that I can see for you to feel kindly disposed toward me." Lynden paused. "Will your relatives be angry if we don't go to meet them in London right away?"

"No. I'll send them very tactful letters and they will understand."

Like an old, fat bulldog worrying a mouse, Monroe Downpatrick made a snorting noise with his mouth and throat, then protruded his lower lip and twitched his mustache. "You'll do as you see fit, I suppose, My Lord, but you'll find it won't do to take a light hand on this filly's reins. You'll spoil her and then she'll be wilder yet."

Lord Melbrooke's gaze deepened in intensity, the ash-gray eyes noncommittally encompassing Lynden; suddenly he smiled.

If Lynden had the illusion that the next four days would be a period of nervous introspection and mental girding for her imminent marriage, she was soon relieved of that erroneous notion. No sooner had Lord Melbrooke left for Buckinghamshire than Lady Eleanor cornered Lynden and demanded an item-by-item inventory of the twins' wardrobes to determine what of their clothing would be appropriate for their new (and more elevated) stations. That inventory took Lynden and Lorraine the remainder of the day and the better part of the next to complete.

Lynden's wardrobe at first appeared to be extensive, but closer examination showed it to consist of such articles as a flannel day frock with a ripped shoulder seam, a frilled muslin nightcap with stained lace, a pair of scuffed kid boots with a loose heel. Over the years it had not been Lynden's habit to cull from her wardrobe items either outgrown or abused. By the time the fourth mateless, left-handed mitten was listed, even the loyal Lorraine went so far as to comment, "Really, Lynnie, you take shockingly bad care of your clothes."

"We're to inventory your closet, next, Raine, and we'll see if it's in any better shape" was Lynden's retort. But Lorraine's closet, to her sister's disgust, proved to be a model of organization. Outgrown clothing had been neatly folded and placed in *labeled* boxes, a touch that Lynden found particularly obnoxious. Not a seam needed mending, and frayed laces and tired ribbons had been systematically repaired or replaced.

"Changeling!" muttered Lynden.

Lady Eleanor's response to the inventories was a disgusted sigh. "We shall all be made to look like fools if Lynden prances around as Lord Melbrooke's wife dressed like a penny-pinched country dowdy." She had detailed measurements taken of both girls; informed Lynden smugly that she was too thin and had a little nothing of a bosom; and ordered for them both, from a topnotch London tailor, a fashionable trousseau to be delivered to Melbrooke's Lake-country home.

Mama recovered from the exertions of hysteria sufficiently to take what was for her an exceptional interest in the wedding preparations. She ordered Mademoiselle Ambrose to go to the attic where she would find the wedding gown, wrapped in tissue paper and stored in a trunk, in which Lynden's mother had made her own vows. It was to be altered for Lynden's use. Mama then requested Lynden's presence for a long, depressing lecture on the duties, intimate and otherwise, of a new bride to her husband. Lastly, the invalid announced that she would rise from her sickbed to attend the wedding of her beloved daughter. This last was a Maternal Sacrifice. Though the church was only three cottages away, she had not considered herself well enough to attend services there since her husband's funeral five years earlier.

There were the bride's visits, too. News of Lynden's approaching marriage swept the parish like a wind rippling through a wheat field. The local gentry came calling to bring hastily purchased wedding gifts and to gossip and exclaim over Lynden's good fortune. Despite the twin's popularity in the neighborhood and Lorraine's acknowledged standing as one of the prettiest girls in the county, no one had thought to see either of the Downpatrick twins make so exalted a match. One simply did not expect the future Lady Melbrooke to spring from one's own backyard. Lynden, or Miss Ruckus, as she was known in the parish, had always been the uncrowned queen of the local younger set. To the girls she was a trustworthy confidant and cheerful companion, guaranteed to enliven the dullest gathering. She had been a prime favorite with the boys since, as a wild nine-year-old, she had accepted a dare to mount the squire's half-broken stallion and refused to cry when she broke her arm in the inevitable tumble. Her friends gathered around her now, full of excited, teasing questions; demanding to know how she could have been so sly as to have been engaged to the famous Lord Melbrooke for six months and not told a soul. Where had she met him? Had he wooed her with love poems? Did she think she would like being so horribly rich? Lorraine could only hope that Lynden's evasive stammered replies could be attributed to the natural nervousness of a bride-to-be.

Lynden's wedding day dawned too soon, and she huddled, cold with despair, under her blankets, her thoughts chasing each other in frantic circles. Justin, Lord Melbrooke. Lynden had tried desperately to avoid all thought of him. What thoughts she did permit herself had been of the legend: poet, aristocrat, Lothario. It was safer to think of the legend than the man. He was back in Yorkshire, that Lynden knew. He was not staying in Downpatrick Hall, though. Last night he had sent Uncle Monroe a short note, informing Downpatrick that he could make himself comfortable in the local inn, that there was no need for Lady Eleanor's household to be put to further trouble on his account. He would see them tomorrow at the wedding.

The wedding. It seemed incredible to Lynden that Melbrooke could make so casual a reference to an event that was to her a major shift in her life's fortunes. How detached he must be, how poised. She envied him that. The more she thought about it, the more she decided that a façade of equal nonchalance was the only dignified course left to her. And yet . . . he was as foreign to her as a Hindu god of love, with the mystically remote smoke tones of his eyes and the subtle curves of his lips. Then, there was the barely explored thought that she might be expected to share a bed with him, perhaps that very evening. The idea fairly shriveled her with apprehension. Lynden sat upright and gave a shriek that would have aroused the household had it not been muffled by a hastily gathered double handful of bedclothes.

It was to be a morning wedding. The twins had little time to dress and fix their hair before the family coach would arrive to carry them the fifty yards to the church. Lynden's bedroom became a disordered scene, with a light fog of talcum powder floating in the air and creeping to rest on every flat surface. Strands of ribbon and torn pieces of tissue paper from Lynden's wedding presents were trampled underfoot. When Peg brought the news that the carriage had left with Mr. Downpatrick, Lady Marchpane, and the twin's mother, Lorraine quickened her arrangement of Lynden's coiffure and gave a hopeless moan.

"Oh, no," she cried. "The carriage will be back for us in a cat's wink, and we aren't nearly ready. And the room is in such a muddle, and we haven't even begun to pack Lynden's things! We're supposed to leave for the Lake country right after the ceremony!" Unconventional though it might be, there was to be no festive breakfast following the wedding. February weather was unpredictable; a delayed trip might have to be postponed indefinitely due to roads made impassable by snow or fog. The wedding principals would take advantage of the day's clear weather to leave immediately after the ceremony for Lord Melbrooke's estate.

"Don't fret, Miss Lorraine, Mademoiselle Ambrose and me'll see to your packin' and straighten up th' room besides," Peg reassured her. "It'll be no trouble a'tall. And since you was packed last evenin', we only have to worry about Miss Lynden."

Lord Melbrooke had been at the church long enough to exchange a few civil words with Lady Marchpane and bow formally over Mrs. Downpatrick's limpid hand before Monroe Downpatrick could monopolize his time with a series of ostentatious introductions. Politeness forced him to shake hands in quick succession with a country squire, a rustic knight, and a justice of the peace. Downpatrick's heavy voice boomed at his side, introducing him as "my good friend Melbrooke." Lord Melbrooke assumed a fixed, vague smile and thought his decision to stay the night in a nearby inn rather than under Downpatrick's roof to have been well taken.

There was a stir near the doorway, followed by the rustle of silk as the guests took their pews. Lady Eleanor Downpatrick entered, beaming like Mother Nature. Lord Melbrooke saw that she was followed by a tall, dark-haired girl whose da Vinci eyes were misty with tears. Nice effect, thought Melbrooke; that must be the twin. Her gown was a deep burgundy with a half train. Flattering. And yet its cut and color marked it as inappropriate dress for a girl in her seventeenth year. Melbrooke guessed it had been hastily converted from Eleanor's wardrobe.

Monroe Downpatrick left the sanctuary and returned a moment later with the bride on his arm. Now that Melbrooke had seen her sister, Lynden looked smaller still and infinitely dainty. She wore a winter-white silk wedding gown in floating empire lines, with an overdress of gauze embroidered with silver thread and tiny lustrous pearls. Her hair was done in curls atop her head; two small French locks rested at the nape of her neck. A wreath of wild roses had been settled cleverly among the dark curls, and she carried a tall bouquet of hothouse lilies. Her heavily lashed eyes peeked uncertainly to the right, then across her uncle's wide body to the left, scanning the rows of wedding spectators. Melbrooke thought she looked like a curious earth sprite entering the Cave of the Mountain King. The thought amused him, and he smiled.

The vicar was elderly, and slow of speech and movement. The words issuing from his wrinkled mouth came in dry, intermittent rasps, like the hollow smack of wood-chopping on a windy day, leaving his audience waiting for his words with irritated, resigned suspense. Melbrooke began to mentally recite lines memorized from Homer, and then glanced down when a slight movement in the small figure next to him caught his attention. Lynden leaned toward him and whispered, "Do you know what these lilies mean?" She crossly indicated her bouquet.

"No," he whispered back, cautiously.

"Virginity!" returned Lynden in a whisper so loud that Lord Melbrooke was forced to resist an impulse to clap his hand over her mouth. "Aunt Eleanor said I must carry them. It's so embarrassing."

"Don't worry. You can fling them in the ditch at the first crossroads. And lilies symbolize many other things besides virginity," whispered Melbrooke. He immediately regretted his comment because she asked him, in a voice he was sure carried to the farthest pew, what the other symbolic uses for lilies were. He was relieved that the vicar had reached the point in the ceremony that required them to recite their vows.

At last the vicar pronounced them married and advised Melbrooke that he might kiss the bride. During the last moments of the ceremony, Lynden had divided her time between tapping impatiently on the stone floor with one small foot and glaring alternately at the offending lilies and the equally oblivious vicar. It was plain to Melbrooke that she had innocently forgotten this final part of the ceremony; she started, gave a hasty step backward, and dropped the lilies. He caught her shoulders in a firm, steadying grip, brushing her cold, soft lips with his own. Her liquid brown eyes were wide with surprise; her red, curved underlip quivered nervously. She was scented of lilies and talcum, and he could see, on a creamy cheek and barely reflected in the light from the stained-glass windows, the dried course of a tear.

Lynden's breath caught in her chest as Melbrooke pulled her to him in a powerful move. She felt her head falling limply back into the support of his broad hand, and he kissed her so deeply, so passionately, that her lips felt swollen, pulsing under his. She was afraid of falling and clutched at his hard shoulders, searching anxiously for a hold as his lips searched for her soul. Then he released her, and she stood alone, looking at her dropped bouquet, afraid to raise her eyes to him.

"You have trod upon the lilies," she said, shaken.

Melbrooke laughed softly. "I see I have. But we were going to toss them out at the first crossroads, after all."

CHAPTER FOUR

The coach thundered north, taking the frozen road through Ripon where children playing in the snow at the roadside pointed excitedly at the Melbrooke crest. The twins were seated side by side in the rear of the coach, kept snug against the encroaching cold under mounds of furs. Lorraine occasionally freed one mittened hand to scrape a sparkling oval in the hard frost invading the glass window to her left.

The twins would not see Lord Melbrooke again until that evening. He had ridden ahead with the stated purpose of preparing his household for their arrival. The sisters had been discussing the wedding in exhaustive detail when Lynden's voice trailed off in midsentence and she stared abstractedly at the upholstery button set into the plush fabric of the seat cover opposite them. Lorraine waited patiently, but in vain, for Lynden to finish her sentence, then shrugged and searched in the wicker basket by her side, lifting out a slim, leather-bound volume. The book's title page boasted its purpose: "Guide or Companion for the Minds of Persons of Taste, and a Feeling for Landscape, who might be inclined to explore the District of the Lakes with that degree of attention to which its beauty may fairly lay claim." Lorraine studied the book for a while before Lynden's eyes refocused.

"What were we talking about?" said Lynden. She looked disapprovingly at the book in her sister's hands. "There. If I don't watch you every moment, you go poking your nose into some fusty old book. What an ugly cover. What's it about?"

"It's a guide to the Lake country. And it says, 'There are three approaches to the Lakes through Yorkshire; the least advisable is the great north road by Catterick.' "

"Well, we haven't taken that one, at least," said Lynden cheerfully. "What does it say about the road we're on?"

"Well," began Lorraine, "it says, 'this tract leads through an avenue of rocks that must be of interest to the geologist.' "

"And dull as boiled yams to anyone else, I'll wager," sniffed Lynden. "If you've been wasting your pin money on stupid guidebooks that take pains to memorialize in print every boring feature of the countryside, then I must say, Rainey . . ."

"But it does tell some interesting things, Lynden. For instance, it says, 'one may turn off the main road at Masham to visit the Jerneaux Abbey.' The book says it's a noble scene."

Lynden brightened. "Well, we're not to Masham yet. Let's take the turn and see the thing."

"I don't think we ought, Lynnie," said Lorraine, setting her book aside. "Lord Melbrooke wished us not to stop so that we would be sure to reach his home by nightfall."

Lynden was already pulling the rope that was connected to the small silver bell by the coachman's seat outside. "Fiddle! If Lord Melbrooke wants obedience then he ought to train a greyhound instead of taking a wife." She clamped a hand on her sister's arm. "How dreadful! I've just realized that I'm a wife." Her grip on her sister's arm tightened. "We are going to the abbey!" she said with determination.

It was not so easy to convince Mr. Coniston of this. A fatherly, gray-haired man in his forties, he had been in service to the Melbrookes all his life, first as a groom, now as coachman. He explained kindly that Lord Melbrooke had given him orders to come direct, a diversion of this type would mean traveling partway in darkness, the northern roads could be bad at night, and he had only two grooms with him and one of those a mere lad.

But Lynden's mind was so fertile with inventive and intricate counterarguments that he soon perceived that Her Ladyship was prepared to keep them in their present stationary position by arguing until nightfall. He yielded, saying that he hoped nothing bad would come of it, but she should know it was against his better judgment.

"Fiddle!" said Lynden.

But when the coach arrived before the noble abbey, the twins found to their dismay that it had been demolished centuries earlier in the Dissolution, leaving only a motley collection of crumbling ruins.

"The writer of your guidebook ought to be arrested," said Lynden indignantly as she and her sister marched resolutely through the rubble. "Mr. Coniston must think we're a pair of nodcocks, wanting to come out of the way to traipse around in a heap of rubble." To save face, the twins spent a full hour exclaiming with forced enthusiasm over an indistinct bas-relief, an indecipherable inscription, and an unidentifiable fragment of a statue. They returned to the coach almost frozen into statues themselves. Mr. Coniston hid his smile and drove on.

Thus it was that within five miles of their destination, two hours after sundown under a distant, indifferent moon, the dozing twins were awakened by the sharp scrape of the carriage brakes. The coach horses halted in stamping confusion. There were shouts cut by the crack of a pistol shot. After more stomping and more shouts, the carriage door was wrenched open and Lynden and Lorraine were confronted by a masked man who waved a pistol and growled, "Come out and deliver!"

As they scrambled out, Lorraine clinging weakly to her sister, they heard a soft chuckle from a dark figure seated on horseback before them.

"That's stand and deliver, oakhead," said the dark figure in a youthful voice that was mellowed by an Irish lilt. The speaker wore a black chapeau-bras, tipped back on his head and angled in the French manner. A patch covered one eye and the lower half of his face was obscured by a strategically tied neckerchief. His powerful shoulders bulged beneath a soft leather cloak attached at the neck with a chain; he wore tight whipcord breeches tucked into high leather boots. His horse wheeled and danced beneath him, but he brought it sharply under control as the twins came into view. He sat back in the saddle and said, with a huge measure of surprise, "My God! It's ladies!"

"Of course it's ladies, you villain!" said Lynden angrily. "And if you've shot Mr. Coniston or one of the grooms, then I shall have to live my life knowing it was my fault for stopping at the Jerneaux Abbey!"

The figure swung a long, well-formed leg over the back of his horse and dropped to the ground. "I may be a villain, but I ain't stupid enough to stop at the Jerneaux Abbey. Everyone knows it's just an old pile of stones. And if you look behind you, you'll see your coachman and grooms sitting up on the box. I only fired my pistol to get their attention. They were squawking like cooped hens."

Lynden turned to look at the box. To her relief, Mr. Coniston and the grooms were in their places atop the coach, staring warily at the third highwayman, a rugged-looking scamp guarding them with an old Brown Bess musket. The horses were nosing impatiently for forage through the pile of brush which had been used to block the roadway. The steam rising from their backs made a silvery mist in the moonlight. Lynden, ready for battle, took a step toward the young highwayman before her.

"If you're not stupid, then why did you become a

57

highwayman instead of entering one of the professions?" asked Lynden sternly.

"Lynnie, please," Lorraine interrupted in a shaking voice, clinging to her sister's elbow. "Don't, I beg you, stir an argument with these men. You can have no idea of the circumstances. Perhaps they have wives and hungry children at home. Perhaps they've not been able to get work. What good purpose will it serve to anger them?" As she spoke, she stripped off one of her buff-colored kid gloves, removed a small pearl ring from her index finger, and, in a gesture of conciliation, held it out to the tall cloaked highwayman standing before Lynden. "Sir," she said, addressing him, "will you take this please and leave us in peace? The stone is small, I know, but the quality is excellent. My father told me so when he gave it to me as a confirmation present."

The highwayman took a hasty step backward and shook his head emphatically. "Oh, no! Here, child, put that thing back on your finger before you drop it! 'Twould be the devil to find it in the dark. We don't want your baubles. Lord knows, we'd never even have stopped the coach if we'd known there'd be women in it. Thing is, we saw the crest and thought that Melbrooke'd be traveling within. Well, what I mean is, it's fair game to hold up a fine swordsman like Melbrooke, but the lads and I wouldn't touch things belonging to a lady."

"Dunno 'bout that," mumbled the highwayman who had yanked open the door. "Wouldn't touch nothin' o' the tall, pretty one's, but Oi wouldn't mind to lift the gee-gaws o' the little feisty one. A proper sauce-bucket she is!"

"Well, if that doesn't beat the Yankees!" flashed Lynden, bridling. "You are the most uncivil robbers I've ever met! It is one thing to hold us up, shooting your pistols off in that irresponsible manner, but it is quite another to force us to stand in the night's chill listening to your insults! Also, it's all very well to say that you don't hold up women, but could you not have anticipated that there might have been women traveling in Melbrooke's coach?"

"Aye," said the slender man before her, shaking his head in rueful self-reproach. "I ought to have thought of that, especially when you consider his success with the ladies." He walked to Lorraine and took her pretty chin lightly in his gloved hand. "And I must say, I admire his taste. What a beauty you are, sweeting. Though I had thought Melbrooke's mistress was a blonde, which shows you how rumor can lie."

The artless and almost avuncular delivery of this speech caused a slight delay in Lorraine's comprehension of its precise meaning, but it in no way weakened the strength of her reaction. The last days had been difficult for her; she had a painful awareness of her sister's misery. There had been the flurried excitement of the wedding that morning, and then the long carriage ride culminating in the current frightening ordeal. Whether it was the shocking implications of the highwayman's words or the unexpected caressing gesture of his hand on her chin, Lorraine felt her temperature plummet sharply and she knew with humiliated certainty that she was going to faint. She gave a soft sigh as the strength left her knees and she swayed forward limply into the highwayman's arms.

"Rainey!" cried Lynden. "Oh, my poor Rainey! Have you caught her up firmly? Please hold her carefully! Oh, yes, that's good, you know to support her head! How dreadful! Sir, you cannot know how poor Rainey hates herself when she swoons. You see, our mother is the most dreadful hypochondriac and Lorraine worries, I think, that she inherited Mama's weakness. Though, of course, that's nonsense! Oh, yes, bring her into the coach out of the wind. Thank you. Wait, let me fix this pillow. So!"

An interior flambeau spread a golden stream of weak light through the carriage. Lynden watched anxiously as the highwayman laid her sister carefully amongst the furs and saw with approval that he took great pains not to jar or bump Lorraine's unconscious form.

"Haven't you any . . . What are those things females are always carrying around?" He fumbled for the word. "Smelling salts! Have you any of those?"

"Yes!" answered Lynden. "In the portmanteau beside Mr. Coniston."

He nodded and made as if to leave the carriage. "I'll find them."

"No, you can't," stated Lynden flatly. "The portmanteau is filled with . . . items of a personal feminine nature. I shall get the smelling salts."

The bemused highwayman found himself alone in the coach interior, his arms supporting the most beautiful woman he'd ever held. He drew a plush fur across her body, gently untied and removed her bonnet, and loosened her cloak about her neck. He saw that she still clutched the offered pearl ring in one tightly closed white hand; he carefully uncurled her gripping fingers and slipped the ring back onto its proper place on her finger. It alarmed him that she lay so still, and he tried softly to rub some color back into her blanched, smooth cheeks.

Lorraine returned to consciousness with a distressed whimper. She lifted her head and looked about, starting in fright at the sight of the masked figure leaning over her.

"No, love, don't be frightened, it's only a mask," said the highwayman softly. He pulled down the kerchief to reveal his face. "See, dear, I'm an ordinary fellow, after all."

Lorraine blinked in the dim light and his face came slowly into focus; the light was too diffuse and shadowed to perceive colors, but the form was there, the contours as clean and attractive as its owner's voice. It was a marvelous face, with high cheekbones and a gracefully bridged nose. The mouth was wide and sensitive, the corners curled slightly in a smile. His hair was long and as dark as Lorraine's. He was so near that she could smell its crisp, healthy fragrance. She wondered briefly and without fear whether his right eye was patched to answer the demands of disguise or deformity and decided that he was so perfectly made otherwise that it did not matter.

"Better now?" he asked her, his finger light against her cheek.

"Yes. I—I fainted? I'm sorry for it. But where is Lynden?"

"Lynden. The hot-blooded brat with the curls? She's outside hunting through her undergarments for smelling salts. And the fainting was my fault. I shouldn't have handled you so roughly. I fear my manners are better suited to the taproom than the presence of ladies. I make you my apologies, Little Delight."

She turned her face away from him, the soft white lines of her profile resting against the sable blanket. The weak interior light caught in the dense warmth of her long eyelashes, so thick and silky that they appeared to have been plucked from the sable.

"I accept your apology," she whispered, "but pl—please, you mustn't address me in that manner."

"Mustn't?" replied the highwayman softly. "Aye, but you needn't worry, I haven't forgot that you belong to Melbrooke, though it would be easy enough to do. Lord knows, you're soft on the eyes."

A soft "whish" of velvet on velvet and a draft of sharp night air indicated Lynden's return to the coach during the highwayman's last speech.

"What a flirtatious tongue," said Lynden tartly as she climbed inside. "You ought to try your hand at writing syrup sonnets instead of robbing coaches. You could hardly do worse than this, and if you were brought to book, you wouldn't be hanged unless it were by the literary critics. Raine, I'm so glad you've waked up. I couldn't find the salts, and then I remembered I'd thrown them out at the last minute because having them along reminded me too much of Mother." She brushed past the highwayman to sit on the edge of the seat near her sister, then looked up at him. "Oh, and I've a message from your rascally friends outside. They say they're clearing that brush barricade away from the carriage path and then they're leaving, so you'd better come along and be off with them. Which advice I heartily echo."

The highwayman reluctantly drew his gaze away from Lorraine's lovely profile and grinned at Lynden. "Do you, hornet? Well then, I'm off. Tell Melbrooke not to come and hunt me down. I haven't harmed you."

"That," said Lynden sharply, "is a matter of debate. And let me tell you one thing more before you leave, *Mister* Highwayman. About your wicked, detestable insinuations. My sister, Lorraine is not Lord Melbrooke's—that is to say, Lord Melbrooke and my sister are not—are not . . ."

The highwayman's smile widened. "Is 'mistress' the euphemism you're stumbling for? Lord, child, spit it out. I won't tell your mother."

"Very well then, mistress!" returned Lynden with dignity. "And Lorraine isn't Lord Melbrooke's . . . Lorraine isn't Lord Melbrooke's *anything*. Because it is I . . ."

"It is?" said the highwayman, quirking an eyebrow quizzically. "I wouldn't have thought—though you're pretty enough but . . . what did you do, lock your sister in the closet 'til you had your man leashed?"

Lynden answered this sally with a glare that might have sent a lesser man to bed in his britches. "Before you continue making vulgar jests, I think you ought to know that I am *Lady* Melbrooke! Lord Melbrooke and I were married this morning," announced Lynden frigidly, suppressing a very unladylike urge to add "so there." She noted with satisfaction that she had at last succeeded in impressing the fellow. He gave a low, surprised whistle.

"Truly? It must have been a late moment match, then. And Silvia waiting in her castle, itching like a

62

first-skin snake to be at Melbrooke, by all accounts . . . I wouldn't be in his shoes for twice his fortune!"

Lynden's satisfaction evaporated abruptly. She studied the highwayman, her brows knitted, and asked, "Who's Silvia?"

"Don't you know, then, little hornet? Here's innocence!" The highwayman's handsome countenance became a study in contrite dismay. "If ever there was an addlepated gabblemonger, I'm he! I shouldn't have said anything—but Lord, wherever you're from, well, the gossip must be staler than the dark side of the moon. Still, the Bard of the Lakeland is a master catch. Your people must have baited a devilish cunning trap!"

Since this last remark was not only highly unflattering, but also far too close to the unhappy truth, it was not surprising that Lynden lost the final tatters of her temper. "You—why, you are the horridest, rudest person I've ever met! Including my cousin, Elmo, and he's so ill-behaved that Aunt Sophronia has been forced to hire a former prizefighter as his tutor! You can say what you like about me, at least *I'm* a Christian citizen. I don't go about robbing and insulting folk at night on the King's Highways!"

"Well, you shouldn't be about *at all* at night on the King's Highways," retorted the highwayman, giving a quick, teasing tweak to one dark soft curl escaping Lynden's bonnet. "Ain't safe, child, and so I'll bet you were told before you decided to give a drop by to the Jerneaux Abbey. It's my belief that you're a ballad that likes to compose itself. Learn prudence, hornet. It's best to have a care. The nights are full of rogues!" He smiled at her again, and cast a brief, almost wistful glance at Lorraine before leaving the coach. The sisters heard the brisk tempo of his retreating footsteps as he rejoined his companions, and the highwaymen melted into the forest's thick blue shadows.

CHAPTER FIVE

"As every English schoolboy knows," claimed the guide book, "Fern Court is the residence of our Poet Supreme, Lord Melbrooke. The graceful stone-and-timber dwelling nests within the fair bosom of Westmorland in the peaceful dale below the awesome crags of Loughrigg Fell. Few pleasure-travelers care to brave the Lakeland winters; those who stream to the site in summer hoping to glimpse Lord Melbrooke en reverie beneath an ancient oak, or on a contemplative walk through the fellside, will be disappointed; the poet is in residence at Fern Court only during the winter season. However, summer tourists making the pilgrimage thence will be well rewarded for their efforts, for the surrounding aspect of dour cliffs with their gaily throbbing brooks and the nearby sparkling mirror of Grasmere Lake are sights that will at once humble and uplift the visitor."

Contrary to the guide book's pronouncements, the twins arrived at Fern Court more quietly depressed than either humbled or uplifted. The author of the invaluable guide book would have been disappointed to know that they attributed their melancholia to the stern lecture delivered to them by the coachman on the imprudence of their behavior with the highwayman, rather than to the disobliging darkness that prevented their viewing the surrounding aspect.

The carriage made a slow, rocky descent down a potholed mountain pass and into a valley; then, suddenly, the coachman pulled the carriage neatly through a right-angled turn and the road became smooth. Lorraine commented that they must have entered Melbrooke property; only a private roadway could be so well maintained. Lynden drew back the leather curtain and opened the carriage window to peer into the darkness. For a while she could see only the occasional blur of a roadside fir tree as it caught the coach's flambeau. Restless black shadows filled the distance as the coach entered a thicket and then a clearing. Now, some one hundred yards ahead, Lynden could see the groping form of a long, two-story building, its many windows glowing into the night like staring cats.

"Fern Court," whispered Lynden.

Lorraine looked over her sister's shoulder.

"But, Lynnie, he said it was small, didn't he?" she said wonderingly. "And it's twice the size of Downpatrick Hall. Why, I shouldn't wonder if we found it had twenty bedrooms! If Lord Melbrooke thinks Fern Court is small . . . Lord Melbrooke must be fiercely rich!"

"Well," said Lynden, tossing her head and trying bravely to swallow her awe, "if he thinks that I shall be intimidated by his fortune, he's wrong!" She was silent a moment and then added hopefully, "Perhaps it's shabby inside."

But shabby it was not. Lord Melbrooke had called the furnishings "old-fashioned" and it was true that their style proclaimed their age as some fifty years—but old-fashioned? Fern Court had been furnished from the sketchbook of Adam and bore the style of the Neoclassical Revival. Not a table, nor a chair, nor a bookcase existed that was not gracefully formed and delicately detailed. Indeed, as Lynden entered the warm, walnut-paneled foyer, she saw before her a demilune pier table so enriched with gold inlay that she was sure it must be worth more than all the furnishings of Downpatrick Hall together.

They were met in the foyer by a tall, pretty woman in her thirties. Clad in a neat brown frock, she wore her light hair in a tidy chignon. Her green eyes were warm with maternal concern.

"There, come in now, bonnies. And you must be Lady Melbrooke," she said, taking Lynden's hand. "How cold your hands feel! I'm Mrs. Coniston, Lord Melbrooke's housekeeper. Such a grand surprise it was to hear that My Lord took it upon himself to marry!" She busied herself taking the girls' wraps, stacking the wintry capes in the arms of the diminutive chambermaid standing behind her. "And this must be Miss Lorraine, isn't it? Such rosy cheeks! It's been cold this night, indeed." She looked behind the girls, her gaze meeting with the coachman's, who had followed them in and stood near the door stamping his feet. "And how is my John tonight?" she said to him. "Lady Melbrooke, Miss Lorraine, you've met my husband, Mr. Coniston, of course, as he drove you here. But how late you've come! We were beginning to fear some misadventure."

"Aye, May, there's been a bit of an incident," answered her husband, stripping the heavy leather gloves from his hands. "That's why I've put th' grooms to carin' for m' horses whiles I come in t' talk t' His Lordship. I must tell him myself what's passed on the lanes here tonight and the explainin' wouldn't wait 'til tomorn. But first thing is to put these lasses before a fire. They must be fair chilled from the ride."

Mrs. Coniston gazed anxiously at her husband and gave his hand a quick squeeze before ushering the twins into a spacious drawing room, its walls hung in a soft golden cloque silk. The chairs and side tables were decorated in polychrome designs painted on a cream ground, and faced a generous marble fireplace, its chimneypiece carved in bands of honeysuckle ornament. Fanciful paintings of mythological subjects were tastefully arranged along the walls; there was one small aureate portrait of a lovely plump lady at her bath that Lorraine reverently identified as a Rubens.

Mrs. Coniston pulled a cushioned bench with out-scrolled sides in front of the fireplace and invited the twins to sit down. She then turned to the attendant housemaid. "Jill, please have the footmen carry the luggage to the rooms we've prepared——I shall be up to assist with the unpacking in a moment——and have Cook send up tea for the ladies. Oh, and you may inform Lord Melbrooke that Her Ladyship and her sister have arrived."

"That won't be necessary, Mrs. Coniston," said Melbrooke, entering the room on her words. He was formally dressed for evening, Lynden noted that he must have arrived well enough in advance of them to have had time to change his riding clothes. She could not avoid the rather rueful reflection that if he had been worried by her late arrival, he certainly gave no sign of it.

Melbrooke favored the room's occupants with a remote, yet charming, smile, nodded kindly to Lorraine and crossed over to Lynden, taking her hand for a welcoming kiss that brought an odd little skip in her heartbeat.

The twins sat listening guiltily while Mr. Coniston told Lord Melbrooke the story of their journey, not omitting Lynden's insistence on the inadvisable stop at Jerneaux Abbey. Melbrooke made no comment until Mr. Coniston related that Miss Lorraine had swooned. The poet's expression had hardened and he looked down at Lorraine's fire-flushed cheeks. "As Mr. Coniston couldn't hear your conversation with the highwayman, perhaps you would care to tell me what he said to you?" The words were gently said, but imperative.

Lorraine sent one quick, scared glance to her sister and stared fixedly at the tips of her kid boots.

"He was horrid and . . . familiar," said Lynden vehemently. "Lorraine and I don't want to talk about it! And if you mean to give us a bear-garden jaw about stopping at the abbey or about the imprudence of letting the highwayman carry Lorraine into the coach, let me tell you that Mr. Coniston already has! You may as well know that I am *not* very much in the mood to be lectured any further!" She looked challengingly at her husband.

"Yes," said Melbrooke, with what Lynden regarded as maddening calm. "So I observe. I'm not trying to harry you, Lynden. But I think that even though nothing was taken, we should send a groom into Keswick tomorrow to report what happened. It appears that you and Lorraine were close enough to identify this man. Can you describe him?"

Lorraine was silent a moment. "It . . . it was so dark. And I was distressed at the time. Quite . . . *not* quite myself, you see. I'm afraid I can't recall . . ."

"So," said Melbrooke, studying the pair thoughtfully. "And were you too distressed to recall also, Lynden?"

"Not at all!" replied Lynden, with spirit. "*I* remember him perfectly! He was the most ill-favored ruffian I've ever seen, with huge scars crisscross his face . . ." She faltered to a stop, flustered by Melbrooke's skeptically cocked eyebrow. "Well, that was all I noticed about him. I don't know how to describe people. *I'm* not a poet. That hateful highwayman has already caused us enough trouble today. I don't intend to trouble myself further with him. Lorraine and I," she announced, "will retire for the night!"

It was three-quarters of an hour later that Lynden, robed and bedgowned, padded down the hall to Lorraine's bedroom to bid her good night.

"Rainey, are you awake?" whispered Lynden, tapping on the door. There was no answer, so Lynden gently lifted the latch and pushed open the door.

Lorraine was seated cross-legged on the floor, facing the desultorily burning fire, a hairbrush idle in her lap. She did not look up as Lynden entered, but continued to stare mesmerized as the flame left one ember after another, orange and white tongues of fire disappearing into glowing red coals. Lynden leaned for the poker and stirred the fire into a semblance of life.

After a moment, Lorraine spoke. "Is your bedroom pretty, too?"

"Yes. It's like this one, rather, but done in cream and white. It's a little longer, perhaps; there's a part at one end with a dressing screen. Would you like to look at it?"

"Tomorrow." Lorraine lifted the hairbrush and began to draw it through her unbound hair. "Lynnie . . .?"

"Hmmm?"

"I—well, my bedroom door was opened, and I couldn't help overhearing . . ." Lorraine ventured hesitantly, ". . . Mrs. Coniston say that your bedroom was next to Lord Melbrooke's."

"Yes," said Lynden bleakly. "And there's a connecting door between the rooms."

"I guess you're really married now."

"I guess so."

"It's hard to believe," Lorraine said softly.

"For me also."

They lapsed into sisterly silence. The rhythmic sigh of the brush on Lorraine's hair was puctuated intermittently with the pop of the fire.

"Why didn't you describe the highwayman?" asked Lorraine dreamily.

"Because *you* didn't describe him. Why didn't you?"

"I don't know. But he's not *bad*, Lynden, I'm sure of it. What do you think Lord Melbrooke thinks?"

"Lord knows. Probably that we're both escaped Bedlamites."

What did Lord Melbrooke think? The thought continued to occupy Lynden's mind as, back in her lovely tent bed, she rubbed her feet against the brass warming pan at the foot of the bed. How little she knew of his emotions, his thoughts. They were a frightening mystery to her. She wondered what was behind his cool courtesy toward her. Only detachment? What did he intend for the future? She wondered if there was a basis for friendship in their odd marriage.

How funny she had felt when he kissed her hand downstairs, warm as if she had just blushed, though she had not. She remembered with embarrassment her soft, breathless excitement when he had kissed her that morning in church. She did not know enough about him to guess what it had meant to him: had it been convention, an impulse, or some strange practical joke? Did it mean he found her attractive? How much of a real marriage did he intend to make with her? Suddenly it occurred to her that she did not even know if he intended to consummate their marriage. The idea frightened her. Intimacy with a stranger? She wondered if she had made a strategic blunder by immediately announcing her wish to retire. What would he make of that? Would he think she was eager to be intimate with him? Lynden cringed, her cheeks burning with mortification. Perhaps she had committed an obscure breach of marriage etiquette. Perhaps he would think she was unmaidenly. Hateful, thought Lynden. Hateful! Her most powerful impulse was to present herself before Lord Melbrooke promptly and disabuse his mind of whatever false notions he might have formed of her desire to share his bed. She rolled out of bed, pulled on a quilted cotton robe, and began to pace up and down the rectangle of cream carpeting beside her bed. An ornate Cressent table clock on the mantelpiece chimed eleven times as she heard footsteps in the hall followed by the muffled scrape of a wardrobe drawer in Melbrooke's room.

She walked to the door connecting their rooms but hesitated as she raised her hand to knock. After a moment's thought, she went into the hallway and knocked on Lord Melbrooke's hall door.

Melbrooke's voice answered the knock: "Come in." But whoever he had expected to admit, it was not his teenaged bride, clad in a worn robe with a singular childish print, an expression of high drama on her face.

"Lord Melbrooke, I want you to know that I haven't

been waiting for you to come to my bed!" Lynden announced, and then regretted it immediately, because no sooner had the last words rushed from her lips than she noticed Lord Melbrooke's valet. The man had been to her left, bending to fluff the bedpillows. But he straightened now, his jaw dropped with amazement.

Melbrooke watched as Lynden's cheeks tinctured pink, and pitied her forlorn confusion. What an infant she was.

"You relieve my mind," he said evenly, and then nodded to his valet. "Harley, I won't need you further tonight." His words produced no effect on the hypnotized valet, who gave no sign of even having heard them. "Harley?"

Harley turned reluctantly from Lynden and began to fuss with the bedclothes. "Yes, My Lord, but I must finish turning down the bed. You and Her Ladyship would like to talk, I know. Don't mind me, please."

Melbrooke grinned in appreciation but took the arm of his palpably interested valet and propelled him gently toward the door. "Somehow I think I'll manage without the bed being turned down for one night, Harley. Good night."

"Very well," said Harley, crestfallen. He had nearly reached the door when an idea struck him, and he brightened hopefully. "But perhaps My Lady would like a drink . . .? I would be happy to fetch it!"

"I don't want a drink," said Lynden, recovering her tongue, if not her temper. "And I wish you would go!" Harley left, with a last injured glance to Melbrooke. Lynden watched as the door closed behind him, then turned to Melbrooke and said, with a sniff, "What a nosey little man! Really, you have let your servants get out of hand—they are the most familiar . . ." Suddenly the memory of her aunt's voice came back to her, saying almost the same words she had used to Melbrooke, only the reference had been to her relationship with Peg. "Oh, well, then, never mind about that. Why did your man stare at me so? It was because what I said was dreadful, I suppose!" She finished, looking adorably guilty.

"Not at all," extemporized Melbrooke. "I'm quite sure that Harley paid not the slightest attention to what you said. In truth, he is a man of somewhat conventional habits—very fashion conscious—and he was rather amazed to see that you are wearing a nightgown printed in . . . lollipops, I believe they are? I'm afraid that it may have offended his sense of propriety."

"Well!" said Lynden, impressed and swallowing the story whole. "Not that I'm surprised because Mademoiselle Ambrose says often, oh, and often that servants of fashionable people are far more fastidious about such things than their masters themselves. I couldn't help it, though, because this is my only robe. Great Aunt Penelope gave it to me for my thirteenth birthday, and even my uncle remarked at the time that he thought it a trifle young for a girl my age—though one must take into consideration that he and Aunt Penelope have been at each others' throats since—well, but never mind that. The thing is, the wretched robe wore like armor and Aunt Eleanor would never buy me a new one because *this* one never wore out. You don't have to be afraid I'll embarrass you much longer by going abroad in it," continued Lynden, seriously. "Aunt's ordered Rainey and me new clothes to come from London and . . . But that isn't what I wanted to say! You've got me quite off the subject!"

"That was very bad of me, indeed," agreed Melbrooke, a smile sweetening his plush gray eyes. "Would you like to sit here by the fire? You'll be more comfortable then . . . and I'll try to refrain from distracting you further."

He took her arm and led her across the bedroom. Lynden scanned the room with some unease, taking pains to avoid observing the bed with its ominously dark hardwood headboard. The room was not large, its furnishings drawing their beauty from the fine patina of their burr-grained surfaces. There was an impression of masculine reserve which Lynden identified to herself as Melbrookeness.

Melbrooke set her down gently on a mahogany settee with cabrioles that was placed at a comfortable distance from the fireplace where a shiny brass mesh screen reflected the active reds of the fire. Melbrooke sat opposite her in a stern armchair with a plain, curving crest. Lynden had obviously interrupted him as he was undressing for bed, as no jacket covered his white lawn shirt and his neckcloth had been removed, leaving his collar open at the throat, the skin tawny gold in the firelight. The informality of his attire, now coupled with the potential intimacy of their relationship, made her feel a nervous constraint. It occurred to her, too, that barging into his bedroom on their wedding night might appear to him as the impulsive act of an excitable juvenile, more panicked than poised. And the more she tried to find something adult to say, the more tightly her jaws seemed to be clamped shut, her tongue frozen. She would never be able to speak again and would have to move about with a painted sign draped around her neck: MUTE. If he says "cat got your tongue?" thought Lynden, I shall know without a doubt that I've married a man devoid of sensitivity.

Fortunately Melbrooke was a man of great sensitivity and he sat gazing dreamily into the fire. At last Lynden recovered herself enough to remark, "You misrepresented your house."

"Have I?" he said without looking at her.

"Yes! Because you said it was old-fashioned, which may be so, as it hasn't been recently redecorated, but the furnishings are of the first stare—even *I* know that and I know almost nothing about being first stare! And then there's that picture in your drawing room that Lorraine says is a Rubens . . . or perhaps a Rembrandt, I forget which. You can't pretend that such pictures are found in *common* houses, because if an artist is so famous that I've heard of him—well, there you are. You made this sound like a tiny, cozy sort of place, but it's enormous and elegant," finished Lynden on an accusing note.

"You've been grievously ill-used," said Melbrooke amicably. "Do you think you'll ever be able to trust me again?"

Lynden curled her legs under her and sighed. "You're laughing at me, I can see, but I shall try to be a good sport about it. Still, if your other houses are even more elegant than this, I don't know *how* I shall go on. I don't believe I was cut out to be a great lady. And then there was that dreadful guidebook!"

"Was there? You must tell me about it," Melbrooke said sympathetically.

"Lorraine got it to learn about the Lake District, but it is filled with the fustiest, most erroneous information! It said the Jerneaux Abbey was a noble sight, which is the most bald-faced distortion of the truth I've ever heard and I am sure that the local merchants there about bribed the writer to put that in to increase trade in their area! There was a section on Fern Court, too. It said that many tourists come to look at it in the summer, which I think is the vulgarest thing. Imagine having people come to gape at your house! Oh, and there's worse yet! The guidebook called you 'Poet Supreme'—as though you were some nasty dessert to be served at a ladies' luncheon! I think you ought to sue the publishing company! But what I'd like to know is this: Do you intend to consummate our marriage?"

Her last question came too quickly even for self-disciplined Melbrooke. He looked at her and exclaimed, "What!"—not so much because he had not heard what she had said but because he could not believe that she had really said it.

"I said, do you intend to consummate our marriage?" shouted Lynden and promptly dropped her curly head to her lap and covered it with her hands. There was a short silence before she heard him rise and join her on the settee. She felt the touch of his fingers, light as a

74

dove's feather as they played thoughtfully in her hair.

At last he spoke, his voice soft. "Poor Lynden. Do you know much about it?"

"Not much" was her muffled reply. "Mostly what Mother told me."

His fingers traced a gentle pattern around the edge of her ear. "Your mother? I'll bet it was gruesome."

He was rewarded by a watery giggle. "It was."

Melbrooke stretched one arm around her shoulders and slid his broad hand down her trembling back in a motion that she found both reassuring and unsettling. The caress drew from her, like a poultice will draw poison from a wound, a single, tragic sob, a sob that so overcame her with its intensity that she bent her head further to rest it upon her knees. She remained in this position for a few moments until he was driven to investigate. Softly he slipped one hand underneath her hidden cheek and felt a tear drop from the silken moist lashes onto his waiting palm. With firm, deliberate pressure he lifted her face from her knees to gaze with interest into the brown eyes now luminous with tears. With one forefinger he smoothed the little furrow of anxiety which had formed in her brow. The smoothness was temporary, however, and the anxiety returned as he spoke to her.

"Lynden, tell me this. Do you credit what your mother tells you about other subjects? No, don't look away from me again, little courageous one. You can say these things as well to me as you can looking away. Don't you think it's possible that your mother might have a distorted view?"

"Of course," said Lynden, giving another woebegone sniff. "My mother has distorted views on how many folds to put into a handkerchief! But even taking that into account, I'd rather visit the dentist for a tooth extraction than bustle about under the covers with someone I barely know!"

Melbrooke hid a smile. "Do you think that getting to know me better will moderate your sentiments?"

"Might," said Lynden fairmindedly. "But you'll be angry, I suppose, and humiliated. At least, *that's* what Mother says."

Melbrooke made a very rude recommendation for a manner in which Mother might employ her time and was again rewarded by a giggle, this one considerably less waterlogged and more bell-like than the last.

"I think you've been very kind," said Lynden generously. "I was afraid you wouldn't be. It would be nothing strange if you weren't, being as you were horridly tricked into having to marry me. I wasn't sure, but I thought perhaps you might think that I was a willing part of the plot."

Melbrooke had been cradling Lynden's small chin between his thumb and forefinger; he let his thumb wander to caress the curving line of her jaw, watching the emotions flow through the warm depths of her eyes. "If I had thought that, Lynden, I wouldn't have married you," he murmured.

"You wouldn't have?" inquired Lynden, considerably startled. "Well! But—well, but I don't see how that would have altered the situation any, except for making me the sort of unsavory character that no one in his right mind would want to marry. Not that I doubt I'll be anything but a very bad wife as it is. But—I mean, they forced you to marry me, didn't they?" Lynden tried to read the thoughts behind his impenetrable gray eyes. It was impossible.

Melbrooke shook his head slightly. "My little kite-flying friend, this is 1817, not the Dark Ages, and no one can force anyone to marry, especially not a trio of, forgive me, marplots like your guardians." With an almost imperceptible movement his hand left her cheek, and he leaned back to look at her, his hands resting on the arms of the settee.

"Oh," said Lynden, taken aback. "Then—then why *did* you marry me?"

"I've told you once before, in the library at Downpatrick Hall, though apparently you didn't catch it."

Melbrooke's voice was cool. "Do you remember, Lynden, I said that the world was a censorious place . . . ?"

"Oh, *that,*" returned Lynden, her tone expressing her surprise that he should again raise so trivial a point. "Because people will talk about me? I don't care about that, not a fig!"

"No, I can see that you don't," said Melbrooke grimly. "Very well, Lynden, if you don't care what people say about you, then perhaps you would be more interested in what people say *to* you. Shall we discuss the highwayman who stopped the carriage on your way here? No, I'm not going to quiz you further for a description of him. If you and your sister choose to protect him, that's your affair. I'll not play the tyrant on those grounds." He paused, then continued in an even tone. "How did you describe the highwayman's manner? Horrid and familiar, I believe. You were traveling in my coach; news of our marriage isn't common property yet. Lynden, it doesn't take the wisdom of Solomon to figure out what assumptions the highwayman must have made about your status, and I'm sure he remarked accordingly, which certainly makes understandable your reluctance to repeat his words. I know you won't like to hear this, my fiery friend, but that is but a very small taste of the treatment you would have received had rumor spread you were my discarded mistress."

"I wouldn't care a snap!" said Lynden gamely, her eyes misty with unshed tears.

"No? How little you know about it. Within a sevennight of Lady Marchpane's return to London, half the rakehells in London, bent on making their reputations, would have posted to Yorkshire in hopes of succeeding me in your affections," said Melbrooke bluntly. "With wagers made in every betting book in the city on the outcome. Who would have protected you? Your aunt and uncle? Your mother? They are more likely to have fed you whole to the sharks and washed their hands of the matter. Frankly, I think your aunt would have done so with relish. I don't imagine she had any great fondness for you before I arrived, little one, but after she thought you and I might have an attraction for each other, I think she would have gone to great lengths to see you hurt. I don't know whether you are aware of it, but we have a little history, your aunt and I. She has some bitter feelings toward me, as well."

Lynden's complexion had fluctuated sharply from rose to milky white as she listened to Melbrooke's cool, emotionless voice. "In short," she said wretchedly, "you married me out of pity!"

The hard grayness of his eyes softened to silver. "Not at all." He perjured himself unhesitatingly. "Let us rather say that I offered my support to a new friend in the only way I was able."

"It sounds awfully noble to me," said Lynden doubtfully. "But perhaps you are that way on account of your being a poet?"

"I suppose that would explain it," agreed Melbrooke, keeping a stern command over his attractive features.

"You can't go marrying every woman you want to help, you know," pursued Lynden.

"I shall contrive never to do so again," offered Melbrooke, finding it impossible to contain his smile any longer, even at the risk of offending her. "But I think that you ought to go back to bed now. You've had a very long day. You must be tired."

"I am a little," said Lynden, rising promptly and starting for the door. She had no wish for his polite dismissal to be restated more bluntly. He arose from the settee and opened the door for her. As she passed him, he reached up a hand to touch her cheek, gazing at her reflectively as she paused in the doorway.

"Don't stay awake worrying whether you'll be a 'good' wife," he said softly. "You'll find my expectations can be most elastic."

CHAPTER SIX

The morning was well advanced before Lynden and Lorraine were able to rouse themselves and appear in the morning parlor where they breakfasted together upon fluffy scrambled eggs and fresh oranges. To Lynden's secret and not quite acknowledged disappointment, she learned from Mrs. Coniston that Lord Melbrooke had ridden out earlier to visit several of his tenant farmers. After the twins had eaten, the conscientious Mrs. Coniston was at once ready to conduct them on a tour of the house and outbuildings. Lynden was perfectly ready to peek about in the several old hay barns, laughing at the plump ducks and chickens and searching the lofts for kittens. She spent a pleasant half hour in the stables, cheerfully renewing her acquaintance with the grooms and Mr. Coniston; but as for the scullery house, the bake shack, and the cold cellar—those could wait for another day, couldn't they? Mrs. Coniston reluctantly agreed and took the sisters inside where she showed them the most important rooms, explained that the house had been decorated by His Lordship's grandmother on the event of her marriage, and made a futile attempt to interest Lynden in the more mundane details of household management.

"*You* keep the keys to the linen closet, Mrs. Coniston," insisted Lynden. "I'm sure I'd lose them, and then a merry fix we'd be in with no clean sheets or dry towels. As for showing me inventories of tablecloths and canned jellies and china plate—I haven't the faintest idea what to do with them. In my opinion you ought to go on as you have been; you do a much better job than I could!"

Mrs. Coniston had saved the kitchens until last. Here she introduced Lynden to the French chef and the idea that Lynden, as the lady of the house, was called upon to approve the menu for this evening's supper. Here Lynden was more in her element, and Mrs. Coniston was able to appreciate in full the pitfalls of having a seventeen-year-old mistress. Lynden immediately canceled the vegetable dishes, announcing that she was *not* partial to them; and, on hearing that *le sauté de ris de veau à la provencale* meant sautéed calves' sweetbreads with tomatoes and garlic, informed the already inflamed chef that they would not have it—it sounded nasty! Her pièce de résistance was a demand for the addition of no less than two extra desserts. Lynden found herself bundled in her cloak and mittens and out the door in record time with Mrs. Coniston's fervent wish that the sisters might enjoy a walk on the fellside and her admonition—certain to pass unheeded—that they be sure not to leave the path.

Lorraine observed her sister's air of smug satisfaction as they set off on the northbound pony trail, and said, "I'm sure you're pleased with yourself, Lynnie, but you behaved dreadfully. 'Tis your classic way to avoid doing what you don't like by pretending you'll make a botch of it if you're left the task. What poor Mrs. Coniston must be thinking! You'd be well served for your mischief if you found yourself taken at your word and the chef served no green peas or apricot fritters this evening when you know you are so partial to them!"

"Ho! They won't take my advice for a minute, and you know it!" returned Lynden triumphantly. "Mrs. Coniston and I understand each other better now, I think, and she won't feel she must consult me every time the tea cozy needs an airing."

"No, she won't. But she must think you a very odd sort of female for all that."

"Fiddle Mrs. Coniston! We'll help her sometimes, Raine, but I won't walk around with a heavy jangling knot of keys at my waist like a gaol guard! What do you think of Fern Court?"

"It's a wonderful place, Lynnie! Such an extensive library! The piano in the music room is an exceptionally fine instrument, and the art—why, a walk down any hallway gives one the feeling of being in an elegant gallery." Lynden looked unimpressed as Lorraine continued. "But what I enjoyed most was seeing Lord Melbrooke's study, where Mrs. Coniston says he spends his afternoons writing. Think, Lynnie. That comfortable-looking oak desk is the very surface he used to write his 'Ode to Agamemnon,' his 'Songs from the Northern Shires'! I find it hard to believe that he is actually my brother-in-law. Not a month ago I spent an entire Sunday in my room reading his collected works! You are married to a genius, Lynnie. You should read some of his works, then you could perhaps appreciate that."

"And start to lick the dust from his boots like everyone else, I daresay," exclaimed Lynden. "That's not what I care for! But, Lorraine, look at the view. Did you ever see anything like it?"

They had been following the rugged course of an ancient pony track on its wandering path from the valley, up the side of Loughrigg Fell. The air was mild enough for February, with some sun, though the ground was frozen; the path's crisp, dry surface was pleasant. Their track had traveled north, then northwest, and, looking south, Fern Court was no longer in sight.

A hushed valley bed stretched west, its surface a quilt neatly patched with small woods, square fields, and quiet whitewashed farms resembling tiny embroidered patterns. More mountains rose in dull blues from the horizon, like lumpy pillows heading an enormous, homely bed. Ice-covered Grasmere Lake loomed to the northwest in silent, crystal slumber. A pebbly beach confined the lake. From there a slope, silver with winter-bleached grasses, ramped to where Lorraine and Lynden were standing.

The massive, rounded summit of Loughrigg Fell dominated the east. Lavender and gray tones dappled its sides, and copper swatches appeared where the sun struck. At the remote peak lay a dazzling vein-work of snow. Above it a few secretive, wispy clouds drifted in the soft blueness of the sky.

"The valley is just as Wordsworth described," cried Lorraine. "Do you recall? 'Behold! Beneath our feet, a little lowly vale, a lowly vale and yet uplifted high Among the Mountains . . . Urn-like it was in shape, deep as an Urn; With Rocks Encompassed'!"

"I suppose it is," conceded Lynden, "though how you've managed to commit so much of that stuff to memory will always be a mystery to me! Are you cold or shall we go further?"

Lorraine immediately denied that she could be daunted by such a niggling annoyance as the chilly temperature in so magnificent a surrounding. The pair walked on.

Presently the path split, one branch continuing further along the fellside through a pair of barbed stone columns, the other angling sharply to the right where a level limestone shelf looked toward the valley. Lynden walked onto the stone platform, and in a movement that made Lorraine's stomach pitch, she sat fearlessly on the very edge, dangling her legs over the side.

"Come sit, Raine, you'll be able to see forever!"

Lorraine came cautiously to join her sister, dropping to her knees a safe four feet from the edge and crawling the remainder of the distance. Below her, the cliff dropped a sheer two hundred feet to end on jagged screes. There was a road at the foot, its surface smooth enough for horses, perhaps even a coach-and-four.

Lorraine's gaze followed the road, which led up a long, gentle slope to the walls of . . .

"A castle!" breathed Lorraine. "A real castle!"

The castle stood high on a natural mound, its rear protected by a mammoth wall of rock. In their innocent enthusiasm, the medieval builders of the castle had unsuspectingly added every element to its taciturn form that later generations would come to view as romantic. There was a high stonework curtain, supported at intervals by splendidly crenellated round towers. Pilaster buttresses streamed from the great tower, and, miraculously, a heavy planked drawbridge spanned the fifty feet width of a moat.

" 'A fair pavilion, scarcely to be seen, / That which was all within most richly dight, / That greatest princes living in it mote well delight,' " quoted Lorraine reverently.

"I don't know how that fits," objected Lynden. "After all, we can't tell if it's rich inside, and as for greatest princes delighting in living there—why, I think they'd remodel it right off!"

"Certainly not!" exclaimed Lorraine stoutly. "Now, Lynie, close your eyes and make a picture in your mind. Listen! Can you hear the sweet tones of a mandolin? A knight serenading his lady! And the clatter from belowstairs? A squire cleaning the honorable stains of battle from his master's armor. Now sniff the air. There! Do you smell pure fragrance of the fresh rushes the loyal maidservants spread on the floor?"

"No," said Lynden, with a sly glance at her sister's dreamy countenance. "I do smell something, though, but what . . .? Ah, yes, 'tis—'tis the stench of the moat, where, so cousin Elmo says, the gallant knights found it convenient to . . ."

"Stop!" cried Lorraine, clapping her hands over her ears. "Horridest of sisters! And how Elmo could have been so indelicate as to tell you anything of that sort is . . ." She broke off, staring at a pair of riders who had been coming toward them on the valley road. They had been a featureless, animate couple until now. One was a woman unknown to Lorraine. Beside her rode a gentleman on a particularly beautiful bay stallion with a striking blaze on its forehead. She heard her sister stir besides her.

"Melbrooke!" exclaimed Lynden. She changed position, swinging her legs back from the edge to lay flat beside Lorraine. "Do you think he saw me?"

"No. But does it matter?"

"Of course it matters. Who knows what he'd think? Probably that I was spying on him or something."

The woman, who was almost below them now, was clad in a mink-trimmed riding habit of a particularly lively shade of crimson, an elegant plumed bonnet perched on her ornate curls. The twins were too far away to make out her features, but her style and self-confident bearing bespoke the genteel beauty. The two riders were moving at a walk when the woman suddenly turned her horse to block Melbrooke's path, and his stallion reared slightly and pawed the ground. She rode back to him and pulled her horse beside his so that the horses were facing in opposite directions. As the girls watched, the woman pulled so close that her leg was touching Melbrooke's leg full length, and she leaned over to place her hand on his chest. They were evidently having a conversation, but from the stone platform overlooking the road the twins could hear nothing, not even a murmur. After a moment the pair rode on out of sight.

Lorraine turned her head to look wonderingly at Lynden. "Who was she?"

"*Not* one of his tenant farmers," said Lynden grimly. She rested her chin thoughtfully in her cupped hands. A robin's song drifted incongruously from the twisted branches of a bare mountain ash on the slope nearby.

"Do you think she's from the castle?" asked Lorraine.

"The castle," repeated Lynden slowly. "The castle!

Silvia in the castle! Lorraine, don't you remember? When I told the highwayman that Lord Melbooke and I were married he said something about Silvia waiting for him in her castle. And then he had the audacity to refuse to explain what he meant by it. And she was blonde, too! The highwayman said Melbrooke's mistress was blonde!"

Lorraine sucked in her breath sharply, watching her sister with worried eyes. "Do you feel bad?"

"I—I'm not sure how I feel. I mean, Lord Melbrooke hardly pretended to be in love with me when he asked me to marry him, and everyone says he has a reputation as a rake."

"They say that all gentlemen in the first rank of society have mistresses," said Lorraine in an uncertain attempt at consolation. "I'm sure it doesn't mean anything."

"I suppose not," said Lynden. But somehow the robin's song took on a mournful ring and the placid valley had lost some of its magic.

If Lynden could have decreed her thoughts, she might well have decided to banish all traces of Lord Melbrooke's blonde companion. Unfortunately, it seemed that the more she tried not to think about her, the more vivid were the pictures her wayward imagination drew. Again and again on the walk home she saw the woman place her hand on Melbrooke's chest, in a gesture at once intimate and flirtatious—a lover's gesture.

Well, thought Lynden. Am I to be that most pitied of women, a deceived wife? How clever Aunt Eleanor has been, and how complete was her revenge, to have matched me with a man whose libertine propensities would cause his wife endless humiliation. Drearily, Lynden decided that the only respectable course would be to model her behavior after that of her favorite fictional heroines; to withdraw virtuously into a gentle shell, never betraying a glimpse of her travail. How proud she is, the world would say. How noble! Through all her husband's philandering, no matter how public, she would bear herself with dignity! At least this was Lynden's plan until she was half dressed for supper. Then, as a cheerful young maidservant was laying out her tired gray dinner dress, a new and vastly more appealing scheme danced brazenly into her mind.

"Not that one," she announced in a markedly decisive voice. "Not the gray, Alice. Tonight I'd like something more . . ." She rushed to her cabinet and began searching energetically through her wardrobe. At last she found the very thing: "This!"

"This" proved to be an ankle-length ball dress in a shade of peacock blue, which had an undeniably flattering effect when combined with Lynden's lush black hair and fresh complexion. She had worn it only once; in Yorkshire, at a small evening ball given in honor of one of the twins' particular girl friends on the occasion of her seventeenth birthday and so arranged that the young ladies in the birthday girl's set might attend, even those not yet out. The ball had been a great success, but Lynden, in her peacock blue, had been an even greater one.

The gown's neckline was rather daringly décolleté, especially for one so young as Lynden, which was, of course, one of the reasons she was so particularly pleased with it. Frowning at her reflection in the gilt-framed dressing mirror, Lynden regretted for a moment that she had no necklace to wear—of course her tiny gold heart-shaped locket would not do; but she then decided that perhaps a plainer effect might be more gracious. As an experiment, she asked the maid to pull her hair straight back from her forehead, leaving a few locks to fall from the crown in long Grecian curls and brush teasingly against her shoulders. Yes, she looked older!

So, appropriately costumed, she had only to put herself into the proper mood for her new role—that of the gay, heart-whole sophisticate. It would be better, so much better than her previous plan, not only because she had strong doubts about whether she would be able to maintain an air of virtuous resignation for more than a quarter hour running, but also because she had the uncomfortable feeling that a martyred withdrawal might be misinterpreted by persons of little sensibility as a teenage sulk, or, worse yet, as the sign of a broken heart! Intolerable! Instead, vowed Lynden, she would show The World (and her unfaithful husband) that so little did Melbrooke mean to her that his extramarital affairs were a matter of unconcern to her. No, better— amusement. Lynden dismissed her maid and practiced in her mirror.

"Why, Lady Marchpane," she exclaimed brightly to her own flushing image, waving her hands with great animation. "What ever do you mean? Oh, was my husband seen entering the apartments of Lady X last night? Really, it is *too* naughty of him. Not that I care a penny pepper, of course! Oh, Lady Marchpane, didn't you know? I'm surprised at you. I thought *you* knew everything! You see, Melbrooke and I have an agreement—we each go our own ways. We're quite the modern couple!" She blew the mirror a flippant kiss and went to see if Lorraine was ready to go down to dinner. Lorraine was not. She had gotten involved in reading a new poetry anthology and somehow the minutes had slipped away unheeded. She eyed Lynden's ball gown askance, but said nothing about her tomboyish twin's sudden fancy for fashion and urged her to go along to the dining parlor. She would join Lynden there presently.

The dining parlor was small and formal, its walls miraculously hung in strong blue damask, forming a very pretty background for Lynden's gown. Over the mantel hung a large, Louis XVI tapestry which depicted Venus directing a come-hither look at a handsome mortal Adonis. Adonis was gazing back at her with wary speculation, leaning his broad shoulders against a leafy olive tree. He was tall, slim, and blond —in a word, Melbrooke-like. As Lynden looked at the picture, fantasy replaced Adonis's loincloth with knee-breeches and a formal dinner jacket, and Venus's mantle with a mink-trimmed crimson riding habit and fashionable bonnet, Adonis abandoned his lazy posture against the tree and, walking over to Venus, took a firm grip on her shoulders. Suddenly Lynden was back at the church altar in her wedding gown and Melbrooke was leaning toward her, holding her shoulders. In the tapestry the nineteenth-century Adonis brought his lips slowly to Venus's waiting mouth, and she closed her eyes, pressing closer against his body. Lynden felt again the pressure of Melbrooke's kiss, the gentle intensity, the insistent caress.

Behind her came a soft metallic click as the dining-room door opened. Lynden turned to see who had entered and found herself confronting the cool gray stare of the flesh-and-blood Melbrooke. She gazed back at him numbly; so real had been her fantasy that she was sure anyone of Melbrooke's perception would have seen it as well. Lynden stammered a greeting, blushed furiously, and turned away from him toward the tapestry. To her relief, she found that Venus had again assumed her conventional, classical garb and Adonis had returned to lean languidly against the olive tree.

I meant to appear sophisticated, thought Lynden ruefully. A fine beginning. She raised her hand to her cheek and found it still burning. She heard Melbrooke come beside her.

"Did I startle you? I'm sorry," he said. "I was looking for you, you know. I have something I wanted to give you."

Lynden turned to look suspiciously into the gray eyes. "What?"

He smiled at her, curiosity in his expression. "Nothing so alarming, Lynden. I'm afraid that sometimes my presence seems to exercise a rather unhappy effect on you. May I have your hand?"

Lynden held out her hand, saying nervously, "If you like. Though I've *already* bestowed my hand on you at the church so what you want with it now is more than I . . ." She stared down at her index finger as Melbrooke slid a delicately sparkling ring on it, then carried her small hand to his lips and placed a light kiss on the fingertips. Lynden withdrew her hand with some haste and examined the ring where a flawless, deep-red ruby blazed like a comet amid the brilliant, starlike fire of a dozen diamonds.

"Is it for me?" whispered Lynden.

"Well, yes," admitted Melbrooke. "However, don't let that deter you from telling me if you don't like it, because than I'll get you something else."

Lynden's eyes became as wide and challenging as the stone on her finger. "If I don't like it . . . ? It's the most beautiful thing I've ever seen! But I don't understand! Why have you given it to me?"

Melbrooke sighed. "For some reason, Lynden, you persist in investing my actions with a subtely of motive that I cannot recall ever having possessed. Please try not to look so shocked. There is nothing improper in a husband's giving his wife an engagement ring, though, I admit, it is more generally done before the wedding."

"Oh! An engagement ring?" So, it was only a conventional gesture. Lynden deftly managed to swallow her disappointment that it had not meant something more without really admitting to herself that she had wanted it to mean something more. But if he wanted to play the thoughtful husband, then she would show him that she could play the dutiful wife with the same emotionless ease. She smiled at him in a way that she hoped approximated her Aunt Eleanor's brittle artificiality. "That was very kind of you, My Lord. Indeed, I don't know *why* you should bother, but since you have, why, I thank you."

"Very gracious," he noted, looking a good deal more amused than Lynden would have liked. He went to the small, highly polished dining table and drew out a chair for her. "Is your sister coming down for dinner tonight? Why don't we sit, then, while we're waiting for her. I could ring for wine, if you like. No? Very well." He sat opposite her, the diffuse yellow candlelight lending a luminous, internal sheen to his wheatcolored locks. "How was your morning? Mrs. Coniston told me at breakfast that she was going to show you around Fern Court. You must have been heartily bored."

"Not at all," said Lynden, resting her crossed arms on the table and leaning forward. "Especially I liked your stables and the barns. Do you know we counted over twenty-five kittens in the lofts? And I met your chef as well. French, and very emotional. Oh, and I oversaw the linen closets," said Lynden, thinking to herself that "overlooked" might have been a better word.

"So. Is all in order?"

"Order!" exclaimed Lynden. "Lord, it shared the order of the cosmos, from the alpha of the hand towels to the omega of the bed sheets. One can't help but be impressed, though I wonder, Lord Melbrooke. Are you *really* rich? No, what I mean is, are you really, really rich? Are you rich rich?"

"Lady Melbrooke," he answered smiling. "Vulgar as it may sound, I am really really rich rich."

"I am very glad to know that," confided Lynden. "Not that I care for riches, because I don't. I might as well warn you that my political sympathies are almost Republican, you know, but your house is most extravagantly run, and I thought that in case you weren't really rich rich, I ought to go on record as pointing it out to you." She sat back in her chair with the air of one who has nobly acquitted her duty.

"Is it?" said Melbrooke in a shocked tone, though his lip twitched suspiciously.

"It is," said Lynden firmly. "Though it looks as though you may be laughing at me again. Why, this chandelier for example." She pointed at the glittering piece above the table. "Rock crystal, I believe? Nobody owns rock crystal these days, except for kings and emperors."

"I didn't buy it," he said apologetically. "I inherited it from my grandmother."

"As though that makes it any better," said Lynden severely. "And even if we did give you credit for that, what of the twenty candles for family dining? Ten would have been sufficient, generous even. And you needn't think that you can cozen me into believing they aren't made of myrtle wax. At Downpatrick Hall tallow is burned everywhere except the salon and the guest rooms, of course."

Lord Melbrooke was about to deny the slightest desire to cozen Lynden into believing any falsehoods when Lorraine entered, looking very pretty in her best puce dinner dress. He greeted her and asked her politely if she, too, disliked his chandelier.

"Your chandelier?" she said, dazed. "This one? Dislike it? Oh, no! I should never presume—no, indeed. What has made you think that I might?"

"Nothing," he replied. "But Lynden did say that she thought we were burning too many candles in it."

"Lynnie! That was too bad of you," said Lorraine reproachfully. "There must needs be a lot of light. How could the diners enjoy these beautiful tapestries or this graceful epergne?" She indicated the large silver serving piece set at the table's center.

"The tapestries look very well if one cares for that kind of thing, I suppose," replied Lynden. "But this epergne? Why, one ought rather to dim the lights on its behalf. Observe the side facing me. Look at this small figure! The top half of his body is a human boy's but the bottom half is like a goat's, which I must say casts a particularly unfavorable light upon the character of his mama."

"Even so," said Lorraine firmly, "you ought not to be discussing such a thing at the supper table. 'Tis monstrous improper."

"Well, I *might* point out," said Lynden, "that you are inconsistent. How can it be perfectly proper for the figure to be there *and* be monstrously improper for one to talk about its being there? I might point it out, but I won't. Instead I will very civilly change the subject." She turned to smile very civilly at her husband. "My Lord, Lorraine was quite, quite taken with your study this morning when Mrs. Coniston showed it to us, and was not even put off by the messy pile of papers on your desk. I don't know if I've told you before, but Lorraine is very partial to your poems. In fact, she quotes you all day whenever she has exhausted her store of quotes from Wordsworth and Spenser."

Lorraine shook her head modestly, disclaiming. "But I am a great admirer of yours, Lord Melbrooke. Is your work in progress to be epic poetry?"

He leaned back in his chair, sipping his wine, his eyes shining. "It's possible, though I entertain some rather well-founded fears that it may only turn out to be a very *long* poem. But I am flattered that you quote me in company with Spenser and Wordsworth."

Lorraine was staring at Lynden's hand where it lay cupping the stem of the wine glass. "Lynnie, what have you got on your hand?"

"You don't have to say it as if I had a worm sitting on me. Lord Melbrooke gave it to me," said Lynden, as casually as she was able.

"He did?" said Lorraine, almost forgetting his presence in her excitement. She took Lynden's hand and examined the ruby. "One can only echo the lines of William Dunbar: 'Hail, redolent ruby, rich and radious! / Hail, Mother of God!'"

"Nothing like that," said Lynden, dismayed to find herself blushing. "It's an engagement ring, is it not, Lord Melbrooke?"

He studied her enigmatically. "Yes," returned Melbrooke. "And now that our engagement has been officially announced, perhaps you will be able to bring yourself to call me Justin."

"Fiddle!" said Lynden, and the footman brought in the first course.

CHAPTER SEVEN

Eleven o'clock the next morning found the barn kittens harrying the local rat population, the scullery maid polishing the dining room's epergne, and the twins in the music salon where Lorraine sat before the grand piano trying to master the first movement of Beethoven's Concerto no. 3 in C-minor. Lynden sat at a large desk trying to compose a letter to her mother. For more than twenty minutes she had been frowning over a page inscribed with the words "Dear Mama," but now she stood and joined her sister on the piano bench, pointing to a line on the sheet music before them.

"What does this mean?"

Lorraine stopped playing to look. "That? Where it says *'allegro con brio'*? That means fast with vigor. I seem to have plenty of *brio* but I'm afraid I'm not *allegro* enough yet. Wait, was that a knock on the door? Come in! Oh, Mrs. Coniston, hello!"

"Good morning, ladies," said Mrs. Coniston briskly. "Lord Melbrooke wishes you to come to the drawing room. There is company that His Lordship would like you to meet."

"Why, Mrs. Coniston, there's a note of . . . of something in your voice," said Lynden. "Who is the company? Don't you like them?"

Mrs. Coniston shook her head in unconvincing reproach. "Really, my dear, you are much too quick in your judgments. It's not my place to judge His Lordship's associations!"

"Ah! You *don't* like them!" cried Lynden triumphantly. "I knew it! Are they some of Lord Melbrooke's shocking rakish friends?"

"They are that, in all faith, My Lady, but it would hardly be fitting for me to say so. You ought to meet them and make your own mind up and that's all I've to offer!"

Lynden put her hands on Mrs. Coniston's shoulders and at once surprised and charmed that lady by giving her a quick hug and whispering, "Thanks for the warning. You're a dear, you know."

Thus, when the twins entered the drawing room, it was not the surprise it might have been to see Lynden's husband sitting on the settee next to a spectacular blonde who could only have been yesterday's lady of the crimson riding habit. She was tall, generously endowed where nature had treated Lynden with economy, and the natural blonde hair framing her handsome features had caused countless of her acquaintances mistakenly to seek a similar triumph with the dye bottle. Today she was dressed, not by accident, unless Lynden missed her guess, in a clinging gown of lemon amber that looked exceptionally well against the gold drawing-room walls, imparting the distinct impression that the lady had some special sense of belonging there. She smiled graciously at the twins when they entered, as though she were the hostess putting at ease a pair of not terribly important guests.

Before this moment Lynden had been unaware of even the most minute feelings of ownership connected with Fern Court, its lovely rooms, or its beautiful furnishings. It had been a place owned by Melbrooke and only remotely and accidentally connected with her, and yet, now, Lynden found within her a strong and unsettling desire to drag this usurper in lemon amber from her settee, order a carriage, and bundle the blonde beauty back to her castle.

Lord Melbrooke was at his most reserved and least communicative. He gave Lynden a smile that would have frozen water at twenty paces, and introduced her first to the woman beside him, who, it came as no surprise to Lynden, was called Lady Silvia, and then to the gentleman, her half brother, Lord Crant. Lynden had been too intent on Lady Silvia to notice him, but as he bowed over her hand, she realized that, while Lady Silvia was the more well-favored of the siblings, Lord Crant had much the more interesting aspect. His hair was darker than his half sister's, in fact, almost black; and his face was more sharply set, all angles and plains, with a wide, clever mouth. But none of that mattered, really, when you looked at his eyes which were the oddest and most arresting Lynden had ever seen. Extraordinarily, as though by some whimsical act of God, each of his eyes was a different color; the right one was the deep sky blue of his half sister's eyes and the left was brown. It rather took Lynden aback for a moment —but only for a moment, because the expression in his eyes began to make a greater impression on her than did their unusual color. Crant was smiling—not a friendly, benign smile, but a mocking one, with edges of cruelty.

"But, Justin, she's devastating!" he murmured, with precisely enough irony to rob his words of sincerity without making them an insult. "Small wonder you were tempted at last into matrimony. She's a Venus."

"Indeed," drawled Lady Silvia, coming forward to take the hand that Lynden had jerked from Lord Crant's grasp. "A vestal virgin."

There was enough truth in that to hurt. Lynden colored and wondered how much Lady Silvia knew. Surely Melbrooke wouldn't have told her that their marriage had not been consummated? Lord, if that had been a guess, it had certainly been shrewd!

"Justin shows taste in this as in all things," suggested Crant suavely, directing a sneering smile at his half sister. He returned his gaze to Lynden, made a cursory examination of her slender figure, and said, "Justin tells us you come from Yorkshire," in the same tone as he might have said "Justin tells us you have less brain than a peahen."

"I do come from Yorkshire," said Lynden angrily, and then defended herself as best she could by adding, in a manner that would have driven her ailing Mama into strong hysterics, "and I've never seen anyone before with two different-colored eyes."

Lynden heard her sister gasp at the calculated rudeness of her statement and Lord Melbrooke, at Lynden's side, acquired a sudden and intense interest in plucking a microscopic speck from his elegant coat sleeve, a look of stern concentration on his attractive features.

Meanwhile Lord Crant was rapidly revising his initial impression that Melbrooke's new bride was a shy, banal schoolgirl. Good God, had this infant actually some wit? If she had not, would Melbrooke have married her, no matter what the inducement? Melbrooke was, of course, no fool.

Crant favored Lynden with his ungentle malicious smile. "A trait that passes through my family. But, no, you wouldn't have seen it, because, my dear, Crants never travel in Yorkshire."

"That," replied Lynden tartly, "is the Crants' loss."

"So I am beginning to believe," said Crant.

Two o'clock that same afternoon found the barn kittens catnapping in the lofts, their stomachs full; the scullery maid sitting before a warm kitchen fire gossiping with the chambermaids; and the twins, muffled in scarves and winter bonnets, stomping along the valley road to Grasmere Lake. Of course, there are some that might take issue with the charge that Lorraine's graceful strides could be called stomps, but there could be no other description for Lynden's gait.

"And did you see her face," that young lady was saying, "when she leaned over Melbrooke and positively mewed in that high, sugary voice, 'So, Justin, *dearest,* you stole your little bride from the schoolroom! How very romantic!' "

Lorraine grinned in reminiscence. "I did see her face then, but *that* look was nothing compared with the look she gave you when you said, 'The schoolroom romantic, Lady Silvia? How could you think so? Only because it's been so many years since you were in one.' It was not fair of you, either; you know she can't be a day over twenty-five."

"That I can believe. There was the faintest suspicion of a blemish starting on her chin, though she had tried to cover it over with masking powder."

"There's nothing wrong in that, Lynnie. You've done the same yourself!"

"Used to, but *I* haven't had a blemish in years—or at least since Christmas last when Aunt Sophronia sent us that box of aniseed comfits," said Lynden judiciously. "Thing is, I don't mind that she uses masking powder on her blemishes."

"One almost invisible blemish," corrected Lorraine, who had a penchant for accuracy.

"Oh, very well, I don't mind her using powder on her *one* blemish. I don't even mind her having blemishes . . . in fact, I wish she had more of them! It's that brother of hers, Lord Crant. I hate the way he stares at me, as though he were trying to guess whether I'd tried to improve my figure by stuffing goose feathers into my bodice. And that's one thing at least that I've never done! Especially after last spring when Allison Fitzcrystal took a spill as we rode in her father's meadow and the feathers flew out like thistledown!" Lynden kicked an unoffending stone from her path. "That was lesson enough for me! What did you think of Lord Crant?"

"Of his manner? That he was intelligent, self-confident, and so . . . so very hard. So sardonic! How I admired you for having the nerve to match wits with him, Lyn, but you must be cautious. I feel that he might have been much more cruel had Melbrooke not been by."

"Melbrooke! How can you say so? He stood there

and did nothing, absolutely nothing, to defend me! If I hadn't stuck up for myself, those Crants would have torn me to pieces!"

Lorraine thoughtfully tidied a wisp of hair that had escaped from under her fur-lined bonnet. "I think—well, I was watching Lord Melbrooke this morning, Lynden, and I thing that he was more aware of everything fhat was going on than you know. It might well be that if you hadn't been able to defend yourself, he *would* have protected you." She saw that Lynden looked frankly skeptical. "I suppose it's a moot point. But Lynden, there was something else I noticed about Lord Crant. There was something—Lynden, did he remind you of anyone?"

"Lord, no!" said Lynden, surprised. "Except maybe a snake I saw sliding away in the grass once. No, of course he didn't remind me of anyone. He's the oddest-looking man I've ever seen, particularly with those exotic eyes, although I do think his eyes might have been very attractive, unusual as they are, if only they'd landed in a less grim visage. Listen, you can always think of a fragment of verse for everything. Why don't you think of one for Lady Silvia?"

Lorraine chuckled. "Actually, I have already. It's from 'The Rime of the Ancient Mariner': 'Her lips were red, her looks were free, / Her locks were yellow as gold: / Her skin was as white as leprosy, / The nightmare Life-in-Death was she, / Who thicks man's blood with cold.' "

"Well done!" applauded Lynden. "That's her to a tee, though she doesn't 'thick men's blood with cold,' at least not Melbrooke's."

There was a forlorn note in Lynden's voice that wrenched her sister's heart with pity. They walked together in silence, Lorraine absorbed in serious thought. Finally she spoke. "Lynnie, perhaps I oughtn't to bring it up but—Lynnie, you—you did tell me that you and Lord Melbrooke hadn't . . . oh dear, that your marriage was in name only?"

Lynden stopped dead in path center, put her mittened hands on her waist, and turned around to glare at her twin. "Yes!" she said grimly. "I know I told you that and I hope very much that you are not about to say anything that will make me regret that I did!"

Lorraine stared down at the tips of her leather boots. "Dear, dear Lynnie," she said gently. "You know that I would never want to do anything that would make you regret confiding in me and I don't know very much about being married but . . ." She hesitated, screwing up her courage. "I *feel* that it might not have been right to, um, discourage Lord Melbrooke from claiming his marital rights. I—somehow I seem to have gotten the idea that gentlemen place great importance in such things, and if Lord Melbrooke isn't sharing that . . . that sort of intimacy with you, then perhaps he feels it is quite proper for him to pursue that kind of relationship with someone else? Especially as yours wasn't a love match?"

Lynden stared angrily at her sister, opened her mouth as though to speak, shut it again, then whirled around and marched off. Lorraine watched her in sympathy, deciding to say nothing more; she had already given Lynden quite enough to digest.

They walked under a grove of snow-covered boughs, Lynden's head down, Lorraine looking up at the day. A sharp breeze whistled by, causing a fine mist of snow to settle down their necks and up their sleeves. The snowy mist disappeared when they came into the sunlight; the sun shone with a hint of warmth from a sky that was a deeper blue than its late steely hue. The path widened, and ahead the twins could see the flat, snow-covered surface of frozen Grasmere Lake stretching featureless to the opposite shore, punctuated near the shoreline by spiky dead pond sedge and hare's-tail.

The path dwindled to nothingness at the end of a long spit of land which reached fifty yards into the lake. Here they stopped to rest, their breath making short-lived puffs in the air and streaming away in the stiff breeze. The snow on the lake surface was arranged in long, tiny rippling drifts which reached toward the center of the lake; here and there, in places where the wind was able to course unhindered by shore-bound growth, the exposed ice was gun-metal gray, unscored, and pristine. The sun reflected wildly from the millions of ice and snow crystals, so powerfully that the twins had to shield their eyes from the piercing sight.

"It's so bright, so blank," murmured Lorraine.

"Raine? See there across the bay?" Lynden was pointing with her free hand, not across the lake, but across the bay formed to their left by the spit of land on which they were standing and the curve of the lake's end. "Do you see those weathered gray rocks there on the fellside? One of them moved. And another. Do you see them?"

"The light is probably making you see things," answered Lorraine. "Let me look." She peered where Lynden pointed. "You know what those are? Those are Herdwick sheep!"

"The rugged sheep of the Lake country, suppliers of wool and staple mutton! I know. We read about them in that fusty guidebook of yours. Let's cross over and see what they're like close up. Remember the guidebook says they have white faces and wide, wooly shoulders like lions?"

"Yes, but let's walk across the ice. That sheep track across the rocks looks too rugged to scramble on this afternoon."

They set off across the bay, Lynden in the lead, skating on the soles of her boots. Lorraine trudged behind, absently examining the double track Lynden was impressing on the thin layer of snow. The exposed ice was opaque and dark, spotted with tiny frozen bubbles and an occasional trapped, frozen leaf. The color of the ice slowly lightened as they neared the middle of the little bay; at the center there was a long patch the wind had bared of snow. Lynden slid across it, whooping gleefully. Lorraine, walking behind, noticed that she was able to see down through the ice to the bottom of the lake, where green waterweeds waved in emerald spirals. It seemed to Lorraine that she was privileged to see a hidden underwater world through a thin viewing glass.

How thin the viewing glass proved to be! As she watched, Lorraine noted hundreds of tiny cracks radiating outward from her feet, and before she had a chance to move, she cried out in pain as the icy water rushed to cover her ankles; then, with a dull crack, the ice finished its division into three separate islands, and she fell among them. She screamed as the frigid water clamped ruthlessly about her.

"Lorraine, grab my scarf!" Lynden was coming back across the ice, unwrapping her scarf from her neck; the ice cracked threateningly under her feet as she drew near Lorraine, forcing her retreat, the short scarf dangling uselessly from her hand.

"Lynnie! Go back toward shore," said Lorraine hoarsely, trying to tread water. "It's no good, you'll fall in, too. You've got to go for help . . . Cottages back up the path."

Lynden's eyes were frightened and desperate as she cast about for an aid. There was a thick, fallen tree limb, thinly glazed with ice, at the frozen edge of the water; Lynden yanked it free and returned. "I'll push this limb to you; try and put your arms around it and I'll pull you out." She pushed the end of the limb to Lorraine, who tried futilely to follow her sister's instruction.

"I don't know if I can . . . so cold. There." Lorraine succeeded in hooking one arm around the limb. Lynden strained on the other end, fruitlessly.

"I . . . can't lift you, Lorraine . . . too heavy."

"Go, Lynden, now . . ."

"Yes, yes, I will. But you must hook your elbows over the limb on either side—it will hold you up." Lynden's voice was breathless with exertion and fear. "I'm going now, Lorraine. Please, please hold on." And she was gone, flying along the shore, over the rocky sheep path, her skirts billowing.

Lorraine was alone. The sky loomed overhead like an inverted blue bowl, pressing down upon her, suffocating her; her limbs were a great weight. There were no sounds other than the crisp, slow slosh of the thick water. Time slowed, stopped, then started again. A tall distant figure was standing on the shore, and a male voice came to her, booming and unintelligible. She could not follow his movements. If he was moving rapidly, agonizingly slowly, or wavering in and out of reality, Lorraine could not tell. Suddenly, a broad, flat, lightning-split tree trunk was sliding ominously toward her, a slithering dark mass, and the figure, man or spirit, was leaning cautiously, stretching an arm low over the surface of the ice, his hand reaching closer, across an eternity of time and an infinity of space . . .

As she was dragged out of the water, Lorraine felt the savage bite of the wind on her soaked skin and clothing, and the sharp, stinging suck of her icy skirts. She felt heavy and sick and aching, then light and numb. She looked up, blinking her ice-encrusted eyelashes, trying to focus on the face of her rescuer. She saw only a bright blur, a harsh white light—and then nothing.

Lorraine's seventeen years had been filled with books, music, and Lynden. There had been no sweethearts, no stolen kisses, no flirtations. Thus, when she awoke in a man's arms, it was the first time she had ever done so.

But it was long after light had pierced the darkness before she was aware of that. For a while she knew only, and in a dim way, that she was being moved, lifted, turned, rubbed, and comforted. At last she was lying still, with a gentle arm encircling her waist. Someone was stroking a towel through her damp hair and from time to time the hand would leave her waist to tuck a coarse woolen blanket closer around her. There was a fire; she could hear its strong, snapping voice and she lay near it, quiet, content.

Gradually the deep, aching coldness began to leave her body, and as her well-being returned, so did her curiosity. Lorraine opened her eyes. Immediately she was taken by the shoulders and lowered carefully, until her head rested on a rag-stuffed pillow. Above her, bathed in the soft, rusty firelight, she saw the wonderfully chiseled features of her highwayman, his lips curved in a light, caressing smile.

"Welcome back from the underworld, darling," he said. "But tell me, is your life always this eventful?"

"N—no. Was it you who pulled me from the water?"

He shrugged. "I thought it was a touch cold for lake bathing, and your white little teeth were chattering so hard that I couldn't get your opinion. Was it presumptuous of me? I'll throw you back in, if you like. Lie peacefully, child, I want to get you something hot to drink."

He rose and left her, walking to the wide hearth in long, graceful strides. Lorraine lifted her head to examine her surroundings. Her overwhelming impression was of dark, fragrant wood everywhere; it seemed that she was in a small cabin. A square, frost-whorled window in the wall opposite the hearth let in a cold, gray light which contrasted with the warm blue-and-yellow of the fire. As her eyes adjusted to the light, she considered the other features of the room: a beamed ceiling, a leather-strapped trunk in the corner, a round cricket table on which were scattered a few books, a simple oak bed with hay mattress, and a country-copy Hepplewhite chair in elm with a brace of pistols slung over one arm. The pistols seemed an incongruous detail, though she was aware of her rescuer's profession.

The man ladled liquid into a cup from an iron pot hung over the fire and carried it to her, lifting her so she might drink comfortably.

Lorraine sniffed it uncertainly, and looked up at him. "What's in it?"

"Better that I don't tell you, you might not drink it." He put the cup to her lips and tilted it, and she drank. "No, don't stop. Have some more."

She took two more swallows, and he set the cup down. Lorraine tried to smile.

" 'Tis very tasty," she said. "I—I'd like to thank you."

He laid her back on the pile of blankets. "No need. Actually, I bring a different lady home every night, feed her some broth, and if she doesn't expire in five minutes, I know it's safe to eat myself. Is the blanket scratchy against your legs? I could wrap a sheet around you."

"My legs? No, the blanket is soft but—oh, why is it that . . . Sir, are my clothes off me?" she asked plaintively.

"Yes, but they haven't strayed far. See, princess, they're on the hearth there, drying rapidly, not a mite worse for their adventure. Except your boots—the leather's ruined, I'm afraid. Why, poor darling, don't look so distressed. What's one pair of boots, after all?"

"It isn't the boots," whispered Lorraine with horror, her face beginning to sting with color. "It was—did you—oh, could *you* have removed my clothing?"

The highwayman ran a hand through his hair. "I'm afraid so. My lady's maid is on vacation. And since I've begun confessing, I suppose I'd better admit that I molested you while you were unconscious. Too bad you weren't awake to enjoy it, but I thought it would be just the thing to warm you up."

Never in her young life had Lorraine been the recipient of any remark quite like this one. She stared at him for a mortified, panicked moment and then said, "You haven't really, have you?"

"No, child, my tastes don't run in that direction, I'm afraid, not that you don't look damnably seductive there in my shirt that's seven sizes too big for you." He put a lazy finger under her chin and traced her lips with his thumb. "But now that you're awake and thawed, perhaps you might like to try . . ."

"No! Oh, please, no!" Lorraine interrupted him hastily.

He removed his hand and patted her cheek kindly. "No's enough, sweeting, you don't have to beg me. You haven't been around much, have you?"

"I suppose not," she said shyly, "not in the sense you mean. Well, I haven't in any sense, really. And I'm sorry, truly sorry, to have seemed so . . . mistrustful of you. I could see that you didn't like it at all. But it wasn't that. You misunderstood. It overset me to think what you must have seen."

"What I must have seen? Of all the prissy notions! You were comatose from the cold, child. Ought I to have left you in wet garments?" He stopped, a thought occurring to him. "Have you ever been with a man before? No? I suppose that accounts for it. Listen, princess, the last thing you need to worry about is letting anyone see your body. Believe me, I've seen plenty, but nothing ever that compares with yours." He watched her closely, his sensitive mouth gathering into a grin. "What a blush! If nothing else, I've succeeded in raising your body temperature. That must be good for you." He lifted her head, brought the cup again to her lips, and ruthlessly fed her the remaining broth.

As he helped her settle back once more against the pillow, it occurred to Lorraine that to be rescued from peril by an outlaw, and to lie upon his cottage floor exchanging risqué riposte, was an adventure that might, more conformably, have befallen her sister Lynden. She was about to remark so to the highwayman when a frightening thought intruded.

"Lynden," she said, trying weakly to sit. "Lynden will come back to help me and I won't be there! She'll think I've drowned! Oh, please, I must dress at once and go to her. She'll be in agony!"

He shook his head and sat back on his heels. "I've

thought of that, so I pulled the branch you were holding back to the bank, with your scarf wrapped around it and your bonnet perched on the end of a twig. Come to think of it, I wrote 'safe' in the snow there, as well. She'll put it together. If you'll close your eyes for another half hour, you'll feel much stronger and your clothes will be dry. I'll ride you home on my mare then, if you like."

Warm before the fire, Lorraine shut her eyes and wished that she was Lynden. Then, surely, she would have had the courage to talk to him, to ask him the many questions that were shining in her mind. His beautiful, lilting accent—was he indeed Irish? What need forced him to cover one eye with a patch? And why must he pursue his living as a criminal? His speech and manner were that of an educated man. She nerved herself to ask one small, experimental question.

"From what was the broth made?"

The highwayman was sitting in the elm chair, tipped back against the wall, sipping broth from a chipped, handleless cup. He smiled into Lorraine's eyes over the cup's rim and said, "Polecat."

CHAPTER EIGHT

"Polecat?" repeated Lynden, several hours later as the twins sat together in Lorraine's pretty bedroom at Fern Court. "I wonder that you weren't poisoned!"

"After he told me, there was a moment or two when I felt a trifle weak inside," confessed Lorraine. "But I didn't want to be such a Poor Thing—which I could tell he was *already* thinking I was. So I mastered myself."

"And after that?" asked Lynden eagerly.

"He told me to be still again. After a bit, he said he was going out to saddle his mare and that I should dress. I did, and when he returned, he wrapped me in the blanket. He set me in front of him on his horse."

"That's dandy!" cried Lynden. "Did you talk on the way home?"

"No. But, Lynden, there was the murmur of the wind, the sparkle of the stars . . . and the warmth and strength of his arms around me."

"Rainey, it's the oddest thing, isn't it? Here am I, the ill-behaved, wild twin making the most envied match of the year, while you, the good, quiet one, have fallen in love with an outlaw!"

"I'm not in love with him," protested Lorraine, perhaps without the degree of conviction she would have wished. "Indeed, I hope I'm not so impressionable and flighty as to fall in love with any gentleman on so brief an acquaintance."

"No," agreed Lynden. "But if you'd been alone with him for another quarter hour, Lord knows what would have come of it. Did he say anything before he set you down from the horse?"

Lorraine stretched out her palms toward the fire. "I asked him if I might see him again, and he said it wouldn't be right, he liked me too well to see me in the kind of trouble *that* could cause."

"Didn't you argue?"

Lorraine crossed her arms, hugging her waist. "No, I was afraid he would think it much too coming and you know I'm not much of a hand at it, anyway. I thanked him again for rescuing me, but he'd have none of it, and said that from what he'd seen of *you,* Lynden, you'd have had me out of the ice in no time, anyway. Oh, then he frowned, rather, and said that it might be better if I wasn't to tell anyone that he'd taken my clothes off, because if he knew anything about people, ten to one they'd be making something of it that it wasn't."

"If that isn't just like a man!" said Lynden in disgust. "He tells you to fib, but does he help plan a convincing lie? Not a bit! And as a result, you walk into the house and announce you were saved by a tinker and his wife!"

"I thought it was clever," objected Lorraine, rather hurt. "After all, I could hardly say it was one of the local farmers. Mrs. Coniston knows everyone about and she'd be bound to figure out the cheat. Besides, what if she sent them a fruit basket in thanks and they denied it? Lynnie, you know I couldn't say that it was the highwayman."

"No," agreed her sister. "But you might as well have, if you were going to make up something as flimsy as a tinker! Only imagine how it looked. I was standing by the window with Mrs. Coniston, hoping you'd be home soon. After I'd found your bonnet and scarf and the word 'safe' written in the snow, I assumed you'd been taken to someone's home to dry off—but, anyway, there we stood by the window when Melbrooke walked in. He'd just come back from riding. They had told him in the stables about your accident, and he took my hand in the kindest way and said he was very sorry it had happened."

"It was good of him to be so concerned!" said Lorraine with sincerity.

"Daresay it was, but I wished him at Jericho not thirty seconds later. Consider, you arrived slung over the saddle front of a young gallant like fair Ellen Netherby and then trip happily into the house, to announce you've been rescued by a tinker and his wife! Not only was there not a whiff of a wife, but tinkers *don't* ride away into the moonlight with their capes flying out behind them; nor do they ride thoroughbreds, carry holstered pistols over their shoulders, or salute ladies with their hats in farewell. Nor do ladies throw them kisses in reply!"

"Oh, dear," said Lorraine in a chastened tone. "I don't know what possessed me. I would never have done it if I'd known anyone was watching."

Lynden wiggled her bare toes in the silky plush of the carpet. "Very likely not, but in the meantime here's Melbrooke supposing us a pair of lunatics! Of course, he didn't say a word of doubt about your story, but he had that look—I know it now—the look that says if you want to pretend this is the truth, then I'll pretend it's the truth but we both know it's a lie."

On the bedside table, a half-empty teapot in Chinese blue and white peeked seductively from under its quilted tea cozy, tempting Lorraine to wander over and pour herself a scant cup. A small worried pucker disturbed Lorraine's smooth brow as she stirred in sugar with a dainty silver spoon.

"Lynnie, perhaps we've been wrong about this. Perhaps we should have confided everything to Lord Melbrooke. Deception is such a—a squalid and cowardly business, and, really, isn't that what we're doing, when you think of it?"

"I suppose it is," said Lynden. "But you take much

too dim a view of deception. According to Uncle Monroe, politicians and diplomats engage in it constantly, and those are quite up-in-the-world persons so it can't be completely without merit."

Lorraine perched on the edge of her bed, balancing the teacup on her knees. "This is different, Lyn. Lord Melbrooke is your husband. What of your vows?"

"My vows, my vows! What of them? If you'll recall, I agreed to love, honor, and obey, not to tell the truth, the whole truth, and nothing but the truth!"

"No, but deceiving Lord Melbrooke is hardly showing him love and honor!" reproved Lorraine gently. "And I'm covered with shame to think that I was the first to tell Lord Melbrooke an untruth and you were forced to back me! Lynnie, I've been wrong! Let us at once repair to Lord Melbrooke's library and divulge all, throwing ourselves on his mercy."

"Of all the grandiose, play-acting, fidgety ways to talk! Lorraine, what has gotten into you?" exclaimed Lynden. "If we tell Melbrooke the truth, then chances are that within the clock's tick he'll be out, rousing the sheriff to arrest your highwayman! You can't tell the whole story without revealing that you know what the highwayman looks like and have a fair idea where he lives, can you? They'd hang him, I'm sure, and you wouldn't like that to happen to . . . Oh, it puts me off to forever be calling him the highwayman. What's his name, Raine?"

"I don't know. He didn't tell me," Lorraine said and then burst into tears.

Lynden came hastily to sit beside her twin, putting an arm about her trembling shoulders with a suddenness and protective ferocity that made Lorraine's precariously balanced teacup rattle a threat.

"There, you shan't cry, Rainey, you shan't! Dearest of sisters! Don't think about Melbrooke, not for a moment. So what's a lie? It's in a good cause, isn't it?" Lynden leaped to her feet, her hands clasped in excitement. "I have it, Raine, I have it! A good cause! That's what it is!" She sat down quickly again and the teacup rolled to the floor.

"Lynnie, the tea!" cried Lorraine.

"Never mind it, you oughtn't to have been soaking down tea in a crisis, anyway. Besides, this is my house, isn't it, and if I choose to spill and break teacups in it, I've a right, haven't I? But never mind that! I have a plan! Lorraine, do you recall the Ladies' Benevolent Society back home that the vicar's wife always pushed Aunt Eleanor to patronize? The one that made the squire's footman marry our parlor maid after he got her in an interesting condition? Well, Lorraine, you and I could form our own Ladies' Benevolent Society and induce the highwayman to reform his criminal ways!"

"Why, Lynnie! But . . . but that was quite a different thing," said Lorraine, rather aghast at the idea. "And he may not like to be reformed!"

"They never do," said Lynden knowingly.

"No, perhaps not," agreed Lorraine. She dampened her handkerchief in the water basin and kneeled to dab at the tea spot in the rug. Then she gathered the shards of the teacup in her palm. "Lynnie . . . I wonder, did you happen to *notice* anything particular about the highwayman? In the way he carried himself? I mean, in his manner?"

"Of course," said Lynden promptly. "He spoke like a gentleman. At least he spoke in the *way* of a gentleman. The manners of a gentleman and the mouth of a . . . oh well, I know what you mean. But of course I noticed it. Anyone would have. Why?" Then her eyes sparkled excitedly. "Ah, yes! I take your meaning. What if he was not just aping the manners of a gentleman, but was really one such fallen on hard times?"

"It wasn't just apery, it was his natural manner," said Lorraine seriously. "Lynden, I think—no, I can't say it, 'twill sound so foolish."

"Don't mind that, Rainey. Heaven knows, and so do

you, that I've been the world's first fool more times than the bunny's sought clover. Go on."

"All right. Don't laugh. I knew today who it was that Lord Crant reminded me of. He looks quite, quite —bizarre though it sounds—like the highwayman!"

Lynden placed an open palm on her cheek. "Marry come up, Rainey, you're right!" She sprang up from the bed, poured two cups of cold tea, handed one to Lorraine, and raised her cup in a solemn toast. "To the Ladies' Benevolent Society for the Reformation of Highwaymen!"

Lorraine's misadventure was to have its logical consequence. By the next morning she had developed all the symptoms of a severe head cold and sore throat. Mrs. Coniston, a medical conservative, was fearful that it might turn putrid and prescribed an exhausting regimen of mustard foot baths, teas of potherbs with lemon, and bed rest. When Lorraine was awake, the sisters sat together on her bed plotting schemes for the benefit of the highwayman that, had he been privileged to hear them, would have both touched and alarmed that young man. Lynden took her meals with Lorraine, as well, sending a message through Mrs. Coniston to Lord Melbrooke that she wished to keep the invalid company, admitting only in the most secret corner of her heart that this noble resolve was partly based on shyness at dining tête-à-tête with her elegant husband. As a result, Lynden saw nothing of him over the next week, save a few short encounters in the hallway. If Melbrooke disliked this arrangement, he gave no indication, but continued on his even, independent path, dividing his time, as close as Lynden could tell, between his writing and riding out-of-doors. Visiting his mistress, thought Lynden, as she watched him cantering across the rocky valley floor on his stallion with its long flowing mane and tail.

One such afternoon Lorraine was napping so Lynden, rarely at a loss for occupation, pulled a traveling chess set from her drawer and retired to the stables, where she most improperly engaged in an absorbing attempt to teach the younger groom chess. She spent several happy hours letting her pupil beat her at no less than three games and left only when he was called off by Mr. Coniston to change the bedding of the carriage horses.

Lynden drifted back to her bedroom and stowed her chess set. She then noticed that the connecting door to Lord Melbrooke's bedroom had been left open, apparently an accident by one of the chambermaids.

Lynden walked over, resolved to close the door, but instead found herself standing still, her hand on the doorknob, gazing into her husband's room. She had not seen it since her first night at Fern Court, and then had hardly noticed it; she had been too full of the day's excitement to draw more than an impression of neatness and understated beauty. The furnishings were of richly grained hardwood with brass inlay and ornaments, the upholstery thick, matte-surfaced, and deep green. Beside the bed a dwarf bookcase sat beneath an exquisite Cotman watercolor landscape. Lynden came closer to study the painting. She recognized its subject as a bridge not far from Downpatrick Hall in Yorkshire. Leaning down, she tried to read the titles of the books in the bookcase but soon gave up, finding most of them to be in French or Latin.

The massive, silent rectangle of Melbrooke's bed lurked to Lynden's right, seeming to inspect her alien, feminine presence in its domain. It was a sober, puritanical furnishing, the Brazilian rosewood frame cut at the head in high unpainted relief with the Melbrooke coat of arms. A stickler for irreverence, Lynden crawled toward the middle of the great bed and poked her finger insultingly into the mouth of a ferocious dragon quartered within the shield. As she withdrew her finger, she saw with dismay that she had left a prominent fingerprint to mar the immaculate, waxy polish. Never mind, she thought, and tried to repair the damage with a corner of her skirt, but merely succeeded in increasing the damage, rubbing off more of the delicately applied finish. The effort left Lynden feeling curiously incompetent and cross, so she rolled over on her back and glared at the frugal plasterwork ceiling. A fine unpretentious view, she felt, and wondered how it would have appeared to her had she shared this bed with Melbrooke. Would the ceiling have hung low over her, oppressive and eerie, or would it have drifted toward heaven, shining and celestial like a silk altar-hanging? And the act. Would it have been painful and shocking as her mother had hinted, or would it have been like his kiss in the chapel, only longer and more intense?

A rift in the clouds allowed a broad beam of winter sunlight to pass, and a golden layer of light from the high window appeared on the middle of the bed. Lynden rolled into the amber rectangle, enjoying the shimmer it imparted to her butter-colored bombazine day dress and the penetrating warmth to her winter-chilled muscles. She stretched like a sleepy puppy, her arms generously outflung.

There was a soft click and a swish as the door opened, and Lord Melbrooke entered the room, staring down at his pretty, dark-haired wife and registering no less surprise than she did herself.

"Lynden, for God's sake, don't move," he said, and Lynden, convinced by his tone that a single movement would jeopardize her welfare, if not her life, lay petrified. "Close your eyes," he ordered, and she obeyed.

Lynden felt the bed give to each side of her and then came the touch of his lips on hers. The suddenness with which the kiss was offered caused an inadvertent response within her, and she shivered with soft surprise. His hands were on her back, lifting her to him, fitting her body to his as he placed firm, burning kisses on her neck. Her lips fell open as she drew in a deep, sighing breath, and he covered them again with his own, filling her with a deep, penetrating kiss, a gentle, probing exploration of her silkiness, her moistness. She shivered again, involuntarily, and he spoke her name, bringing a hand up to steady her, his fingertips brushing cool against the fevered skin on her cheekbone. His mouth followed the path of his fingers, and then kissed her eyelids. Steady lips brushed against her forehead; she felt his breath in her curls, and the tender caress of his hand was on her back, on her shoulder. Lynden's heart beat painfully under his hand's gentle pressure at the quiet slope of her breast, and her body began to feel confined, swelling and ripe, closed in by the butter-colored gown, as though the dress would flame and dissolve under the heat and touch of his hands.

Frightened, she pushed against his chest. "Don't! I— I don't like it." She lied.

He released her immediately and sat back to watch her trembling and sparkling beneath him, like a proud, pouting child who has refused dessert and at once repents and defends her gesture.

"I wasn't trying to torture you," he said softly.

"I know that." Lynden turned her burning cheek to the pillow.

"I'm relieved," he answered drily. "Your response left me in some doubt."

Lynden turned back to make a shy study of the calm gray eyes, unsure whether to convict him of irony. With his experience perhaps he was only too well able to determine her response, to see through the shallow surface of her resistance. Then he might think her easy, as women were usually easy for him, so the rumors said. And he had his mistress, the deep-bosomed, catty Lady Silvia. Must he come to kiss and confuse Lynden, too? She tried to stoke the angry fires within her but their response was sluggish and unenthusiastic. What would have happened if she had not pushed him away?

"You didn't like my—well, my response?" questioned Lynden cautiously. Let him reveal some of himself for a change.

Melbrooke shrugged slightly. "It isn't for me to like or not to like, Lynden. It only *is*. I'm sympathetic, if that's what you want to know. It must be very hard to spend seventeen years as a child and then overnight be expected to turn into a woman."

The corners of Lynden's eyes tilted reproachfully. She was not sure that he was not accusing her of immaturity. "I suppose you think we know each other better now," she said, attempting a sarcastic tone.

He smiled. "I suppose you think we don't. All right. How does your sister feel today?"

Nonplussed by the sudden change of subject, Lynden said, "Lorraine?" and then thought, That was dumb, as though I have several sisters. "She's quite well, and Mrs. Coniston says that we might go out tomorrow, of which we are glad! At least I'm very glad," she amended. "Lorraine is not as committed to the out-of-doors as I am."

Melbrooke placed his hand in the shaft of sunlight, examining it. "I hope this doesn't make me sound too much like your Uncle Monroe, Lynden, but I wish both of you will develop a commitment to stay off the ice. There may not be another conveniently placed peddler the next time one of you takes the plunge."

"It wasn't a peddler," protested Lynden, chewing her lip. "It was a . . ." For one sick moment she forgot what Lorraine had said he was, then it came back to her. "Oh, yes, it was a tinker."

"A tinker," Melbrooke repeated dutifully. "And his wife. But tell me, do you think I believe that?" he asked on a note of passive inquiry.

Able to make nothing of his expression, Lynden asked him, "What will happen if you don't believe it?"

"I'll pretend I do until you confide in me—I hope, shortly. Frankly, it's a strain on my powers of dissimulation, being such a—forgive me—such a poor story."

"Pooh!" said Lynden, deciding quickly that aggressive dishonesty and spirited deceit were the only ways to combat Melbrooke's rather disarming openness. She had the feeling that if she didn't set him back sharply, he would have the truth from her in two minutes flat.

"It isn't a poor story. It's a fine story! Oh! What I mean is, it's the truth! All tinkers needn't look the same, need they? Some might be young and—and quite dashing! And I'm sorry if I made you angry by pushing you away just now, but really, *you* shouldn't have tricked me—I mean, to say 'hold still' like that as though some huge hairy spider were about to hop on my nose. It was too bad of you, and it was *the only reason* that I didn't get up straight away when you came into the room."

He placed his fingers lightly, lightly on the side of her neck. "I'm sure you would have, and it would have been a pity because, you see, I wanted to kiss you. It's not an unnatural desire, little one, no matter what you might think." His fingers touched her cheek once more, and he stood and held out his hand to her, as if to help her up. "I hope now that once you've found your way into my room that you will make it a habit to come."

Not very likely, thought Lynden, allowing him to help her from the bed. She wandered toward the door to her bedroom behind Melbrooke, who turned the doorknob and pushed the door open for her. Instead of leaving, however, Lynden paused in the threshold, crossed her hands behind her back, and leaned against the door frame.

"Umm . . . Lord Melbrooke?"

"Yes, Lady Melbrooke?"

"Oh, very well, then—*Justin*. I was wondering about Lord Crant . . ."

The shuttered gray eyes scanned her. "You wouldn't be the first. You have a specific question, I take it?"

"Yes," said Lynden, wishing it was not his habit to make such intimidating withdrawals. "I wondered if he had any children."

His eyes lightened for a moment, as though her question had surprised him. "Children? No, he's never been married."

"Not married? Oh. But what about illegitimate ones?" asked Lynden with studied casualness, hoping

118

he would attribute the high color in her cheeks to his recent kisses.

"I don't know, Lynden, that's not the kind of thing I discuss with other men. It's possible." He took her chin between his fingers and tilted her face slowly into his cool gaze. "But I'm curious. What's made you interested in that?"

"Nothing! That is . . . oh, nothing. He seems like the type, perhaps," Lynden faltered nervously.

"Very perceptive. He's no companion for anyone your age, but I don't have to tell you that, do I?"

"Certainly not!" said Lynden, slipping out of his hold and into her room. "*I'm* not stupid enough to become enamoured of a Crant!"

CHAPTER NINE

The southerly breezes carried a thaw that kissed the fellside with the craft of a coaxing lover and melted the snow, enticing its moisture into the silver air or luring it to swell the mountain becks until they overflowed their mossy banks and roared helplessly under the spinning weight of white water. The clouds had dropped to listen, floating in dense blue bunches around the fell peaks, where ice still glittered in the ebony shadows.

A golden eagle shrieked and wheeled in the gray sky, a swift amber spot against the clouds, while far below, two small figures toiled their way up the ancient peat trod that climbed the fellside from the shores of Grasmere Lake. The winter frost had lifted the trod's surface and now its softening caused it to give and shiver underfoot. The wet squelch of the steps mingled with feminine voices, rising together through the active air.

"I can't agree, Lyn," said one voice. "I think his telling you that he didn't believe in the peddler bespeaks a nature of good breeding and gentlemanly candidness. It's *our* behavior that's stealthy and . . . What was the other thing you said?"

"Trickish," replied Lynden shortly. "Are you sure we are going right, Lorraine? We're halfway to the tip peaks and there's no sign yet of anything resembling a highwayman's get-safe shack."

"It was different by moonlight," admitted Lorraine, tramping resolutely, if a trifle breathlessly, beside her sister. "But I did mark the way as carefully as I could in my mind. If only I could find that row of firs . . ."

The trod grew thinner and less distinct as it roped toward the high cliffs through a twisting complex of jagged ridges and desolate mountain passes. It maintained a curiously smooth and level course the meanwhile; even at its narrowest it was wide enough for a careful horseman to make his way up or down it at a walk. They were approaching a flooding brook, its deep rustling moan booming louder as the track ran a shallow upgrade, then made a sharp, right-angled jog.

The twins had arrived at a highland plateau, a dwarf crater trembling with the thundering bawl of a steep waterfall smashing its churning burden of thaw into a deep foaming tarn. The tarn drained violently into a chilly beck that glistened down the fellside like a strand of diamonds. A magnificent red stag had been drinking the sweet aerated brook water on the far side of the plateau, but he soon sensed the human presence and, trumpeting his disapproval, turned to ramble down a secret mountain trail.

"This way!" Lorraine cupped her palms and shouted to help her words reach Lynden over the water's crash. "Follow me!"

At its narrowest reach, the beck was four feet wide, spanned haphazardly by five flat, slate-gray boulders submerged below a translucent film of frigid water. The footing was further complicated by dark patterns of slippery lichen inhabiting the stepping-stones, causing the girls to balance with care, attentive to the possibility that more than just the hems of their skirts might be dampened.

Some fifty feet beyond the beck was a tall plantation of silver firs, stretched across the plateau curve, dark green and white needles resting on a thick undergrowth of black thorn and hazel. Only at one point was the underbrush partially cleared and it was through this passage that Lorraine led her sister, both girls exclaiming as large, glassy drops of melted snow fell from the tips of needles and branches to pelt frigidly on the backs of their necks. After a few more steps they came out in a snug platter of open land, about a half acre surrounded by trees and backed and partially shaded by an escarpment that concealed the tiny hanging valley from above. Tall dried shards of purple moor grass provided a scratchy, rasping floor for the small plateau, and off to the west side of the clearing, a lone oak stood, several winter-withered russet leaves still clinging modestly to its naked branches. A bright green growth of holly wound up the trunk, the scarlet berries providing an audacious accent to the umber scene.

The mountain cabin where the highwayman had sheltered and dried Lorraine stood in the center of the cleared half acre. The rough-hewn walls of the squat, boxy little structure begged for a coat of whitewash; one shutter had come loose from its hook and swung gently in the southerly breeze.

Lynden gave a boyish whistle. "This is it? I'm nutty about it already! If only we'd had it in Yorkshire—wouldn't it have been a capital place to sneak off and hold secret meetings!"

"I'm not sure, Lynnie," said Lorraine cautiously. "I believe this is a smuggler's cabin, a place to store their goods until they can be sold. I've read about such places, and they're much frequented by desperate felons."

"As though we'd have let anything so paltry deter us! We could have kept them away with barking dogs or deadfalls and hauntings. Think of the stories we could start. Someone had stayed in the cottage overnight," continued Lynden, making her voice low and spooky, "and his remains were found in the morning, seated in a corner chair, tattered flesh hanging from a bleached skeleton . . ."

"Rubbish," said Lorraine, laughing. "There's nothing so ghoulish. I have the prettiest thoughts here. It's like the line from Spenser: 'Into that forest farre they thence him led, where was their dwelling in a pleasant glade, with mountains round about environed.' Shall we go knock on the door?"

They walked across the rustling grass, and Lynden rapped on the weathered door. It swung open quietly under her fist.

"Hello?" Lynden was answered only by the whisper of emptiness. She stepped inside. Lorraine followed her. They crossed the slate threshold, leaving behind the windswept, piny outdoors to enter an indoors scented pungently of smoke and damp wood. Light filtering through the thick glass window created a water-colored interior of gray and sepia shadows, and from a catch-bucket set in the corner came a light, steady plunk of dripping water. A tiny whistle of wind down the chimney stirred the pewter ashes in the fireplace.

"His things are still here," observed Lorraine joyfully. "The books on the table, yes, and that old trunk! He must be near."

A tall, slender shadow appeared in the square frame of light cast on the far wall by the open door.

"Very near," the shadow agreed. "Won't you come in?"

Undaunted by the lack of warmth in his tone, Lynden grabbed and then shook the highwayman's unresponsive hand, asked him how did he do, and said, "I've come to thank you for saving Lorraine's life. You can't object to that."

"Apparently not," replied the highwayman sardonically. He smiled at Lorraine, his wide mouth curling attractively at the corners. "Though I thought you wouldn't be able to find your way back here."

Lynden noted the shy warmth in Lorraine's answering smile. "Lorraine has an *excellent* sense of direction and knows where she's going all the time. At least she used to," Lynden added pointedly.

"It was nothing, really," said Lorraine, looking

flushed. "We only followed the trod, and whenever it forked, we chose the less rocky branch, the one smooth enough for a horse."

"That was clever," the highwayman said resignedly. He came in, swept the door shut with one hand, and glanced censoriously at the soaking, muddy hems of their capes and the splashes of damp on their shoulders. "It's too bad you don't seem able to make a trip out without soaking yourselves to the skin. Since you're here, you might as well dry off before you start home. Sit down."

He hung their cloaks from the pegs driven into the wall above the hearth, spread blankets for them to sit on, and started a fire. When the fire was burning strongly sending sparks up the chimney and heat into the room, he hung a good-sized soot-blackened pot from the hearth crane and pushed it over the fire.

"If that's polecat," Lynden said, "I'm not having any."

"No, Lyn, smell. It's *smouch*, tea mixed with dried leaves of the ash tree. Don't you recall, Peg made it for us once to drink."

"Yes," said Lynden. "It's very economical. Only a few pence per pound, isn't it? I remember it made me heartily grateful that I wasn't poor!" Encouraged by the highwayman's grin, she offered to work the bellows for him; the offer was civilly refused, so she said, "I've been thinking, sir, that perhaps you are a very famous highwayman? Like . . ." She scrutinized him for a moment. "Like Cutthroat Kelly. No? Or Gentleman George, who robs coaches with full dress toggery beneath his capes? Or the Galloping Ghost, who robs in the dark of the moon?"

"Certainly not," objected the highwayman, evidently irritated at his involuntary placement in that company. "My name is Kyler, and I am *not* famous! In fact, I've only stopped two coaches in my life, and robbed neither of those. What's more, I never intend to do it again."

Lorraine curled her legs underneath her, arranging

her skirts modestly. "One carriage was ours, I know, but the other . . .?"

Kyler grimaced. ". . . had three schoolboys and a governess, who promptly had the vapors and refused to exercise the slightest restraint over her charges. They swarmed out of the carriage, shied my mare, asked dozens of ridiculous questions. Each demanded to discharge the pistol, and it was blasted hard to reload three times in the dark, let me tell you! One of the brats nearly put a hole through my hat! Then, in order to assuage their disappointment when I ran out of ammunition, the little demons made me take each one in front of me for a gallop on the mare before they could be gotten rid of."

Lynden giggled. "It must have been very funny. What were you before you tried being a highwayman?"

"A smuggler."

"Now that's real adventure," exclaimed Lynden with a note of envy in her voice. "Is that how you knew about the secret cottage, because smugglers use it? Lorraine thought so! Were the friends that helped you hold up our coach smugglers, as well? Yes? What were you before you became a smuggler?"

"A soldier."

"Before that?"

"A schoolboy. You ask a lot of questions, don't you?"

"I wouldn't have to if you'd volunteer something about yourself," said Lynden, showing him her dimples.

Kyler ladled out two cups of smouch and handed one to each sister. "Be careful, it's very hot," he admonished, filling a chipped cup for himself. "All right, let me see. I'm twenty-two years old; no, twenty-three last month. I was raised in Ireland by my stepparents, Tom and Grania Miller. My stepfather died when I was twelve; my stepmother, when I was seventeen. I served HRH for three years in the infantry, was discharged honorably and broke. Unemployment being what it was, and the connections you make in the army not being particularly relevant to legitimate employment . . ." He shrugged. "Maybe if my parents had apprenticed me in trade instead of insisting on sending me to school, things might have worked out differently."

"Could you not have gone to your real father for help?" asked Lorraine before she could stop herself.

The highwayman took a long sip of the smouch before speaking again. "My real father is dead, I believe," he said without expression. There was quiet for a moment, broken only by the hollow drip of water in the bucket and the muted roar of the waterfall.

"I have a theory," said Lynden slowly. "But it is—well, do you promise you won't be offended if I tell you?"

"No."

Lynden put her finger in her cup and brought it to her mouth, sucking it absentmindedly. "No? But I must tell you, anyway. You wear an eye patch, do you not? To conceal that your eyes are colored differently? Because I don't doubt that such a marked coloring would make you very conspicuous in your profession; that would be a handicap. But I must say you handle it clumsily, because I recall when you stopped our coach your right eye was patched; now your left one is. And I see from the way that you're glaring at me that you think it would be more polite not to have mentioned it, but, really, someone ought to tell you."

"I'm honored," he snapped, "to receive your observations." He tilted his head to take a large swallow of smouch.

"If you didn't like that, you'll like less what I'm going to say now," predicted Lynden. "I think you're Lord Crant's natural son."

Kyler set the tin cup down so fiercely that hot smouch slopped over the side and ran down his hand. "Damn." He plunged his scalded hand into the water bucket. "You're lucky you're not a man, Lady Melbrooke, or I'd horsewhip you down the mountain."

Lorraine brought a scrap of cotton cloth from the

table and gently patted Kyler's hand dry. "It was my idea, not Lynden's," Lorraine said quietly. "You are so like Lord Crant, you see, in the way that only a brother could be, or a son."

Some of the hard anger lessened as the highwayman looked into Lorraine's honest brown eyes. He turned to gaze out the window, the silver light etching the flowing pattern of his cheekbones. "Or a nephew," he said, almost to himself. "But it can't be, it's too incredible."

Lorraine went to the window beside him, the light lending an aura of blue fire to the rich black waves of her hair. "There is a story, then," she said softly. "Perhaps it isn't something you tell people in the general way of things, but you might tell us. I should like very much to listen, if you would be willing to talk about it."

With a slight smile, he reached up to touch her cheek, and then led her back to the fire. He sat down between the twins, crossing his legs, and stared into the flames as he spoke.

"First I'd better tell you that it's more than possible that none of this is true. I was away at Dublin University when my stepmother died of the flux, and it happened so quickly that by the time the news got to me that she was ill, she was gone. She left the priest a letter for me . . . God knows, the letter sounds clear enough, and yet it's hard to know. She had some fever and pain, too, so I don't know what state she was in when she wrote it. But let me show it to you, and you can read it and judge for yourself."

He uncoiled himself from the blanket, and from between the leaves of a large, heavy book on the table, took three flat yellowed pieces of parchment, handing them to Lorraine, who moved closer to the fire and peered at the precise, thick handwriting.

"*Kyler, my dearest boy,*" Lorraine read. "*If I am right to tell you this, I do not know, but Truth is God's balm, and His sword, and you have been my joy and comfort these seventeen years so I cannot now carry these shadows with me into my next life but must leave them with you here to do with as you will. You know, dear one, that Tom and I adopted you and that your own parents are dead. But never have I told you the true circumstances of that adoption or those deaths. You might have questioned me earlier, I know, but for your own sweetness which saw that curiosity would give me pain. Should Death reach me before you do, I hereby now—I hereby now . . ."* Lorraine's voice faltered, and a blur in her brown eyes became a sparkle; a tear fell on the soft cheek. She handed the letter to her sister. "You read it, Lynnie, I can't see it," she said huskily.

Lynden looked at Kyler. " 'Tis very melancholy! Let me see . . . yes. It says, . . . *before you do, I hereby now confide your Story.*

"I grew up in England, a Vicar's only daughter, not as I have told you in the Sunny South, but among the bleak mountains of Westmorland, where I met and married Tom Miller, a gardener for the Castle of Crant. We lived there twenty years, watching the seasons pass and the sons of the castle grow to manhood. The elder, Charles, was a cheerful Godly boy and the younger, Percy, jealous, restless, and dwelling in the shameful, secret temples of Sodom and Gomorrah."

"Percy! That's Lord Crant, isn't it?" whispered Lorraine. Kyler nodded and Lynden continued reading.

"The Holy Dove bore Charles's spirit to the Abode of the Blessed while Charles was in Italy on his Tour; the family heard the news many weeks later and the boy's father, the old marquis, was struck ill with grief.

"It was near to eight months later, my dear Kyler, that your mother came to Crant. She arrived past sunset and afoot. Young Master Percy brought her to our cottage, bidding us to care for her for she was a lady and near her time to give birth. Master Percy told us to speak of it to no one and left.

"The lady told us her story in those next few days, how she was the daughter of an Irish miniaturist; reared

128

in Naples and sadly orphaned. She supported herself painting enameled snuffboxes with the eye of their owner; Charles commissioned one and thus they met. They were married within weeks, Kyler, and how I wish that you could have heard her speak of their tenderness and joy in each other. For each, it was as though they had found another part of themselves, before lost and aching. So pitifully, cruelly soon, though, came the fatal sailing accident, and Charles vanished, boat and body, beneath the waves in the wind. She was distraught for some months, cared for by Sisters in a nursing hospice. It was when she learned of her blessed condition that she found again the will to live and bring happily to life this precious token of her Perfect Love.

"She was surprised and worried to have received no word from Charles's family following his death. Charles had written to his father, the marquis, immediately on his marriage, appraising his family of the Happy Union; she could only believe that the letter had been lost before it reached England. Moreover, she had no money and visited Charles's bank in Naples only to find his account there closed."

"Oh, poor, poor lady," said Lorraine, seeking refuge in her handkerchief.

Lynden continued: "Grows worse, Rainey, listen. *I will not sadden you, dearest Kyler, with the struggles this poor lady endured on her penniless journey to Crant Castle. Only believe that she arrived sick, wretched, and weak. Yet how content she was, and how eagerly she awaited your birth, my son and hers. Surely now, she thought, her tribulations would be over. Master Percy had received her so kindly, she said, and with such affection, and called her his dear sister. But the old marquis was so weak—his heart, Master Percy had avowed to her—that it would be better to wait a few days and then break this happy news to him in a gentle fashion—the shock, so Master Percy told her. Trusting and innocent, your mother had given Percy her papers*

129

of identification, her letters of character and introduction, even her marriage license, so that Percy might prove her claim to the marquis."

"Oh, no," cried Lorraine.

"Yes, I'm afraid," said Kyler grimly.

Lynden read on: *"The days went by; we waited for Master Percy to come to establish the lady in her rightful place. There was no news until one day, two weeks later, when Tom came home much troubled, and told me in private that Master Percy had called Tom to his study and asked how did the lady do. He went on to tell Tom that the lady was not who she claimed, her papers were false, investigation showed that she was no more than an adventuress, had never been to Italy, and Charles could not possibly have fathered her child. He gave Tom money—a hundred pounds! And told him this matter must be mentioned to no one; word of it could bring on his father's death.*

"We were shocked, frightened for the lady, for one look at her sweet face had told us that if liar there was, it could never be her. We kept the truth from her, and two days later she gave birth, held you, her son, for one golden moment, and then died."

Lynden stopped to brush the tears from her cheek, and Lorraine sobbed quietly into her handkerchief. The shutter began banging again, and Kyler went outside to fasten it. When he returned, he filled everyone's cup.

Lynden took a deep breath and continued reading: *"How like your father you were, Kyler, even in the first moments of your life: not bald, like most babies, but with dark hair, already with its own shine. More dangerous to you, though, my son, were your eyes. The special Crant colors, one brown, one blue. It was on the very day of your birth that Master Percy came and saw you thus, and then took Tom aside, giving him money, money enough to support us modestly for the rest of our natural lives, telling Tom to take the money and go away to live, but first to smother the infant as it slept and bury it with its mother. There were no mar-*

riage papers, he said, there had been no marriage, the child was born out of wedlock, and it would kill his father, the marquis, and forever tarnish the memory of his brother should the child's existence come to light.

"Such wickedness! What would we not have done to avenge and protect you, my sweet son. And yet we were simple people, without power; and with his father ill, Master Percy ruled our corner of the county like a petty king. If we'd known where to go . . . where to plead our case for you, we would have done it, but we had no proof of Percy's villainy save our own words; would any judge have believed us over Master Percy's word? And if they disbelieved us, might they not take you away from us and put you under Master Percy's guardianship? The risk was more than we could take. We resolved to flee that night, to leave England bound for Ireland, to raise you as our own child.

"The rest of the story, of course, you know, my dearest love. Except that I must mention one curious incident. Before we left Crant on that night, Lady Irmingarde visited us. She was an aunt to Charles and Percy, elderly, eccentric; flower gardening was her life's dedication and she was rarely lucid on any other subject. She lived at the castle and went about her business in her own odd, independent way, never helping, never hindering anyone else's business; she never seemed aware that anyone else had any business. She stood over your crib that night, your great aunt, and told you in her scratchy, broken accent that you shouldn't trust your Uncle Percy with your papers, that Percy was not careful with papers, so she had taken them and hid them for you. I remember well how desperately Tom and I tried to make her tell us where the papers were, to coax her into telling us how much she knew—but it was no use. She would only stare at us in her fey fashion and tell us that she was always hiding Percy's papers. All she said else was that she wrote it on the sundial. We found nothing on the sundial or near it, so we gave up at last in despair, thinking that the shrouds of madness could only be wrapping themselves tighter and tighter around her mind.

"I still wonder if we failed you then, dear one, if there was something we might have done had we been more clever, less panicked. Please know that the love I've borne for you could not have been stronger even had our ties been blood, and I know that your love for me was likewise, so do not worry that I did not know that, after I am gone. Your loving mother, Grania Miller, anno Domini, 1811."

CHAPTER TEN

The twins, in matching dinner gowns of cherry satin trimmed in tatted lace and with cherry ribbons in their hair, were seated before the fireplace in Fern Court's music room. Within reaching distance of the girls a snapdragon bowl sat on the hearthstone, filled with a generous scoop of plump raisins swimming drunkenly in a sea of hot brandy and honey. Lynden dipped her thumb and forefinger in the bowl, and quickly popped a sweet, swollen raisin into her mouth.

"Lorraine, don't be such a hen-heart. Try some now. You always wait until the brandy is cool and the raisins aren't so good."

"I'm not as quick as you and my fingers always get stung," protested her sister.

"Hold your mouth open, then, and I'll bring them for you." Lorraine did as Lynden suggested, and, for her compliance, received many more raisins than she had desired. Lynden watched with amusement as Lorraine attempted to remove with her lace hanky the sticky splash of brandy and honey which had fallen down the front of her gown.

"I didn't understand Kyler's explanation for not pursuing the story directly after his mother died, did you?" asked Lynden.

"I think so," said Lorraine, her statement muffled by the mouthful of raisins. She held up a finger, signaling "one moment," chewed valiantly, and swallowed. "At first there was only the grief, about his stepmother's death, I mean. I don't think he really believed the story in the letter, either; think how strange it would be to be brought up thinking of yourself as a gardener's boy and suddenly find you might belong to a great aristocratic family. It would seem too romantic to be true, wouldn't it? And then, with the war on, I suppose he went army-mad like many boys and joined up. After the war—why, think of how remote the story would have seemed after all he'd done and experienced in battle. There was this, too: even if the story were true, so what? If there had been no proof, while his stepparents were at Crant, what hope had he of finding the proof of his birthright so many years later?"

Lynden took the bowl in both hands and swirled the contents, mixing the ingredients further, speaking as she did so. "But when he came north to deliver that load of contraband with his two cohorts and found that there *was* a Crant Castle and that he had the Crant coloring, the story at last seemed real and he decided to stay on! What I don't like, though, is his attitude, as though this were only a crusade to punish Lord Crant for his treachery to Kyler's natural parents and the agony Crant caused his stepparents. He doesn't seem the least interested in establishing his own inheritance."

"He's not ambitious. I like him better for it."

"Humbug," answered Lynden. She followed, with her finger, a particularly fat raisin floating in a lazy circle on the surface, and then pounced upon it like a kitten on a pull toy. "He's not thinking of the future. Smuggling is all very well when you're young, but barrels of illegal brandy and tobacco bales could get mighty heavy in your middle years. Besides, the best way to pay Lord Crant back is by ousting him from his usurped postion as master of Crant Castle!"

"Oh, I agree," said Lorraine. "But I wonder if that's realistic, Lynden. Wouldn't Lord Crant have destroyed any papers proving the truth of Kyler's birth long ago?"

Lynden sprang from her seat and paced the room thoughfully, coiling a cherry ribbon around her finger. "He might have. But why dismiss the story of Great-

Aunt Irmingarde? If she knew about the papers, perhaps she did take them. Maybe they're still somewhere in Crant Castle waiting to be found." Lynden's voice rose with excitement. "Raine, you and I are going to pay Lord Crant a little visit!"

Lorraine shook her head. "We can't, Lyn. If Lord Melbrooke finds out, he'd be furious. You told me yourself that he more or less forbade you to have anything to do with Crant. And don't say Lord Melbrooke won't find out, because you're always saying people won't find out and they always do. Lord Crant is bound to mention it to Lord Melbrooke and we'd be neck-deep in stillwater."

"As long as we don't let it cover our noses, we're all right," retorted Lynden. "I already have a plan. We'll pretend that you're intrigued with Lord Crant . . ."

"Never!" gasped Lorraine.

"Oh, very well. We'll pretend that *I'm* intrigued with Lord Crant. It can't matter which one of us it is. Anyway, I'll tell Lord Crant not to mention our visit to Melbrooke."

Lorraine carefully tested the temperature of the brandy with her fingertip. "Surely Crant will think you a very odd sort of female?"

"With that hussy he's got for a sister?" exclaimed Lynden. "I daresay he'll think I'm a very *usual* sort of female."

Lorraine at last selected a raisin and gingerly put it in her mouth. "Perhaps Crant wouldn't tell Lord Melbrooke about it, but I wouldn't wager a pieman's tip that Lady Silvia wouldn't have the story of our visit to your husband quicker than hasty pudding."

"Botheration! You're right. I'll have to think of something else." She tapped the piano seat with her palm. "Come, play something from a Handel oratorio. Yes, play *Judas Maccabaeus.*"

Lorraine went to the piano, wiped her fingers clean on the handkerchief. "But I thought you detested *Judas Maccabaeus.*"

"I do," said Lynden, sitting on a sofa, crossing her arms, and leaning her head across the back. "I won't be tempted to listen. I've got serious thinking to do."

Lord Melbrooke entered the room a half hour later to find Lynden, eyes closed, in her place on the sofa and Lorraine attacking Handel energetically. He smiled at Lorraine, and signaled that she should continue playing; she smiled back at him as he crossed the room, leaned over Lynden and kissed her on the forehead. Lynden's eyes fluttered open and she gave a guilty start.

"Oh. Good evening, Lord—Justin."

Melbrooke smiled. "Tired, my dear? You were out so long today."

"Yes, we were—we were walking. On the fellside. But how did you know how long we were gone?"

"I directed Mrs. Coniston to follow behind you and report your movements to me."

Lynden giggled. "I'll bet you didn't. She told us at breakfast that she was overseeing the airing and pressing of the antique lace tablecloths, and she'd no sooner leave them to the laundrymaids than Michelangelo would allow his charboy to finish Moses." She sat up, and Melbrooke took a place beside her, stretching his arm along the sofa back, behind, but not touching, her.

"Actually, I saw you walking out from my study window," he said.

"Did you?" His nearness, combined with the knowledge that he had been watching her, made Lynden's throat feel strangely tight. What had he felt, observing her from the high window of his study? Casual interest? Did he watch her broodingly as she tripped off with Lorraine, bonnet snugly on her head and cape flying out behind, or had he merely glanced out the window and noticed her? Perhaps he had known they were on a clandestine errand; she knew she could not logically fear such a thing, as her thoughts were her own, after all—but his gray eyes were so penetrating.

"I thought you worked so hard in your study that

you didn't have time to gaze out the window," said Lynden against the bright, dramatic background of Lorraine's Handel.

"I should have been busy, but I find myself going a little dry at times, lately."

"Dry?" repeated Lynden, disconcerted by the sudden warmth in his smoky eyes. "Well. Well, I'm not talented myself, so I don't know much about it. What is it that they say—you're waiting for the muse to come?"

"No." He was smiling. "Something else."

Possible meanings for his words multiplied in Lynden's mind. As she stared at him, the color slowly blossomed in her cheeks. It occurred to her that she might ask him to clarify his words. She might have, had she not been so afraid of what her own reaction to his answer might be. Disappointment? Embarrassment? Elation? None felt comfortable. She brought her hand to her cheek, feeling the coolness of her fingers as she fought what she considered a quite wanton urge to discover what would happen if she closed her eyes and lifted her face to her husband.

"I'm sorry your work isn't going well for you." She wished that she might have thought of something less clumsy to say. "I've been trying to stay out of your way since I've come to Fern Court, and not be a distraction for you. That was our bargain, you know."

"And you work so hard to keep it, don't you?" he said, whether serious or satirical, she could not tell. He speculatively fingered a lock of her ebony hair, letting the clean, silky strand slip over his fingers. "Oddly enough, Lynden, it's your efforts to stay out of my way that have been the distraction."

"I—I don't know why they should be." She felt inadequate. He was so confident, so much in control. Lynden found herself resenting the advantage ten years in age gave him, ten years intensified many times by the sophistication that came with his status, his birth, and his genius.

The softening smile left his lips. "Then perhaps you

will recall that we made a new covenant on your first night at Fern Court. We agreed that we would try to become better acquainted. Since that conversation, however, you've limited our contact to the most transitory. It's natural that you should enjoy Lorraine's company, but I think also that you avoid me."

"Of course I don't," protested Lynden, despising herself for the blush that had stayed under her skin, despite all that she had willed it to leave. "Though if I did, you seemed content enough with that."

"If that was how I seemed to you, Lynden, then I've been at fault, and I should be even more at fault to allow you to continue thinking in that mistaken vein. My desire was that you have time to make some adjustment in your own mind to our relationship without pressure from me." There was no cruelty in the gray eyes, but neither was there license. "The result has been for you to grow increasingly uneasy in my company and to misinterpret my motives. Lynden, I would do anything to bring back the natural lack of constraint you showed me on our first meeting at your home in Yorkshire. Circumstances have spun this tension between us, but to go on as we have been solves nothing. I can't allow it to continue; surely you must see that?"

"I'm not sure," said Lynden, feeling an uncomfortable vulnerability.

He let one hand slip gently to her shoulder. "We could talk about it."

There was no pressure in his touch, but she felt as though he was drawing her to him; she put her hand on his chest to keep her distance.

"No, I—oh, that is, perhaps we can. I—I don't know, I . . . I'll have to think about it for a few days first— whether I want to talk about it, I mean. But it's late now." She spoke quickly, the words tumbling against each other. "And I'm tired. From the walk today. I was practically asleep when you came into the room. Raine, Raine, stop pounding that poor old piano to death and leave *Judas Maccabaeus* to rest in peace. We were about to go to bed, don't you remember? Good night, Justin. I hope you find yourself less dry tomorrow."

He shook his head. "In a few days. Then, perhaps."

During the night a west wind rolled in from the sea, as quick and vocal as a jolly old sailor visiting the homefolks. It scattered rain on the fells and lakes like pennies tossed to children, and sang a lively wind-song chanty that echoed through the valleys. Even the tall black clouds might have been puffed from the bowl of a walrus-bone pipe.

Early that morning, having discovered that new wax candles were to be molded, the twins invaded the kitchen and aggressively offered their assistance in the project. Never before had Fern Court seen such candles, tinted ingeniously by experimental dyes into virulent pinks and a livid lime green, and scented with Lynden's special mix of herbs that gave the burning candles what Mrs. Coniston termed "the scent of damp socks." The girls tired of pouring the wax into traditional long, slender taper molds, and sought to achieve unusual shapes by molding with a crystal wine goblet (one of a fifty-year-old set which unfortunately cracked under the hot wax), a teapot (also a casualty, as it had to be broken to remove the finished product, which did, after all, turn out to have an interesting shape), and a soup tureen, Lorraine's pièce de résistance, which produced a candle of large and stable proportions that Mrs. Coniston at once honored with a proclamation that it should be forthwith taken to Lorraine's bedroom and there placed upon her mantel.

Lynden was about to argue that Lorraine's candle should go in the center of the table, replacing the detested silver epergne, when a young chambermaid ran into the kitchen and made the exciting announcement that the men were back. John Coniston and one of the grooms had taken the wagon into Penrith the day before on miscellaneous errands. Despite what had no doubt been an early start home, it had taken him the whole of the morning to make the return to Fern Court, through roads as muddy as a river bottom. The twins elected to join Mrs. Coniston, and the three slipped their feet into wooden pattens, took the big black kitchen umbrellas, and hurried through the rain to the carriage house, their running feet shooting knee-high streams of spray fountaining from the glassy puddles.

The air in the carriage house was warm and humid, smelling sharply of the polishes Mr. Coniston used to keep the coaches shining—beeswax, white wine vinegar, and oils of lemon and linseed. The stableboys had scattered fresh bedding straw on the hard earth floor to absorb the drippings from the wagon's huge ironrimmed wheels, the straw reflected olive and gold in the cloudy light from the four storm lanterns.

When the ladies arrived, several grooms and a stableboy were unloading the wagon, a task punctuated by Mr. Coniston's stringent remarks on the state of the Lake country roads, be they ever so scenic. A respectful audience was gathered around him, comprising the better part of those persons employed at Fern Court including two laundrymaids, the gardener, a chambermaid, a kitchenmaid, and the august person of the French chef himself, who had abandoned the kitchens, as soon as the twins had arrived there that morning, for the quieter environs of the servants' parlor where it had been possible to engage Lord Melbrooke's valet in a companionable game of hazard. But the carriage house held a greater lure for him now, Mr. Coniston having returned with an order of those delicacies, not readily available in the barbarous vicinity of Fern Court, that would provide some challenge to his culinary skills.

The detachable cover had been removed from the wagon, so by climbing to stand tiptoe on the wheel hub, Lynden was able to look into the wagon body.

"Your histories have come, Raine," she called. "I see the name of your bookseller on a parcel there, and oh! there are a thousand bandboxes—inscribed, if you please, with the name of some very fashionable London modiste. Why, Mr. Coniston, without telling a soul, you've ordered yourself a jaunty new wardrobe and you plan to take Loughrigg Fell by storm!"

"You've found me out, M'lady," chuckled Mr. Coniston. "Take the finery t' my chambers, lads!"

Lynden jumped off the hub, laughing, and ran around to the tailgate, where she fell upon an oversized hatbox and began to rip off its wrapping. "Never! It's the clothes Aunt Eleanor ordered for Raine and me from London, isn't it! Did they arrive at Penrith by carrier? And you picked them up for us, you sweet, dear man! Hoo-ray!" Lynden tossed off the hatbox cover and pulled out a fetching cabriolet bonnet with a deep-red velvet brim and curly black plumes that nodded seductively from the side.

"This," announced Lynden, with great satisfaction, "is what I call a hat!" She squashed it down over her hair and peacocked around the wagon, driving the maids and the stableboy into a fit of the giggles by rapping the grooms across the knuckles with an imaginary fan and denouncing them as sly rascals who quite turned her head with their flattery. Then she pulled off the bonnet, perched it on her sister's head, and tore into another parcel, finding it to be filled with a pretty kelly-green morning gown with woven ivory sprig, as well as a quantity of expensive hair ornaments, ribbons, artificial flowers, and lovely dress trim. Lynden promptly declared that there was too much here for her or Lorraine to use, not even if they lived to their eighties. Lynden earned the everlasting devotion of the maidservants by dividing the trim into bunches and distributing it among them. She chose also a particularly attractive spray of artificial flowers and insisted that Mrs. Coniston have it, saying that it would be just the thing for that natural straw bonnet Mrs. Coniston wore to church.

The time was a little past two as the twins walked back to the house. It had stopped raining, but the air was muggy and the wind potent; the drizzle would start again soon. Lorraine and Lynden were walking slowly, speculating on the contents of the many other parcels and bandboxes which Mrs. Coniston had firmly forbidden them to open until they could be brought into the girls' bedrooms. Lorraine was about to mention that she hoped Aunt had not forgotten to order more silk stockings for them when a boy of perhaps twelve years in a thick, gray country jacket ran toward them.

"Please ya, mum," he called, "could ya bide? Ah's a message fer Lord Melbrooke!"

"You could give it to me, if you like," replied Lynden in a friendly voice, trying to remember if she'd seen the boy before. No, she was sure she had not. "I can take it to him."

The boy drew from his jacket pocket a folded gilt-edged paper, set with crested fuschia sealing wax, and tapped it against his hand, watching Lynden with a sly smile. "Dunno if ah ought. M'mistress tole that ah should mind it direct to the Lordship."

"Who is your mistress?" asked Lynden, with an unsuccessful attempt at disinterest.

" 'Tis Lady Silvia. O' of the castle," he said, making no move to hand her the note.

Lynden's brown eyes glowed with indignation. "Oh! Well, I am *Lady* Melbrooke, so naturally you can entrust the letter to me." She put out her palm trying to look formidable and after a short show of reluctance, the boy thrust the paper at her, hesitating only a moment before galloping away across the lawn's brown grass.

Puzzled, Lorraine watched the boy's scampered retreat. "How peculiar! One wouldn't think that Lady Silvia . . . Lynden! What are you doing? Surely you can't be intending to open a piece of Lord Melbrooke's mail!"

"Why not?" said Lynden, retreating inside the open doorway of a grain shed and beginning to pick carefully at the letter's wax seal. "Where in the Bible does it say, 'Thou shall not open thy husband's mail'? And the marriage vows read 'with all my worldly goods, I thee endow.' Mail is worldly goods, isn't it?"

"Of course it is! And as it's from Lady Silvia, there's a chance that it's a length more worldly than most goods! Please, Lynnie, it might make you unhappy. Don't read it."

"I've got to, Raine. If there's something that will make me unhappy in it, why, it's better that I find out now than have it popped on me unannounced, isn't it? And how else will I find out anything, anyway? If we were back in Yorkshire there'd be *dozens* of discreet sources, but here—well, you know Mrs. Coniston's less gossipy than a contemplative nun and if I ask any of the underservants, the whole county will probably know that I did within the hour. But what does Lady Silvia use in her sealing wax . . . ? One practically needs gun powder to blast the thing open. Wait, here it comes! Ah-ha! I knew it. Scented with toilet water! What's more, she dots her i's with circles . . . No, with hearts! It's enough to make anyone toss their tea. Here, Raine, you read it. *I* haven't the stomach!"

"Very well, but I really feel that we ought . . . oh, never mind. Let me see . . . it says: 'Justin, dearest, Whatever is to be done about this dreadful rain? Don't come today, as we had planned, I know you are too much the gentleman to cancel on your own initiative, so perceive me the noble one who declares herself ready to make the sacrifice of a day without your loving company, to save you a soaking!' "

"Bah!" snapped Lynden.

"Quite!" agreed her sister. "I've read enough, don't you think?"

"Certainly you have. *I'll* finish it," Lynden plucked the letter from Lorraine's hand. "It goes on: 'So don't come. There will be many more splendid days and intoxicating nights for us, my Prince Eros.' Upon my word! Who's this Eros?"

"It's Greek for the god of love, and a more snockingly foolish affectation than prefixing it with prince,

I cannot imagine," said Lorraine severely. "What . . . what flubbidubbery! How she had the nerve to address that sort of trifling prose to the Bard of the Lakeland is more than I know!"

"I don't suppose he cares a pinmark about the quality of her prose, Raine." Lynden sank down onto the edge of a sidewise wheelbarrow and rested her chin glumly upon her fists. "It's all those tidy blonde curls that must take her dresser an hour to set—and that enormous bosom!"

"Rubbish," declared Lorraine stoutly. "Her bosom's no bigger than mine and you only measure an inch or two less than me! You've let Aunt Eleanor put that in your mind. And as for the hair—didn't Aunt Sophronia always say that you had the prettiest hair in the county?"

"No! She always said *you* had the prettiest hair in the county, and I had the hair most estranged from a hairbrush." Lynden pulled a wan smile. "It was a very good try, my most sympathetic of sisters, but I believe I'll have to wander down Melancholy Lane for a while before I'm ready to be cheered up."

There was a scythe in the bin, its long, bent handle leaning against the wall, the curved semicircle of the single-edged blade buried a few inches in the musty dirt floor. Lorraine absentmindedly took hold of the handle and hefted it back and forth, not pulling it from the ground.

"Does it say anything else?" she asked quietly.

"Only a closing: 'Believe me, I am, as always, your sweetest lover, S.' "

"Painted words! Whatever else she is," said Lorraine, pulling the point of the scythe from the dirt and tentatively chopping the ground, "she's an intolerable letter writer. Lynnie, I think she chases him."

"Then I wish he would run faster in the opposite direction." Lynden refolded the letter, morosely sharpening the crease between her thumb and forefinger. "And this right on the heels of—Rainey, I do wish you'd put down that blade, I swear it reminds me of Uncle Monroe the night he dressed as Father Time for Lady Isley's costume ball and sliced the feathers off Aunt Eleanor's headpiece with his scythe."

"I beg your pardon, Lyn. This is right on the heels of—what?"

Lynden was staring unhappily into the middle distance. "Melbrooke. He's been trying to—oh, I don't know what he's been trying to do. Make love to me or something, I suppose. He's so careful about it, and so odiously civilized, that I'm never quite sure what he's about until I've had some time to think. Last night while you were dredging Handel out of that piano, he as good as told me, though in the *politest* manner, that I ought to become his *real* wife or have a very persuasive reason why not. At least that's what I think he meant." She jumped up from the wheelbarrow. "It's not fair! Here he is conducting an immoral liaison practically upon my doorstep and at the same time expecting me to submit to him like a ha'penny harlot." She walked away from her sister and looked out the doorway, her slim frame silhouetted against the misty gray light. "It's not only that," she finished sadly, "the truth is that— that I've become rather fond of him. No. More than fond, I think."

"I've noticed that," Lorraine stated softly.

"That's like you," Lynden answered without turning her head. "Rainey, I don't think I've been cast in the mold of the resigned sufferer. I'm sure this is one of those cases that the vicar would have described as being good for the humbling of one's soul. But I'm finding it ever so painful to have my soul humbled. I don't understand why the ladies' journals always make such a virtue out of males conducting their affairs with discretion. Melbrooke is more discreet than the sun in a cloudburst, and I don't find it comforting at all."

"No," agreed Lorraine, coming to stand beside her sister. "Not if you're fond of him. Perhaps, though, he doesn't realize that. Consider the circumstances of your marriage, Lynnie. Perhaps he even thinks that you will feel more comfortable if you are not made responsible for receiving the full measure of his masculine attentions."

"So with great nobility and immeasurable self-sacrifice, Melbrooke has gallantly decided to spare me by pursuing Lady Silvia. Phooey! And if you think I'm going to do anything to help Melbrooke realize he has animated my affections toward him—think of how pursued he has been, and how hanged on, think of the women that thrust themselves at him! If I did, it's likely only to give him a complete disgust for me. I'd rather swallow my foot to the ankle!"

"An unwise choice. That *would* certainly give him a disgust for you!"

CHAPTER ELEVEN

The castle stood above them, up the smooth glacis that was lost under shaggy bushes, gray rocks, and wild beds of withered ferns. The turrets rose from either corner of the castle like horns pointing to the sky. The sun glinted from the iron crossbar of an arched Gothic window, making it a winking eye in the stony expanse of the curtain. The gate was a dark, yawning mouth, and the lowered drawbridge stretched across the moat like a protruding tongue.

It was a cold, windy day, blessed by a cloudless, ultramarine sky. The watery leavings of yesterday's rains were being picked up and carried off in the gust, leaving only a minor, crystalline dampness on the sharp edges of the dry saw grass. At the foot of the hill, Lorraine and Lynden had set up easels bedecked with sketch pads, that, along with watercolors, brushes, and mixing pots, had been laboriously pushed, from Fern Court through the still muddy lanes, in the pit of a rusty wheelbarrow.

Warmly clad in her new astrakhan-edged, high-waisted redingote, Lynden, hands on hips, took two steps back to survey her own painting.

"You know," she said with a considering air, "this wouldn't be half bad if the wind hadn't nipped up the page and made the colors bleed. What do you think?"

Lorraine, frowning in concentration, had been daubing at her own paper, but stopped to give Lynden's effort a fair study. "I think it looks like, um, an inverted sewing thimble in tarnished silver sitting on a liver-brown pillow."

Lynden grinned, pulling a face. "At least it's got *shape,* which is more, least complimentary of sisters, than I can say for yours, which looks like a smashed orange on a mound of potato peels. When Lord Crant appears, I think we had better emphasize our interest in the castle from a historical standpoint, not an artistic one."

"That has the virtue of being the truth, at least. But as for Lord Crant appearing, I only wish he would hurry up about it because my blue paint pot is freezing over," said Lorraine, stabbing energetically at the offending receptacle with the pointed end of her brush.

"Set it away from the shady side of your easel, Raine," advised Lynden. "And Lord Crant's got to come out before long. What sort of gentleman would leave two ladies painting indefinitely in the March wind without inviting them inside for a warming drink?"

"Lord Crant's sort of gentleman! Furthermore, if half we hear of him is true, the warming drink he'd invite us in to would be poisoned. Lynden, we've been here for a quarter hour at least. Have you thought of this. What if he isn't home?"

"Of course he's home. This is the wild north, where is there to go? Besides, there's a flag aloft the left turret. It's his, I suspect, and that means he's in residence. We know for certain that he isn't visiting Fern Court today, with Melbrooke ridden into Penrith."

Lorraine paused in the act of making a bright yellow sun and glanced at her sister. "It's not that I want to criticize, Lynnie, but, really, last night at dinner when Lord Melbrooke told us that his relative, the Duke of Wellington, would pass through Penrith on the way to Scotland today, and that he would be obliged if we came to meet him, do you think you acted wisely in refusing to go? You did it so cavalierly, too, Lyn, you know you did! I'm afraid it must have looked rather obvious, especially when you referred so dismissively to the Iron Duke as one of *your,* meaning Lord Melbrooke's, third cousins, as though the Duke weren't the nation's greatest hero, and then said you felt too delicate to make the ride into town."

"I know it wasn't well done of me," admitted Lynden, wiping her paintbrush on a piece of flannel. "I suppose it means that Melbrooke's put me down to being a tedious, sulky brat. But there was something about the prospect of spending the whole day in Melbrooke's company that . . . well, do you know what I mean?" She waited for her sister's nod, then continued: "He was so cool and civil all evening, too, and it made me feel such a fool when I was seething inside and feeling hurt. When I acted so frigidly toward him and he behaved with such odiously well-bred courtesy toward me, it made me long to dump the platter of *merlans aux fines herbes* in his lap!"

"I think he knew you were snubbing him, Lyn, but he's too much the gentleman to let anything show in front of me."

"Or too little the brangler!" suggested Lynden.

"You can't truly blame him for misliking brangles. I don't like them myself," said Lorraine seriously, watching a tiny chunk of ice as it fell from her paintbrush, slipping rapidly down the paper and bisecting her landscape with a spidery trail of blue. "This worries me, though: What if it comes to Lord Melbrooke that you've gotten the letter intended for him? That boy who brought the letter didn't seem the discreet sort—quite the opposite, I should think. Will Lord Melbrooke find out you have his letter and ask you about it?"

"You worry that he'll ask me for his letter and see I've opened it? Ha!" exclaimed Lynden, with bitter triumph. "The world's most elegant lyricist wouldn't have sufficient command of the language to find prose acceptable for the purpose of asking his wife to hand over a passionate letter from his mistress! I think Melbrooke will sidestep the issue as neatly as he would an

ant pile! Sometimes I wonder if the man *has* a temper."
She put her paintbrush back in its leather pouch,
rubbed her mittened hands together, and shook her
head as though to get Melbrooke off her mind. "Listen,
maybe there's some obscure maxim of social usage we
don't know. Perhaps it's perfectly polite to ignore
painting ladies if they are further than fifty yards from
your doorstep. Let's load the wheelbarrow and move
closer."

Lorraine, who had begun to add doubts of the feasi-
bility of the Crant plan to her already long-standing
ones about the plan's efficacy, wearily agreed and
helped her energetic sister trundle the wheelbarrow
load to a spot halfway to the glacis. Here they stayed
for another twenty minutes until Lynden's patience
gave out and they moved upward again into the shadow
of the castle.

"He'd better come now," said Lynden grimly. "If
we go any closer we'll be in the moat."

Their constant advance upon the ostensible subject
of their watercolors finally had results. Before Lorraine's blue pot could freeze a second time, from the
bailey, onto the drawbridge, walked Lord Crant, a tall,
dark figure clad in a deep-brown coat with tight
breeches and riding boots, his black hair ruffled by the
wind.

"Huzzah!" said Lynden softly. With Crant came a
bowlegged man, whose pink bald pate reflected the
sun's rays brilliantly. As they drew nearer, the twins
could see the white dueling scar on the stranger's
sparsely freckled cheek as well as his pronounced over-
bite, two oversized front teeth of nearly horizontal in-
sertion.

Lynden was prepared to drop a quick curtsy, but
Crant reached her, captured her hand, and shook it
before she had time to whisk it behind her.

"A pleasant surprise, Lady Melbrooke," observed
Crant, looking as though he found her presence be-

side his moat more surprising than pleasant. "And the lovely Miss . . . ?" His voice raised questioningly.

"Downpatrick!" Lynden snapped, as Crant bowed over her sister's hand. Then, since alienating Lord Crant was hardly the object of their visit, she hastily forced a smile and joined Lorraine in an awkward chorus of "nice to see you."

Crant nodded his head, giving them a smile that managed at once to be cynical and lightly curious. "Permit me," he said, "to introduce my cousin . . . and guest, Ottmar Wishke."

Ottmar bowed stiffly from the waist and clicked his heels together with a loud smack that made Lorraine jump.

"Are you a—a military gentleman, Mr. Wishke?" ventured Lynden, repressing a nervous urge to snap her heels in response.

Ottmar bowed again, fixed Lynden with a stare that seeméd to her unnervingly disapproving, and spoke with a rich Teutonic accent. "Indeed. *Major* Wishke. For His Imperial Majesty Frederick William Third's Prussian Army, serving under General Friedrich Wilhelm von Bülow."

Lynden considered, and then thought better of, asking him if he knew that the war was three years over. Instead she turned back toward Crant, attempting to achieve the mien of an ardent medievalist.

"I don't recall if it was mentioned during your visit to Fern Court," she said, "but my sister and I are great observers of antiquities!"

Crant appeared to be amused. "Are you? And which . . . er, antiquity did you come to observe today, myself or my castle?"

If he had meant to fluster her, he failed. Lynden opened wide her pansy-brown eyes. "How can you say so? You've barely entered what my *dear* Uncle Monroe was wont to call the Age of Reason! You cannot be a day above fif—" she hesitated, feeling Lorraine's elbow shoving gently into her ribs. "That is to say, forty- . . . seven?"

"Forty-three, Lady Melbrooke," corrected Crant, apparently not in the least annoyed by her misestimate. "Tell me, is your career as an . . . let me see, ah yes, an observer of antiquities a long-standing occupation?"

"Indeed, yes," she assured him. "In fact Lorraine and I were delighted to be able to stop at the Jerneaux Abbey on our way to Westmorland. Have you had the pleasure of its view? No? What a pity! Lorraine and I found it a most enriching scene. How much we regret that time did not permit our stopping long enough to meditate at length upon its noble aspect." She felt Lorraine's elbow again, decided that she was probably laying it on a bit too thickly, and changed her tack. "My sister and I have been taking the liberty of . . . of making a few random watercolor sketches of the castle for later study. You have no objection, My Lord?"

"None whatsoever. Take what liberties you please," said Crant in a tone Lynden privately characterized as odious. "Would you enrich me with a view of your work?"

"Of course, by all means," said Lynden, waving her brush expansively, wondering if he would oust them from the property at first glance as slanderous caricaturists. "Lorraine, show him yours."

Lorraine glanced nervously at Lynden, stared at her drawing pad, chewed her lip, and reluctantly turned her easel to Lord Crant.

Crant examined the painting. "You have a most unusual talent, Miss Downpatrick," he said, lifting his eyebrows sardonically.

Lorraine tried to assume an expression of modest self-appreciation. "So I've been told. You see, Lynden and I have studied extensively under a master of the Flemish school of interpretative architectural representation. Are you familiar with it?" She could only hope devoutly that he was not.

"I'm afraid I can't claim that erudition, but Ottmar

happens to be an, er, great observer of that very school," said Crant, to Lorraine's horror. "Come, Ottmar, give Miss Downpatrick your opinion."

Major Wishke clasped his hands behind his back, rocked back on his heels, clamped his jaws together, and looked more forbidding than ever. He glared at Lord Crant. "Percy is a great one for the jokes," he informed the company. "I know nothing of pictures."

"I understand perfectly," said Lynden, encouraged by his confession. "I'm sure you had *much* more important things to do in the army, like polishing your sword and shining up your cannons."

Major Wishke, a man unable to imagine himself as the victim of so youthful a satirist, appeared stolidly gratified. "A perceptive comment for an Englishwoman, if I may say so. Women don't always understand such things."

Only Lynden's concern for the plight of the handsome young highwayman prevented her from giving the Prussian a strong shove backward into the dirty waters of the moat. Mentally she listed him in the same league as Uncle Monroe, but aloud said only, "You may find yourself very surprised some day by women, Major Wishke! But it's wrong of us to keep you standing in the cold. Lorraine and I were just saying we should return to Fern Court. Our fingertips were turning numb." She drew the cover over her sketch pad, put it in the wheelbarrow, then began to cover her paint pots.

"You'll honor us with your presence inside for some refreshment first," said Crant, his tone so filled with smug assurance that not only did Lynden feel no triumph in having so cleverly tricked him into an invitation, but found that it would have been more satisfying to be able to refuse. She did accept, however, in a manner that she hoped might pass for flirtatiousness, and allowed him to take her arm in his own. Crant took Lorraine on his other arm, leaving Ottmar to trundle the clumsy iron wheelbarrow behind him. The heavy timber of the drawbridge absorbed their footsteps as they passed into the shadow cast by the machicolation, where the stonework parapet projected from the curtain, its ancient floor slatted with holes from which twelfth-century Crants had poured boiling oil on their besiegers from the north. Ottmar left the barrow inside the ten-foot-thick walls, and they walked down a broad flagstone alley to the massive three-story octagon of the Great Tower. Entering the tower through an enormous pair of studded, lattice-molded doors brought them within a large chamber, bare except for a pair of decrepit fourteenth-century suits of armor standing on rotting wooden mounts. Small circular shafts of sunlight shot in through gun-loops in the walls' masonry to streak across the dim interior. To the right a bold staircase spiraled upward, its width so generous that a cavalry might have charged up it twelve abreast.

The stairs were colored with a soft rainbow of colors, a dancing prism of gentle light falling slanted from somewhere above. The effect was arresting, and the girls, searching for the source of the light, gazed upward to see a beautiful stained-glass dome set' in the center of the ceiling like a fantastic inverted cup twenty feet in diameter. Black leads held together a glowing jeweled mosaic of colored glass, which caught the natural light in decorative configurations of ruby, emerald, sapphire, arfd amethyist. A stem burdened with heart-shaped leaves coiled and twisted about the lip and branched inward in slithering patterns, where it blossomed in golden-yellow lozenges.

Lorraine was about to question Lord Crant about the design of the dome when Crant pointed out the chapel, situated through an arched doorway to their left. He then led the girls to the staircase. Climbing the stairs, they passed small landings and doors that opened into guest rooms, larders, storerooms, and the kitchen.

Crant's private quarters were on a half floor between the second and third floors; it was another gloomy half story later that the stairs ended abruptly at the eastern end of a great banqueting hall. It was a huge room, long without being particularly narrow, the outside wall a bulging curve of herringbone masonry with deep oriel windows framed in trefoil tracery. Most of the hall stood naked, though at the west end a small artful clutter of furnishings huddled before a great medieval fireplace in which enormous oak logs were burning mightily behind an iron screen. Magically, servants appeared to take the twins' winter coats and their orders for tea; Lord Crant must have summoned them, though Lynden had not noticed him doing so. He invited them to follow him to the fire. This they did gratefully, as the frigid draft from the staircase made it seem nearly as cold as outside, especially with their coats removed. Ottmar, silent and stolid, marched stiff-legged behind them across the carpetless stone floor.

The furnishings proved to be a subtly bizarre hodge-podge of periods, styles, and national origins. There was a marble-topped console table that surely, thought Lorraine, must be French and date back more than a hundred years to the reign of Louis XIV. The pieces shared one distinct, unpleasant feature. Their legs were really legs: dragon legs and eagle claws with hideously sharpened talons. There was an odd little stool that terminated in what appeared to be scrawny peacock legs carved in ash; a teak kettle stand that was an exact replica of an elephant's foot, the wood meticulously carved to resemble the baggy, loose texture of elephant skin, and unpolished and dulled to a morbid gray. A manx table with three legs ending in realistically rendered bare human feet supported an oversized terrestrial globe, which stood on lion forelegs with broad, flat paws.

The upholstery had been done in chintz block print, rich dark green and orange on a drab tan ground. Looking closely at the pattern, one discovered a mesh of thorn and thistles backing a large spread-winged bird of paradise landing on its nest, from which a weasel was running, carrying a broken eggshell in its mouth. Lynden caught her sister's attention, discreetly indicated the pattern, and grimaced. Lorraine nodded, her lips set in distaste.

A wizened butler arrived to pour out tea. With studied casualness Lynden queried Lord Crant about Lady Silvia's whereabouts: Would she not be joining them?

"No, she left early this morning to go South to Kendall. She will be devastated, of course," he said, smiling at Lynden with undisguised awareness, "to have missed your visit."

Lynden received this in the cynical spirit with which it was intended, but she was scarcely able to prevent a certain amount of consternation from showing in her face when she realized that Lady Silvia was absent on the same day as Lord Melbrooke.

Crant must have seen her expression of discomfiture; he studied her for a moment, sipped his brandy, and spoke. "She really did go to Kendall, you know. She's decided, it seems, to honor those gentry hardy enough to attend the county in March with a small dinner ball on the fifteenth. So today she's set about placing orders with a butcher, a confectioner, and the fishmonger. Hiring musicians and whatever else had better not be overlooked in advance to assure the evening's success. Justin will have a card, of course. Will you come?"

"Oh, yes, it sounds delightful," returned Lynden, thinking it might provide an opportunity to prowl the castle in greater privacy while Crant and Lady Silvia were occupied with their guests.

The talk became general as the twins asked polite questions about the ball: who would be there and what distances the guests would have to travel. Many would stay until the next day, and Lynden could only feel sorry for those unfortunate enough to sleep even one night in this chill, dismal castle. Lorraine, with her nice sense of politesse, attempted with only moderate results to include Major Wishke in their conversation and at last succeeded with a reference to His Grace the Duke of Wellington's trip northward in which she skillfully managed to express her admiration for the notable general's triumph at Waterloo. This led, in some mysterious manner, to a discussion of Major Wishke's own movements on the day of that illustrious battle. Wishke displayed slight animation and a quite surprising verbosity as he described the courage of the line regiments and the supportive effect of the hidden artillery. Two Prussian corps had begun their approach and the fourth horse had been shot out from under Wishke when Lynden expressed a sudden and unbecomingly passionate desire to admire the view from the oriel windows.

Crant gallantly offered to accompany Lynden, leaving Lorraine to listen to Wishke's announcement that they would stand "until the last man falls."

"Is he really your cousin?" Lynden asked Crant suspiciously.

"I'm afraid so. My mother was Prussian. Ottmar has his uses, my dear."

Lynden looked at him sharply. Had there been a note of warning in his voice? How easy it was to believe the story of Kyler's stepmother when one looked at Crant's bright, glittering bicolored eyes and his slanted smile. She turned from him and gazed out the window. Directly below them and inside the main walls was a triangular courtyard with paths of crushed whitish stone. Against the east wall ran a long, brick-shaped stable, and beside that a squat cylindrical tower with a fine turret top projected from the triangle's apex.

"Isn't that a door at the bottom?" asked Lynden, pointing to the tower's splayed base. "Can one enter it?"

Crant shook his head. "It's been locked since before my father's death. It looks stable enough from the outside, but the masonry inside has been known to crumble on unwary visitors."

"I see," said Lynden, thinking how convenient it would be for Lord Crant to have a section of the castle permanently locked where he might hide his guilty secrets. "And beyond it there, on the hillside outside the wall, how green it is. Has it been planted?"

"Yes, years ago by my mother's sister, my Aunt Irmingarde, whose one unquenchable lust was gardening. The hillside is spectacular when it blooms, but that won't be for a week or so. There are almost three acres of March-flowering plants. Lesser celandine, wood anemone, sweet violets, and snowdrops. I have the list memorized—my aunt used to chant it incessantly. It's almost the only thing that I ever heard her say."

Lynden almost swooned with relief that Crant had mentioned Aunt Irmingarde; she herself had hit upon no unobtrusive way of bringing that lady's name into discussion. "She must have been a most unusual lady . . . I don't suppose she's still alive?"

"Lord, no," said Crant, sipping from the brandy glass he held in one hand. "Dead these twenty years, buried in the family vault."

"Did she write?" asked Lynden with an air of impartial scientific interest. "Most avid gardeners seem to keep logs of their work. She must have left some interesting journals."

Crant shrugged. "They may have been so. I never took an interest in them. My mother had Irmigarde's papers burned some ten years ago during a housecleaning."

"Burned?" cried Lynden with dismay. "Oh, no! I mean, what a pity. One . . . one should save things like that. We never know what will be of historical interest to our descendants."

"Such heat, my dear. And for a pile of ancient rubbish! But then it's nearly part and parcel of your historical fervor, is it not?"

"My historical . . . ? Oh, yes, well, if everyone burned it all up, there wouldn't be any history for us to study, would there? Tell me, is the garden to the right there in the courtyard a planting of your Aunt Irmingarde's as well? Such clever topiary work! And how cheerful the pyracantha looks even in winter with its red berries."

"Yes, that was Aunt Irmingarde's, too. The gardener hasn't the expertise to keep it well trimmed. It becomes a snarling jungle in the summer."

"Mmmm. Is that, um, behind the willow, there, might it be by any chance a sundial?"

"Yes, but it hasn't seen the sun for a generation."

"I don't care for that! I have a fondness, no! a passion for antique sundials," Lynden said with convincing enthusiasm. "Nothing would give me greater pleasure than to study it."

"Nothing?" repeated Crant, a mocking smile in his eyes. "Then you must allow me to pleasure you. Come with me to the garden."

Though they met the idea with quite divergent degrees of enthusiasm, Lorraine and Ottmar were quickly conscripted to join Lord Crant and Lynden. When the small party reached the garden, the twins found the sundial covered with a hard, reptilian scale of gray lichen and veiled with a dry, brittle vein-work of muskrose and hop vines. Lynden parted the raspy growth from the plateau of the sundial face to reveal a half dozen dead beetles, a rusty style—and an illegible inscription.

Ottmar cleared his throat. "I think the sundial is too old to keep very good time," he said, laughing heavily.

Lynden gave him a rigid smile, pronounced him a wit, and announced that she must have charcoal and a piece of rice paper, adding generously that if rice paper was not available, she *could* use some other large sheet of a transparent nature.

"You want to make a rubbing! Lynden, how clever of you," said Lorraine. "Then we can have a—a nice record of its design." Within minutes a pair of yardsmen were found to scrape away what scale they could from the sundial's surface, and a footman appeared with rice paper and charcoal. No more than half an hour later, the completed rubbing was tucked securely in the wheelbarrow which the twins steered together down the hillside, having refused an offer to be returned to Fern Court in Crant's carriage.

Crant and Ottmar watched their downhill progress from a parlor window in the Great Tower.

"A peculiar visit," said Ottmar. "What do you think they wanted?"

Crant crossed his arms and leaned a shoulder against the window. "I honestly don't know. But I believe we haven't see the last of them."

At Fern Court, an hour later, the twins reached Lorraine's bedroom, wedged the door shut with a chair, and rushed to the window. Carefully, they unrolled the rice paper rubbing, each taking a side and pressing it against the glass. The afternoon sunlight pouring through the panes was slowed by the thin gray of the charcoal background, and then leaped through the lines of the engraving. The inscription on Aunt Irmingarde's sundial was no longer illegible. Lynden read it aloud:

> " 'Grave and secret mem'ries
> Clasp'd quietly in my heart,
> Eternally stay nigh me
> And forgotten pasts impart.' "

CHAPTER TWELVE

The following morning Lynden sat before her pretty mahogany writing table gazing thoughtfully at its polished surface, where a stork of fruitwood inlay curved its long neck to peck a slender beak quizzically at a sheet of pressed paper covered with scattered notations.

At the top of the paper Lynden had carefully penned the sundial poem. She had first studied it as a whole; attesting to this were the several elaborate and ill-executed doodles of castle turrets and horses surrounding it. After this, Lynden had been seized by a dramatic inspiration: Hidden in the poem might be a code. She threw herself into the task of uncovering it with the enthusiasm of a spaniel chasing a soap bubble. Reading the poem backward, she found that it was unintelligible. Next she tried reading every other word of the poem:

> *Grave secret clasp'd in heart*
> *stay me forgotten impart;*

or, alternatively,

> *and mem'ries quietly my*
> *eternally nigh and pasts.*

Neither version revealed anything not already explicit in the verse, so Lynden scanned the lines for anagrams. But other than the discovery that the letters of *heart* might be rearranged into *earth*, and that *forgotten* could become *not get for*, no enlightenment was to be gained from this avenue, either. Deep in contemplation, she sat brushing the soft feather of her pink-dyed quill pen across her lips when a knock at the door interrupted her reverie.

Quickly she raised the surface of her writing desk, pulled out a narrow drawer beneath, and whisked the paper into it.

"Yes? Come in."

Melbrooke entered the room, impeccably dressed, as always, in a coat of rich king's blue and breeches that fit without a wrinkle. Closing the door quietly behind him, he crossed the floor to rest one casual hand on Lynden's shoulder, tilting her chin up toward him with the other. He told her good morning and brushed her pink lips lightly with his own. Lynden felt a smarting whip of pleasure lash inside her chest and then, angry with his easy control over her emotions, she slid from his gentle grip and stood, setting her little mahogany armchair between them, her fingers tight on the top rail carved with oval paterae.

"So. You are angry with me," said Melbrooke, surveying her with his calm gray eyes.

Lynden was startled in replying with more heat than she would have liked, "Next time, if you want to know if I'm angry with you, you can ask me! You don't have to experiment with kisses!"

The gaze hardened to tempered steel. "Let me correct that misapprehension, my dear. I don't have to *experiment* with kisses because, unlike you, Lynden, I know what I want!" It was the first time the tight choke chain on his control had loosened in her presence.

Umbrage rose in Lynden's deep-brown eyes as she exclaimed wrathfully, "Well! I apologize for my lack of premarital experience, My *Lord!* And what you want, you can so easily find elsewhere! I won't be sneered at so! Pray, have the goodness to leave my bedchamber."

Lynden spun her diminutive frame and marched toward the door with the firm determination to eject her husband, but he moved forward more quickly than she would have thought possible, and catching her rigid shoulders in his firm grip, he said, "No! Little one, I . . ."

"There's another thing!" cried Lynden, cutting off his words. "Why do you persist in calling me *little*? Are you referring to my lack of size or my lack of significance?"

The tension around Melbrooke's mouth lessened as he studied his affronted bride. She wore a morning dress of rose pink that matched the soft color of her cheeks. The gown was cut high and belted with a wide satin ribbon under a small, pretty bosom heaving with indignation; the décolletage and ankle-length hemline were trimmed with ruffled, snow-white Campaine lace. Her curls were brushed away from her face and spilled from her inkily lustrous crown which was strewn with knots of narrow ribbons in rose pink and white. To Lynden's surprise Melbrooke touched her forehead with a kiss and held her at arm's length, his lips spreading in a smile.

"Whatever, my dear, it couldn't be your lack of beauty. You wear my patience more than you know. Having given you an awareness of that, I will also give you my apology, if you will accept it," he said placatingly.

Lynden had been more indignant than wounded over his actions. She had also been both alarmed and intrigued by the force of his temper, appearing as it did so soon after she had reached the conclusion that he was immune to such strenuous emotions. Her inclination was to forgive him; in truth, she knew that she had provoked him. But there was his larger crime, his intrigue with Lady Silvia, which stood between them with the inflexible, stony finality of the Crant Castle walls. Better for her jaws to be forever fixed shut than to apprise him of that greater hurt. The pain was too private and raw for his sophisticated consumption. It might have been safer to maintain the argument, she knew, and yet how could she when he *would* apologize? Why must he put her in so difficult a position?

She frowned in frustration and said, "I forgive you, of course, if you wish it, because it is one's Christian duty, but I felt I was being pinched by a giant lobster when you grabbed my shoulders! I suppose they are set with bruises now and my maid will be *very* shocked when she helps me undress for my bath. There's no doubt that you might have entered the boxing ring and made your fortune—if you hadn't been born with one!"

One could not tell whether Melbrooke cared for his placement in the realms of professional pugilists *and* edible crustaceans, as the opaque gray shield of polite withdrawal had once again covered the expression in his eyes. He released her shoulders, begging her pardon with no visible remorse.

"But you haven't answered me," he said in a remote, courteous tone. "What have I done to incur your enmity?"

"Why— Can you mean before this morning? Nothing! What could there be?" replied Lynden, checking a question with a question.

"I'm not omniscient, Lynden. You'll have to tell me. I don't flatter myself that you have any special regard for me, but there has been an unmistakable hostility in your attitude since the night I told you that I wanted our marriage to have more intimacy than the occasional greeting in the hallway. The night before last you made it clear that it would be impossible for you to accompany me to Penrith, with such revulsion did you regard the anticipation of a day spent in my company."

"Penrith!" cried Lynden, seizing on that with desperate gusto. "You must have come home late last night—I didn't hear you. Had you a nice day? Did you have a pleasant intercourse with His Grace, the Duke of Wellington?"

"Yes. But it isn't my intercourse with Wellington that I'm trying to discuss," Melbrooke said with careful emphasis.

"Well!" Lynden felt as though the volume of her blood had deserted her internal organs, coalescing in a burning mass on her cheeks. "Well! You're very frank, I think! But I can't discuss anything with you now. Truly I can't! Lorraine and I promised Mrs. Coniston that we'd carry a good-wishes basket of fruit and sweetmeats to Mrs. Robins, the gardener's wife, you know, who was brought to childbed only last night. Though Mrs. Coniston says that, as Mrs. Robins has had twins, it ought to be a sympathy basket! She only said it to tease Raine and me, of course—isn't she sly? We're used to that sort of thing. Why, back in Yorkshire we were used to being called Miss Ruckus and Miss Peace. But Mrs. Coniston said she'd have the basket ready at eleven o'clock and here it is three minutes of the hour. You *will* have to excuse me, you know."

"If you wish," said Melbrooke, his level voice touched with irony. "And to think that I worried that you might be bored here, when you seem to have more to occupy your time than Pomona pruning her walled garden."

After Lorraine and Lynden delivered their basket to Mrs. Robins and had taken turns holding the new babies, the sisters climbed Loughrigg Fell to the smuggler's cabin and found Kyler there, industriously skinning a large hare that he had poached earlier that morning from Lord Crant's property. Lynden at once demanded that he leave off his grisly task and accompany them inside the cottage, where, she said with a theatrical flair, she had Something Important to show him. Kyler laughed and said that he hoped it was not Lord Crant's head that Lynden was guarding so jealously under her cloak. He stroked Lorraine with his warm, brilliant smile before turning to wash his hands in the rain barrel.

Lynden eyed him with disfavor. "I can only hope," she told him austerely, "that you will remember later not to drink the water from that barrel!"

Kyler laughed at her again and tweaked one of her dark curls, saying she was a brat. He accompanied them inside, grinning and teasing, but his good humor ceased abruptly when they told him about their visit to Crant Castle and showed him the treasured rubbing. Full-blown wrath kindled in his exotic, dark-lashed eyes. He grabbed the nearest twin, who happened to be Lynden, and shook her by the shoulders with enough vigor to rattle her teeth. Then, after choking back an old army oath, he proceeded to deliver a lecture of epic proportions on the insanity of women of their young age and innocence embarking on schemes to hoodwink a man of Crant's caliber. Kyler voiced grave doubts about their intelligence, their maturity, and their common sense, and ended by pointing out that on the occasion of their last encounter he had firmly denied them permission to interest themselves actively in his affairs.

Lorraine recognized the source of his anger as concern for their safety and self-reproach for having confided his story to them. But Lynden had already been handled roughly that day, and in much the same tender spots; she glared at Kyler furiously and pulled out of his arms.

"All men are brutes!" she announced with strong conviction. "But I've known that since I was five when Cousin Elmo bloodied my nose with his cricket bat after I beat him in a foot race. You're lucky I don't kick you where Father taught me to kick Elmo so he'd never bully me again!"

"Try it," snapped Kyler, "and I'll make sure you won't sit down for a week."

"That," declared Lynden triumphantly, "would only further prove my point. I don't know why you should be so put out. We were only trying to help you."

Kyler frowned. "Aye. And if you continue helping me that way, you'll soon find *yourselves* in need of help. How stupid do you think Crant is? Don't you realize that a man so quick to commit infanticide would dispatch the two of you in nothing flat? Do you think I want to see you martyred in my cause?"

Lorraine stepped between them, as if physically to block the flow of their disagreement.

"Then you ought to shake me, too," she said to Kyler. "I'm as much to blame as Lynden."

"That I can believe, Little Miss Butter-Would-Melt-In-Your-Mouth. I'll bet you're very adept at letting your other half talk you into things that you want to do yourself anyway." Kyler put his hands on Lorraine's shoulders and rocked her gently back and forth with the slightest of pressures. "You're lucky I'm not mad enough any more. There's only enough viciousness in me to shake one girl a day."

"You can thank your lucky penny for that, Lorraine," said Lynden. "And *Mister* Highwayman, you ought to be more careful what you say about Lord Crant, because evidence bears out that *you* are Lord Crant, and Lord Crant is plain old Percy. Besides, I'll bet you're angry in part because *we* were the ones clever enough to think of taking a rubbing from the sundial and not you!"

"Clever!" Kyler glared at her, then grinned reluctantly. "Little hornet! I could think of another word for it. If you think I'm going to say thank you, you'll be disappointed. But since you've got the deuced thing here, I suppose we might as well take a look at it."

Lynden and Lorraine exchanged relieved glances; they had both secretly entertained the fear that he would have nothing to do with any activity carried out by them on his behalf. But things were moving along fairly well; their initiative, undertaken without his prior consent, had gotten them an expected scold and now they had gained his begrudging acquiescence to a discussion of it. Lynden spread the rubbing out on the table; Lorraine placed clay cups on the four curling corners to keep it flat.

Kyler stared at the page for a good five minutes while the twins waited patiently. Finally he spoke. "I can't make anything out of it. Have you got a theory?"

Lorraine was standing next to him, hands behind

her back, gazing at the rubbing contemplatively. "No theories, but we have eliminated some possibilities. Lynden worked at it this morning. There's no code in it to be broken, nor does scrambling the letters provide a clue. We do think this, though: 'Grave and secret mem'ries' refers to your mother's marriage certificate. Lady Irmingarde must have been using the sundial poem to tell your stepparents that she was keeping the information safe. Unfortunately, they were too overset by all that had happened to understand her."

Kyler nodded, still looking at the poem. "It's possible," he admitted. "According to the poem, though, the grave and secret memories that unfold forgotten pasts 'stay nigh me.' Could 'nigh me' mean near the sundial?"

"I don't see how it could," said Lorraine, her finger thoughtfully tracing a pattern on the cold silver surface of the top button on her cloak. "You see, the sundial sits in the middle of the courtyard garden. It's solid stone—we tapped it—so there's no hollow place inside for anything to be hidden. There are no structures in the garden, either, so the only way to hide anything would be to bury it in the ground. But surely a garden would be the last place to bury anything important, since the ground is always being cultivated and one of the gardeners might have accidentally turned up a buried object at any time. Lynden thinks that the 'me' the memories eternally stay nigh must refer to Aunt Irmingarde."

Lynden, standing opposite, leaned on the table and looked at them significantly. "Yes! At first it seemed to me if she kept Kyler's documents near her that it must mean she kept them with her gardening journals. If they were, then they'd be destroyed now since Lord Crant's mother had the journals burned. But listen, if they were kept in her gardening journals, why would she say 'eternally nigh me'? Eternally means forever, doesn't it? So this morning, when I was in the kitchen getting the basket to take to Mrs. Robins, I asked Mrs.

Coniston where the Crants were buried. Well, they have a mausoleum, in back of that little church at the curve of the main road, St. Andrew's. So I propose . . ."

"No!" said Lorraine so emphatically that her listeners jumped.

"What's no?" demanded Lynden. "You haven't heard what I was going to say!"

Lorraine crossed her arms in front of her and studied her sister with some severity. "I don't need to hear it. I know what you're going to say, and we're not going to do it. Lynden, I've done everything with you: I helped put Lady Shillingworth's London bonnet on the statue of the Magdelene at our village church, I carried the key when we locked Elmo overnight in the gardener's shed, and I even asked Uncle Monroe to explain a newspaper item to me so that you would have time to sneak that can of rove beetles into the pen drawer of his desk, but I won't, Lynden, *won't* stand by while you dig up dead bodies! No and no and NO!"

"Not bodies, Raine, only one body," said Lynden, directing her most appealing smile at her largely immune twin. "You see, I believe that Lady Irmingarde had the documents sewn into the lining of her funeral gown. She probably had it picked out years before her death, you know, as Mama has done, and she decided that would be the one place Kyler's documents would be safe because, bizarre as he is, Lord Crant wasn't likely to fool about with the dress of a dead . . ."

"Wonderful!" interrupted Kyler. "Crant isn't bizarre enough to rifle the garments of a dead woman, but I suppose you think *I* am! I'm obliged to you! Devil take you, hornet, do you think I'm a man to bother my great-aunt's remains on some farfetched purpose? Now this is final, child: We're not going to make a project of exhuming my ancestors, so you might as well set the whole thing from your mind!"

Lynden dropped her chin to her open palms, opened her eyes to their widest dilation and conceded handsomely, "Very well, if it wounds your sensibilities, there's no more to be said. Naturally, if you don't like the scheme, it's forgotten. Eternally."

The Crescent clock on her mantelpiece chimed the last stroke of midnight as Lynden slipped out a side doorway from Fern Court on her way to St. Andrew's churchyard. The night was damp, and the air was thick with a throbbing mist, the light from the blue-haloed moon fracturing silver on millions of tiny droplets. The fog made sounds close, as close as the chill, and Lynden pulled the hood of her cape snugly around her cheeks, both to ward off the creeping dampness and to muffle the magnified rustlings in the dark trees behind her, the high-pitched skittering of unseen bats, and the rhythmic crush of her footsteps on the gravel. Her normally keen vision was neutralized by the glimmer; landmarks were indiscernible, and her only guide was the lighter color of the road beneath her. She kept her head down so as not to miss her step, thinking, as she trudged along, that it was best not to stumble on the stairway to nowhere.

At last the tumorous, spidery growth of bilberry bushes told her that she was nearing her destination. She looked up to a hilltop before her, where, above the slowly circling mist, the steeple and box of St. Andrew's stood black against the luminous purple night sky. It was a small parish, too small to support a clergyman on its own; the Reverend Hewitt rode in from Ambleside to bury the dead, christen the newborn, marry the courageous, and once a week rebuke the faint-hearted from the pulpit. A local shepherd and his sons were charged with the upkeep of the church and yard, but as they lived more than a quarter mile away, no human scrutiny disturbed Lynden's solitary climb.

Reaching the summit, she paused to glance nervously at the fifteenth-century church. Its south doorway lay like a giant keyhole under brick-crenellated offsets. The heavy oak doorway had not moved, of course; surely the slight change in its shadow had been only an illusion of the weak sparkling moonlight. And the soft rustle was only the magic wind rubbing branch on bare branch. Lynden forced herself to walk past the church, down the dark hillside to the churchyard, where sickly greenish mist rolled in quiet wisps between the motionless gravestones. Around her slept the silent, waiting spirits of the long dead . . . and those whose footsteps, until recently, had trod the sandy Lakeland soil. To her right was the dark pit of a freshly dug grave, emitting the musky odor of newly turned earth; behind that lay the sulking, domed Crant mausoleum, squatting in the dark like a malevolent toadstool.

Then, from the yawning maw of the new grave, came the slinking scrape of disturbed rock, and Lynden, the nonscholar who made a point of never remembering poetry, found herself reciting aloud the eerie words of Shakespeare:

> " 'Now it is the time of night,
> That the graves all gaping wide,
> Ev'ry one lets forth his sprite
> In the church-way path to glide.' "

Suddenly a shapeless, glowing mass began to rise from the open earth, spilling toward her from the grave's edge like a creeping vampire!

Lynden sucked in a painful, shuddering breath, clasped trembling hands over her heart, and began backing from the dismal, crouching shape which began to grow to a great height, batlike wings spreading from its sides.

"I'm done for!" cried Lynden in a choked scream. Terrified, she turned and fled from the thing, threading an erratic pattern through the tombstones that blocked her way like giant chessmen threatening a helpless pawn. The breath sobbed in her dry throat, her heart echoed the beat of each running step across the uneven ground. The terror behind her flew in great bounding leaps, lending new energy to her flight. Its unearthly mask uttered her name as if to summon her to the pit from which it issued. It drew closer. She could feel its wicked breath on her cheek, and a great horny claw closed on her shoulder. Dark folds enveloped her, and the scream that rose in her mind tore from her throat. Her face was covered with the claw; she was being smothered. Frantically, she bit at it.

"Ouch! Damn it! What's gotten into you?" the thing said in a surprisingly human voice.

Lynden turned to look at her captor. "Kyler! Oh, thank God! I thought you were a vampire."

"*Me* a vampire," he said, supporting her sagging frame. "You're the one who's nearly bit my hand off."

"I thought you were going to smother me," she said weakly.

"Nonsense. I didn't want you trumpeting our presence here so that we'd have half the county upon us with pitchforks. You squeaked loud enough to raise the dead."

Lynden closed her eyes and shuddered. "Don't even think that, Kyler. I was scared half out of my mind, and then when you came crawling out of the grave like a shimmering ghoul, I thought it was the end of me."

"Silly chit." Kyler gave her shoulders a brotherly squeeze. "It was only my lantern, half-shuttered; and as for crawling out of the grave, the dashed thing's nearly six feet deep. I was lucky I didn't break my leg."

"It was indeed," said Lynden, beginning to recover her spirits. "And why you were so foolish to climb into it in the first place, is more than I can imagine."

"Because I heard footsteps. I thought it might be one of the caretakers and thought it best to drop out of sight. But now, might I ask, what are you doing here?"

"I? It was my scheme to come here, remember? You were the one full of pompous speeches about not wanting to disturb the rest of his ancestors! A fine consistent fellow you've turned out to be."

Kyler's even smile radiated warmly in the darkness. "What was I to do? I didn't want you to think that you could follow me on grave-robbing expeditions at the witching hour. Wait! I think I heard something . . ." There was a padding as of soft leather soles coming from the moon-blue hillside near the church, and a tall, slender phantom floated down the hill toward them. It halted when it came near, and gave a stifled gasp.

"Lynnie?" the phantom whispered tentatively.

"Lorraine!" Lynden went forward to peep under the phantom's hood, and then began to laugh, a happy party laugh anomalous to the stygian surroundings. "Gracious! I thought nothing would induce you to follow me to the graveyard."

"I was lying awake thinking, when I heard someone clunk against the gilt umbrella stand in the side hallway. I knew it was you after I'd checked your bedroom and found your pillows lumped under the covers to make it look as though you were asleep. I *thought* you gave in a little too easily this afternoon. What could I do but follow you?"

Lynden gave a delighted trill of laughter and danced the beginning steps of the seaman's hornpipe, which a groom at Fern Court, a sailor retired from the Royal Navy, had taught her. "Faithfullest of sisters! I wouldn't be surprised if you changed your mind and decided to come because you know I'm right."

Kyler joined the circle hastily and said to Lynden, "Let's not squawk the news to the whole parish. If you'll stop capering around like Puck, I'll walk you both back to Fern Court."

"Oh," said Lorraine. "Have you already been inside the mausoleum, then?"

"No," replied Kyler, "and as much as I like your company, there's no need for the two of you to be here when I do. It'll be no sight for a lady."

"Hen's teeth!" retorted Lynden. "What do you know about the sights ladies see? Ladies attend childbirth and nurse vomiting children. In fact, ladies even lay out the dead."

Kyler tilted his chapeau-bras to the back of his head.

"Maybe so, but I'll bet you've never done any of those things. Besides, laying out a body right after death is a far different story than looking into the coffin of a twenty-year-old corpse. Just now you thought *I* was one of the immortal awake, and ran from me like you had ten bogies on your trail. Lord knows what you'll do when you see the real thing."

"At least I'm not irreverent enough to call my great-aunt a bogie!" said Lynden indignantly. "This is what she wanted—that's why she told your stepparents about the clue on the sundial!"

Lorraine came to stand by Kyler, laying a hand upon his arm. "I think—well, it may be so. How could we ignore the message on the sundial? This may be the thing that she wanted us to do. Surely that makes it right. I want to come with you. Please." She looked down, biting her underlip, her face like pale china in the moonlight, the dark hair curling like a glossy veil from beneath the hood of her cape.

At last he said, "You don't have to do this for me."

Lorraine conquered her shyness and met his gaze. "I know that. And it doesn't matter."

Incredibly, then, he was the one who was shy, or, at least, unsure. "Lorraine . . ." he whispered her name, like a prayer. "This may not work. If it doesn't . . ."

"If it doesn't, that doesn't matter, either," she answered him from her heart.

As though unable to stop himself, Kyler took her, pressing her softness to him with gentle arms, his fingers sliding under her hood to mingle in the flow of her hair. "You're wrong, princess. And so is this," he said, releasing her from his arms in a gesture Lorraine found endearingly noble and Lynden, frustratingly stupid. "Unless I can prove that I'm something more than a smuggler, anything between us is impossible."

"Then we shall prove it," said Lorraine with simple faith.

Lynden regarded the romantic pair with disgust. "If the two of you stand there May-gazing, by morning we won't have proved anything except that it's possible to spend the night in the cemetery without being eaten by werewolves. Kyler, are you or are you not going to let Lorraine and me come with you to the mausoleum?"

He had scarcely heard Lynden's remarks, his attention being occupied by Lorraine's dark eyes; but at Lynden's last question he turned to her. "What? Oh. Very well. But don't say I didn't warn you, if you don't like what you see." He grinned. "I daresay you'll be some use reviving *me* after I faint. To the mausoleum!"

Kyler had abandoned his half-shuttered lantern on a headstone near the grave pit during his pursuit of Lynden. He stopped to retrieve it as they walked through the sighing fog toward the Crant tomb. Steps in native stone sank to the crypt's entrance, a massive arched door of joined-oak surrounded by the mausoleum's facing of dirty grey marble that glistened with fog-sweat. Kyler tried the bulky, four-century-old handle without success before crouching in front of the keyhole, drawing a long iron rod with an angled end piece from his pocket, and beginning, with impressive nonchalance, to work it inside the lock.

Lorraine picked up the lantern and tilted it to throw more of the yellow light on his work surface, while Lynden watched with eager interest.

"I was worried about how we'd get in if the door was locked! You know what to do, though, don't you, Kyler? How fortunate that you're a criminal! What's that device called?"

"Pardon the circumstances," said Kyler, his concentration centered on the lock, "but they call this a skeleton key."

"And it can really open any door?"

"Not every one," he replied, "but most."

Lynden shook her head in wonder. "I wish *I* had one. When I think of the possibilities, well, one can only regard them with awe."

"Or horror, belike, if the thing's in your hands. Promise me you won't use it to get yourself in trouble and I'll give you this one as a souvenir once the door's open. I've got more of them." There were a few tiny, sharp clinks of metal against metal. Kyler swore once in frustration, and then came a hollow clunk and a rusty scrape. The lock dangled free. "There," said Kyler, picking up the lantern. The circle of yellow light surrounding them moved wildly as he swung it to his side. He pulled open the door, which groaned in protest like a zombie about to walk, causing the twins to jump. But no fiend or goblin came skittering and laughing out at them, so there was nothing to do but enter. Kyler went first—the tomb seemed to swallow him and the light.

"I'm waiting." His voice echoed eerily from the confines of the crypt. The twins entered. Kyler was standing in the middle of the tomb, hoisting the lantern high to widen the lamplit sphere. He gazed about him, fascinated. "Nobody in here but us Crants," he said.

The room was small inside, indicating the thickness of the walls. A fetid dampness permeated the air. Ancient Gothic statues of the first Marquis of Crant and his lady reclined on the two massive sarcophagi which stood in the center of the room under a vaulted ceiling. The knight wore a coat of mail over a knee-length tunic; a double-edged broadsword hung from a stony belt at his left side. The lady was clad in a flowing girdled robe. The circular room, walled in white-ribbed sea-green marble, was quartered by four large flying angels sculpted in white marble in a later German Gothic style. Each angel had a long, straight right wing and a curled left wing, and jutted perpendicularly from the wall, to which it was attached by the wide base of its roiling gown. The angels were playing aggressively on the mandolin; a pouting, rounded mouth and bulging forehead were carved into each smooth marble face. The position of the eight wings, the swooping posture of the angels, and their high placement, as well as the curved walls, created an illusion of four celestial troubadours, doomed to fly in an endless circle, trapped for eternity in a charnel house like Lucifer's henchmen. The light from the lantern gave their stony eyeballs an eerie gleam, and spiders had festooned the tuning pegs of the mandolins with a thick, dusty gray webbing.

Burial trays—thirty in all—were lined three high and placed flush into the wall. Each one was faced with a stone marker and bordered with a green marble frieze.

" 'Marble hast a chill which no warmth can kill; / Frigid from the breath of those who supped with Death,' " quoted Lorraine in an undertone.

"A pleasant thought," said Lynden. "This place gives me the green dismay."

"It oughn't to," said Lorraine uncertainly. "Don't you recall the vicar back home told us that Christians have nothing to fear from graveyards? He said that churchyards are no more frequented by apparitions and ghosts than other places, and, therefore, it is a weakness to be afraid of passing through them."

Kyler had been examining the markers in the lantern light, going down the line reading the names to himself, lantern held high; He turned to the girls, a broad smile on his lean, dark face.

"There's your comfort, hornet. There are no more spooks here than anywhere else." He passed the lantern over a few more slabs, the light rising and falling, causing the shadows to shift eerily. "She must be somewhere near here—I've gotten up to seventeen . . . yes, here it is! *Irmingarde Marlene Grubelholtz Wishke. Born 1717, died 1797. Repose in Sweet Gardens.* Why don't you two stand back and I'll see if I can open it."

Lorraine and Lynden gladly obeyed, both of them looking pale, Lorraine leaning on her sister. "Tell us if it's frightful," said Lynden, with a swallow.

Kyler pulled a lever that had been painted to match the marble and cleverly designed to form part of the frieze. There was the squeak of the lever, a long-drawn stony metallic scratch . . . and a sound as of water sloshing back and forth in a metal tub. Kyler gasped.

"Is it too awful?" said Lynden in a shaken whisper. Lorraine's eyes were tightly closed.

"No." Kyler's voice sounded reassuringly normal. "In fact, it's empty, b'God! Empty except for . . . just a minute." The twins watched in some consternation while he went on to open several more of the grave slabs. "The same!" Suddenly he began to laugh—a light ripping laugh that must have shocked the grim angels in their mandolin flight. "This ain't a tomb, it's a sponge!"

CHAPTER THIRTEEN

"A sponge?" asked Lorraine, creasing her smooth brow in puzzlement.

"Has Satan stolen your wits, Kyler?" demanded Lynden. "I wish you would talk sense. Instantly!"

"Very well," cried that young man, his voice still filled with laughter. "Come with me, then, and look. What's this, fighting shy after all the fuss to come with me here? Along with you, fainthearts! Now. Well, open your daylights, you can't see a thing with your peepers shut!"

Lynden was the first to venture a glance, and a second later Lorraine, too, opened her eyes. Kyler had drawn them to the side of the burial tray. They looked down into it and saw that it was filled, not with the grotesquely sunken features of a grinning corpse, but with more than three inches of brackish water. Rust had taken jagged orange bites from the blistered metal lining of the tomb and a queer mossy growth climbed the marble outsides.

"How curious. It's—why, does the roof leak?" Lorraine tilted her face to look at Kyler.

"Like a sieve, m'dear. They couldn't bury anyone here for a Grail. Can you imagine the first marquis laying out his bloss for this tomb only to find the thing was no use once the first rain came? I'll wager there was hell to pay at the next stonemasons' guild meeting!"

"Could they not repair it?" Lorraine asked him.

"For twice the cost it took to build the thing in the first place."

Lynden groaned. "That must have been what Mrs. Coniston was about to tell me then, after she said that there was a Crant mausoleum by St. Andrew's. She said, 'but it's the castle chapel where . . .' She must have been about to add 'where the Crants are really buried' when the chef came into the kitchen complaining that the Penrith spice-seller had fouled the pepper with mustard musks!" She picked up the lantern and went to the end of the row, holding the light on the first tomb head in the line. "Look at these inscriptions —none earlier than 1694. I'll bet they began inscribing these plaques as memorials to impress the tourists! The sexton probably shows them through in the summer for sixpence a head." She returned to set down the lantern and peered into the tray's dripping length.

"What a strange thing . . . how short the drawer is. I've heard it said that people were of a shorter stature in the Middle Ages, but this appears to be no longer than three feet. Surely they couldn't all have been pygmies?"

Kyler leaned over beside Lynden to look. "Whew! Smells like cooked dog flesh, don't it? You're right, though, the length of it does look too short." He reached in and pressed thoughtfully on the rusty metal plate which formed the rear of the burial tray. "What harm can come from us prying around a little here to see . . . wait! I'll be . . . it's going to come off! It's a false back!"

"And there's a box behind it!" cried Lynden, her voice sky-pitched with excitement. "They're in there, Kyler! I know your documents are in there!"

The round-lidded box behind the false back was designed in enamel-on-glass and of a size that might have fit easily on the seat of a dining-room chair. Kyler lifted it to the floor and set it next to the lantern. Rejecting Lynden's eager offer of her flannel petticoat to dry the water scum from the box's exterior, he drew off his own wool tweed muffler and began to polish the smooth surface.

"Maybe a genie will pop out," suggested Lorraine with a nervous giggle as she dropped to her knees, tucking the skirts of her cloak beneath her for warmth.

"More like a frog!" Lynden joined the other two on the floor. She touched the box's side and frowned at the slimy film it left on her gloved fingertip. Deep green fused glass began to sparkle through the wet grime under Kyler's cloth.

"Pretty," said Kyler. Tight, badly tarnished brass hook-and-dot hasps held the lid closed; Kyler released them and gently raised the weighted lid.

Inside lay the musty memorabilia and mystic treasures of the fey and introverted Lady Irmingarde Wishke. There were small parcels tied with faded, fraying ribbon; numerous scavenged scraps of folded paper; a piece of runnered silk stuck with rusty embroidery needles.

Unwrapping the parcels revealed a tiny, empty, Bristol-blue glass perfume bottle; a doll's miniature tea set with pots, cups, and candlesticks in silver etched with flowers; a fan of tortoiseshell sticks painted with carriage fares for day trips in London; and a square gilded tile ringed for hanging and embossed in a flowery print with the words:

> May Peace and Plenty
> On Our Nation Smile
> And Trade With Commerce
> Bless the British Isle.

The parcels contained no clue, so Lorraine divided the papers into three roughly equal stacks and began a careful scrutiny of her pile after handing one each to Lynden and Kyler. The lantern light glowed waveringly on the trio of intent faces; the only sound was the shuffle of paper.

"Nothing," said Lynden at last. "I'm awfully sorry,

Kyler. All I've found are old rent receipts and bills pilfered from Crant Castle. There's a motley assortment of other collectibles, too. Look at this: an old Edwards copperplate that says it's a picture of . . . a yellow water wagtail? The wagtail's about to eat a moth, too. There is a letter to Lord Crant's mother from a cousin who had emigrated to America, and it complains about the size of the stingbugs, the fashions being ten years out of date, and the woods being full of savages. Anyway, its motto reads Our Lives, Our Fortunes, and Our Sacred Honor, and the letter is dated before you were born, Kyler. The only thing that is of the least use is this quarter page that Lady I. must have ripped from a ladies' weekly. It recommends the scent of basil because it 'taketh away melancholy and maketh a man meery and glad.' I ought to have some right now." She glumly tossed the last of her pile back into the casket.

Kyler leaned over and patted her hand. "Don't start tearing up, child. We're not beat yet. *I* didn't find anything relating to me, either, just a lot of dashed bills from merchants. The castle bailiff must have had a marvelous bad time keeping records, what with old Irmingarde stealing the tickets left and right. Damme if I don't dislike looking at the things, too. I mean if it's my money and Crant's been up there for twenty-odd years wasting the ready on a lot of nonsensical gimcracks—here, listen to this: 'paid to Thomas Fentham, carver guilder and frame maker 52 Strand: £30, for A very Large Rich Carv'd Frame Gilt in burnish'd Gold to your own Glass.'—my God, thirty pounds and you have to use your own glass!—and 'A fine Looking Glass—91 by 57½, £160, April 1795.' I don't care how fine it is, one hundred sixty pounds is too much to pay for a deuced mirror which ain't going to make you look any better than one for a twelver. Here's another bill paid to Fricker and Henderson of New Bond Street, which is, mind you, a paperhanging warehouse. Crant's paid the wretches two hundred and fifty pounds. Lord, for two hundred fifty pounds, you'd think the man could buy the entire warehouse!"

"Oh, I don't know," said Lynden. "Hangings can be expensive. I recall my aunt and uncle having an argument about it after she had the drawing room redone in puce and Aunt said the cost of good hangings had risen . . ."

"Wait!" cried Lorraine, voice trembling. "Oh, look. Look! See this!"

Lynden took the folded piece of paper from her, saying, "Good heavens, Raine, you sound like a reading primer. Let me see . . . what curious handwriting. I can barely make it out. It says: 'Feb. 10th, 1794. Saved for baby of Charles, of Crant Castle. . . .'" She unfolded the paper, which was yellowed and stained with the patina of twenty-three years in a damp, tight enclosure. It contained a note written in the same bizarre, boiling script that had been on the outside; a churning design with letters growing from, and sometimes strangled by, idealized flowers, stamens, pistils, stems, and leaves. "It's so strange, but I'll try to read it. 'Percy is . . . hot?' Oh, no, 'not.' 'Percy is not to be trusted . . . Find Baby's mother's papers . . . beneath the . . .' What a queer letter. Is it a *d* or an *s*? No, it must be a *p*. This word must be an archaic spelling of poem: 'pome of spring's floral harbingers.'" Lynden read it through again, trying to concentrate, to block out her rising excitement. *Find baby's mother's papers beneath the poem of spring's floral harbingers.* She stared into the fierce eyes of the sculptured angel hovering nearby.

Kyler exhaled slowly, and shook his head. "Whatever the hell that means," he said.

Lorraine came to kneel beside him. "So we go on, following the path set before us by an eccentric lady twenty years dead. And yet as outlandish as all this seems, 'tis obvious she meant her leads to bring us somewhere, for we've followed them this far. This puzzle was meant to be solved."

"Of course it was," said Lynden, surfacing from her abstraction. "A poem of spring's floral harbingers. It must mean a poem about flowers contains the clue. Lorraine, you know plenty of those."

"Of course I do, there are many, many of them but I'm not sure that . . . oh well, I shall try, of course. The reference would have to be about *spring* flowers, wouldn't it? Shelley wrote about the hyacinth: 'And the hyacinth purple, and white and blue, which flung from its bells a sweet peal anew.' I suppose that might have been a clue if only the castle had a bell tower. What about daffodils? They come in spring and Shakespeare writes admiringly of them in *A Winter's Tale:* 'Daffodils that come before the swallow dares/and take the winds of March with beauty.' "

Lynden nodded. "Yes, and there's a child's verse about daffodils, also: 'Daff a down dill has come to town,/In a yellow petticoat and green gown.' " She brought a finger to her mouth and chewed absently on the tip of her glove. "I can't see the secret in any of those lines. Think on, Rainey."

Lorraine straightened and rested her hands on her knees. "Do you think spring's floral harbinger might be an April-blooming primrose? 'Through primrose tufts in that green bower,/The periwinkle trailed its wreaths;/And 'tis my faith that every flower/Enjoys the air it breathes.' "

"Pretty lines," said Lynden. "Still, I don't think that could be what Lady Irmingarde meant in her note. Kyler, do you know anything to the purpose?"

"Me? Lord, no! The only verses I know which speak of flowers are bawdy ones. 'Now on the grass, where daisies spread,/And decked the spot around,/She clasped my waist, and then she placed/Me gently on the ground.' "

"I don't think Lady Irmingarde would have known that one!" said Lynden primly.

"And daisies don't blossom in spring," added Lorraine, casting a tender smile at Kyler.

He gazed back at her with equal warmth. "There's an old song, then: 'Rosemary is is for remembrance,/ Between us daie and nighe,/Wishing that I might alwaies have / You present in my sight.'"

Lynden was staring intently at the paper in her hand. "Daisies aren't spring flowers, and rosemary isn't a flower at all! We'll never get anywhere if the two of you intend to divert the poetry declamation into a flirtation."

"Pardon, Lynnie," said her sister. "What about these lines frim Robert Burns? 'As I stood by yon roofless tower, / Where the wallflower scents the dewy air.'"

"That might be!" exclaimed Lynden. "Perhaps Lady Irmingarde thought of Crant Castle's great tower as yon roofless tower!"

"She might have," agreed Kyler, grinning and pulling on his gloves. "Except if it was really roofless, even a cold-hearted dog like Sir Percy wouldn't be living there. Even if we can accept that Lady I. managed to find some way of getting the documents beneath the Great Tower, I doubt if Uncle Percy would give his blessing to our tearing down the place brick by brick to find them." Kyler rose to his feet and offered one hand to Lynden, one to Lorraine. "There's nothing for it, children; it's not a riddle that bears solving at this hour of the morning. We'll work on it further, but not now. Let me walk you home before Melbrooke finds you missing."

Lynden took his hand and got up with a grimace of discomfort, rubbing her cold and cramped knees. "That's one calamity we won't have to face. He'll think we've long since gone to bed."

Kyler gathered the parcels and papers, save the one Lynden held, and placed them in the box where they had lain undisturbed for twenty-three years. "Sometimes, hornet, your lack of forethought is a little frightening. He *may* decide to come to your room."

"Well, he won't," said Lynden shortly. She tucked the poem into the inside pocket of her cloak after examining the lining carefully for holes. "Because he doesn't." Lorraine studiously smoothed out the folds of her dress and fastened her cloak more tightly about her, then glanced sympathetically at her sister.

"You're not joking, are you?" said Kyler, looking at her sharply. He frowned. "I don't care much for that."

Incensed, Lynden put her hands on her hips and tilted her face up to his. "Of all the self-righteous meddlers! What right have you to care for it or not care for it?"

"Smooth your feathers, chick. I only meant if your marriage ship is foundering, and Melbrooke finds out about your connection with me, it may end up on the reef."

"Nothing of the sort," retorted Lynden, embarrassed and defensive. "We have an agreement and it's to the satisfaction of us both."

"Those kind of arrangements are to the satisfaction of neither." Kyler lifted the box back into the crypt and pushed it shut, with a long screech of metal against stone. "You can't twaddle me with that line, brown eyes. I'll bet you put him off. Just the kind of thing that a hoydenish, green girl like you would do."

Lynden clenched her fist. She would have liked to deny his accusation, but honesty kept the words to her tongue. Instead, she said, "He doesn't need me. He already has a mistress."

Kyler leaned his broad shoulders back against the tombs and arched an eyebrow. "You're a fighter. Cut her out."

Lynden looked sadly at Lorraine, and then returned her attention to Kyler. "I don't believe I could. I'd end up as number two egg in the basket."

"Humdudgeon! Talking about Lady Silvia, aren't you? I've seen the bushel bubby out riding. The woman's all craft and catlap. Besides, the best way not to give her a challenge is by shouldering Melbrooke away when he's home."

"It's not so simple as you imagine," said Lynden, glaring at him.

"It's not so hard as you imagine," he returned. "What's to stop you? Go into his room, tell him that you're sorry and that you want to sleep in his bed from now on."

Lynden was struggling for a reply that would cut Kyler off at the knees, when Lorraine came to put her arms around her. "Oh, no, how could she? Though Melbrooke seems to be a man of great understanding, how could Lynden be sure he would receive so open an expression of her affection with a degree of tact necessary to save her from chagrin?"

"If he didn't respond properly to an offer like that, he's the one who ought to be feeling the chagrin, not her! Tell you what, though, I won't say another word because from the look of her, the hornet's working up to bite me again. Once stung, twice shy." Kyler pulled the hood closely around the curls of each twin in turn, and took a quick turn about the mausoleum to make sure everything was left as it had been when they entered. "Come along. Let's beat dawn back to Fern Court."

They walked home through a fog which refracted with the pale moon to lend a deep, mineral-blue glow to the tall trees, rough grass, and craggy hillsides that framed the road. A fresh breeze came from the south, morning's waking wind delicately touched with the scent of thawing turf. Lynden was silent, trudging along ruminatively, a few steps in front of the couple. Lorraine occasionally recited a further scrap of possibly relevant poetry to Kyler's admiring audience of one. They came to the crest of the hill overlooking Fern Court and paused to see its long, low shape spread before them, black but for occasional bright pinpoints of night candles flickering behind the gauzy curtains like diamonds on jeweler's velvet. A light burned yet in Melbrooke's study.

Lorraine suggested that they meet soon to further

discuss the night's new mysteries, but Kyler shook his head.

"It can't be for a few days. I promised some lads I'd meet 'em in Broughton tomorrow, so . . ."

"But that's on the sea, isn't it?" asked Lorraine. "Are you to help with . . . I believe they call it a smuggling run? Oh, Kyler, must you go?"

"I'm afraid so, although I don't mind saying that I don't want to leave, either. I have to honor a promise, though, and besides"—his voice was rueful—"I have to earn myself some spangle. If Old Scratch took me tonight, I'd leave nothing behind but my old boots. Anyway, I'll be back by the sixteenth. I don't want you to look for me at the cabin. God knows what kind of thorough-paced villains may be hanging about there! Can you meet me on the sixteenth? Good. Then do you think you could find your way to that copse of aspen and holly-hedge on the upward jut of land above the spot where you fell into Grasmere? That's fine, children, then we'll meet there at two o'clock. Go in now and get in your beds."

The girls had almost reached the side door when Lorraine, seized by an irresistible impulse, ran back to Kyler and, standing on tiptoe, leaned on his shoulders for balance and kissed his cheek. He held her close, then resolutely took her wrists from his shoulders and held her at arm's length; they had a quick, murmured lover's conversation while a barn owl gave a wheezy cry from the yew behind them. Then Kyler turned and, after a few quiet steps, disappeared into the darkness.

Lorraine returned to Lynden and handed her a long, heavy metal piece; Lynden could feel its coldness through her glove. "The skeleton key," said Lorraine. "He said he almost forgot to give it to you."

They slipped into the hall, pausing at the threshold to listen for sounds from the household; hearing none, Lynden carefully closed the door behind them and they removed their wet and muddy boots, wiping them clean on the hems of their cloaks to leave no drips in the hall. "Our cloaks will dry by morning and we can brush the dirt off then," whispered Lynden optimistically. They tiptoed past Melbrooke's study, conscious of the glimmering strip of light that lay at the bottom of his door, not daring to breathe lest he be within working on some wee-hours masterpiece. Then it was up the stairs, one by one, endeavoring to pass over each strip of wood without touching it more than necessary to obtain a steady purchase. At the top of the stairs, they stopped at the landing to listen again. All was quiet. The twins separated at Lorraine's door with whispered good nights.

Outside her own door Lynden made a swift, nervous glance up and down the corridor and put a hand on the latch, still carrying her boots in the other hand. Watchful, she opened the door and slid backward into the room. Safely inside, she rested her forehead against the cool, polished surface of the closed door and gave a long sigh of relief.

"Thank God, no one knows," she whispered.

"Except, my love, for me." The voice came from behind her. She gasped, dropped her boots, and whirled around.

"Melbrooke!" He was standing in the threshold that connected their rooms. The low-flickering firelight glowed golden on the silk of his cravat, where it lay open against his snowy linen shirt, and harmonized artistically with his cream-colored fitted breeches. His shiny blond hair was slightly disheveled, an amber-toned lock fell forward. There was a vibrancy, a tension in the skin over his cheekbones; the gray in his eyes was dense and fluid as though to mask the intensity of his thoughts. Justin's reserve, the sense Lynden had of his remoteness, had always been mitigated by a gentle tolerance; tonight that tolerance was absent, which frightened her more than any solitary walk in a graveyard. Neither was he remote; she felt a new involvement from him. It made him seem somehow more real than he ever had before, and infinitely more threatening. Here was no charming, friendly stranger to be readily handled and dismissed from her presence, if not her emotions. Melbrooke suddenly seemed younger, vividly masculine, and vaguely menacing.

"You look cold," he said. "Come closer to the fire" The words were solicitous. The tone was not. Lynden stayed where she was, watching him warily. He crossed the room, stood above her, encompassing her in a cool survey. His gaze never left her face as he reached out to open her cloak and draw it from her shoulders. She had a momentary, irrational fear that he was going to look in the pockets of her cloak, but he only draped it over the cresting rail of a ribbon-backed chair and then gestured her toward the fire.

She walked before him to the fireplace and stretched her hands to its heat, looking at him over her shoulder.

"I was in Lorraine's room . . . talking." She spoke tentatively, hoping he might at least pretend to accept her words.

"Assuming I couldn't see the muddy hem of your cloak, what of the moonlight mist that dresses your hair like pearls?" He followed the sinuous flow of a curl with one finger, and then lightly cupped her cheeks in his hands. "And the cold touch of the night air on your cheeks? Am I to ignore these things as well?"

Unnerved by his languorous tone as much as by his touch, Lynden shivered under his fingers. He removed them from her face.

"All right, then, if you must know," said Lynden, somewhat intimidated, though managing an air of false candor. "I went out for a stroll. I take a special delight in walking in the fog." He received this with no change in expression. The silence between them lengthened and Lynden began to feel absurdly self-conscious as she stood before him sheathed in the too-tight drape of her four-year-old willow-green satin walking dress. Her hair was indeed wet from the fog. She could feel a cold, damp lock tickling the back of her neck.

After what seemed like an eternity to Lynden, Melbrooke spoke. "There are times, Lynden, when you lie so poorly that the effect is *almost* charming."

She lifted her chin fractionally, wishing that her appearance did not so closely resemble that of a puppy caught in a rainstorm. "If you are determined to despise me for every minor thing, then what can I do? You're furious with me. Very well, you've made that known. I wish you would go away and allow me to retire! I'm sure I don't know why you feel obliged to remain here staring at me in that utterly frigid manner!"

He stepped back, continuing to regard her impassively. "I'm gratified to learn that I have some effect on you. I had been thinking that your scared schoolgirl look was merely due to a fear that I might beat you."

"That you might . . . Oh! How dare you! I'm not afraid of you and I'm *not* a schoolgirl!"

"And it may be that one day you'll do something to make me believe that," returned Melbrooke, more tersely than she had ever heard him speak.

"May bees don't fly all year long!" said Lynden, through her teeth. "Believe as you like, then! I shan't be nosed into being a spinny-ninny to suit anyone's convenience!"

"Well said, my dear, but to the wrong man. You are courageous, resourceful, and independent. Do you think that I would wish you to alter those things? Follow your own path, Lynden, but be grown-up enough to realize that there are certain boundaries of acceptability that you cannot violate. I'm willing to place those limits at the outward bounds of conventional practice. However, I cannot, and will not, give you sanction to court scandal that would destroy your reputation. Do you think that it is my pleasure to play schoolmaster to your schoolgirl? Nothing could be more repugnant to me. I've told you before that I've had no wish to come the tyrant over you. Perhaps it is my fault and I ought to have done so, despite my distaste for it, because you seem to interpret my lack of verbal authority as unconcern and a signal for you to go your length!"

He reached out a long, well-shaped hand to cup her chin in the branch of his thumb and forefinger, drawing Lynden's affronted features further into the dancing firelight. "Lynden, you and I can deal better than this. You are impulsive, but not, I think, flighty. I appeal to your sense of fair play. You've had secrets since your arrival—highwaymen, tinkers, and their wives seem to swim in and out of your perimeter like migratory fishes. However the catch mixes, you must see that when things come to a pass where you are from your bed and probing the countryside at midnight, you must bring yourself to confide me the tale."

It bothered Lynden to reject a plea to her sense of fair play, and Melbrooke's words in praise of her character had not gone unnoticed. It was unfortunate that they had come in the context of a home-felt lecture. There was no joy, either, in being called a schoolgirl, as it had lately been her most unhappy fear that this was how she must seem to him. There was nothing agreeable in appearing unpolished in his cultivated vision.

Then, too, years of living with Uncle Monroe had taught Lynden to react to opposition like Hadrian's Wall standing against northern invaders. She lifted her chin sharply out of his touch and stepped back, her face serious.

"I won't. If you keep asking me, I shall only lie."

The attractively molded features of Melbrooke's face hardened, giving him the impersonal look of an Olympian Apollo. "Sometimes, Lynden, I find you less than delightful. Tonight, were you with a man?"

"A man?" said Lynden. For a moment she was too surprised by the accuracy of his guess to heed its implication. The first thought that occurred to her was that he might have somehow found out about Kyler, impossible though it seemed. "What do you mean?" she asked him, with frightened caution.

The apparent guilt on Lynden's face did nothing to negate Melbrooke's question.

"You were bitterly unhappy to give yourself to me in marriage. You've shied from its consummation, spend long hours away in the daytime—and now at night. Lynden, I'll honor your virtue enough to believe that you're not cuckolding me, but I must wonder if, when you were forced to marry me, there was some man you loved who might have followed you here, and whom you continue to see?"

Lynden stood for a few moments, stiff with disbelief. Then a great weakening wash of anger splashed over her, causing her legs to lose strength under its weight, and she caught the back of a chair to keep herself from being swept away. "You . . . you rake! I'm not the one who is notorious the length and breadth of this country for libertine propensities! Just because you're ready to play Roman candles with half the females in the British aristocracy, don't assume that I'm equally eager to soothe my sorrows with the male half."

"*Much* less than delightful," said Melbrooke icily.

Lynden was nearly breathless with wrath, the hurt welling up in her, bitter tears stinging her eyes. "I don't care. I hate you, anyway."

It was as though sparks were struck in Melbrooke's flint-toned eyes. "I'm tempted," he said, "to find out how true that is."

An angry sob burned Lynden's throat. "You have no right . . ." she began.

He reached for her wrist, catching it in a grip like steel wrapped in velvet, but steel nonetheless. He drew her to him.

"My dear little bride, it's not wise to taunt me with my rights when you know that on that subject I've been more patient with you than is required by the church, the law, or the expectations of society. My rights still exist, even though I haven't chosen to assert them—but you seem to have forgotten that I have any." One hand pressed her waist, bringing her softness against his still, firm length. "Patience has been a spectacular nonsuccess, my sweet. Let's see how you like the opposite."

Holding her resisting body with ease, he brought his kiss to the tender curve of her neck. Her skin burned wherever it knew the possession of his mouth. She sought now in good earnest to free herself from this thrilling contact. Lynden's wrist twisted uselessly against the clamp of his hand as his lips traveled to her earlobe. Sobbing with frustration, she bent her head from him, trying to flee that attentive, insistent mouth, but then his lips caught her sensitive, exposed throat, searing a trail of flame to her chin.

And his hands, his fingers! He touched the swell of her hip and she felt a deep, wrenching internal tremor that reached into her soul. She half-turned her body from him, only to feel his hand flat below her breasts, sending vibrations of warmth and passion into her. His lips moved to caress her thick, still-wet curls, then kissed the tears that fell from her angry eyes.

"Melbrooke, have you gone mad?"

"No. Yes." She felt his clean breath at the back of her neck, felt his broad, burning hand through the satin skirt covering her tautly muscled stomach. "Lynden, little Lynden. Aren't you tired of being curious about this? Don't you want to know?"

"I'm not curious, I'm not!" said Lynden, straining against his grasp. "I don't think about it—hardly ever. Let me go!"

He applied a firm pressure to the side of her hip, turning her back to him, and gathered the luxuriant mass of her hair, forcing her to look helplessly into his eyes. "Why let you go? You're not sure where you want to be." And his mouth met hers in a long, open kiss—a kiss she tried to escape, to turn from, but which held her trembling lips with hypnotic power. His hand imparted a fusing, downward pressure on the low slope of her back, pushing her to him. Finally he freed her from the deep, clinging kiss, and she arched away from him, gasping. It took her a moment to regain her breath, and then she spoke.

"That's not true! I know where I want to go—I want to go to bed! I . . . Melbrooke! What are you doing? Oh! Put me down! I meant I wanted to go to my own bed . . . alone . . . to sleep!"

He had lifted her body with such ease that she felt weightless, suspended, a sensation so unnerving that she gave a tiny shriek and clutched her arms desperately around his neck. Then she was being whirled about on the magic carpet of his arms as he carried her across the room. Helplessly her small fists pummeled his hard chest. Then, like a leaf being carried on an autumn breeze, she was let down rapidly, fragile and trembling, in the center of her lush, cream-velvet draped tent bed. He held here there by her widely flung wrists as she squirmed and wriggled.

"Melbrooke! Get off!" she said, panting from exertion.

"Come, so distant? I thought I was Justin," he said, his voice muffled as he kissed her shoulder.

"Not to me, because Lorraine says Justin is Latin for 'the just,' and you are not! Except that you are *just intolerable.*"

She heard his husky laughter, and kicked at him with new vigor, causing the wooden frame of the bed to shake beneath them as her willow-green satin skirts billowed and flounced around her legs. He took advantage of the disarrangement of her skirts to draw his hand up her prettily exposed outer thigh.

She tried to sink from him, to disappear into the mattress. "Stop!" Her voice was sharp with alarm. "I'm warning you, if you don't release me immediately, I shall scream at the top of my lungs to Mrs. Coniston that I'm being ravished!"

"Fine," said Melbrooke. "But don't be surprised if she doses you with licorice infusion like she does the ewes at breeding time."

Her reply, whatever it was to be, was prevented by

the new pressure of his lips on hers, searching and kissing her resisting mouth; his hands were stroking, massaging her trim body; he pulled the gown from one soft shoulder. She shivered as he traced an intricate pattern on her exposed pale-rose flesh. Again she pulled away, and his fingertips ran softly over her quivering dusky lips, keeping them supple until he could find them again with his own. He pressed her to him, murmuring endearments and love talk, biting gently on her naked shoulder.

Then, suddenly, an unexpected, penetrating throb of pleasure raced through her as he moved his hand from her shoulder, down the swell of her breast. Her skin was leaping, swelling unbidden under his touch, which sent circles of tingling sensation through her. She put one hand on his arm to push him away, but instead found herself holding on to his wrist; and, using the other hand to push against his chest, she was strangely aware of the living, warm muscle beneath his shirt, and then a slight movement of his brought her hand flat against the base of his throat, and she felt the pulse that beat there. He had such beautiful colors in him; she was noticing the amber of his hair, the dappled gray of his eyes, the dark wheat of his brows. The light played over his molded cheekbone as he bent his head to kiss the inside of her wrist. Her hand was taken by his, and she closed her eyes, alone, away from the external world, feeling only the mobile, rhythmic search of his mouth in the cup of her palm.

Lynden's transport was followed by a correspondingly strong reaction of guilt and self-disgust; she had vowed to be strong, she had vowed to resist him. But it happened. She despised herself for being as easy for him as were Lady Silvia, Aunt Eleanor, and the scores of other females whose names had been linked with his through society's gossip. Surely now he would know that she cared for him, too, that she was another marionette to respond desperately to his tug upon the strings. Why must he humiliate her with his lovemaking when he was already in love with another woman? Tears appeared on her lashes and streaked down the side of her face into her thick dark curls.

"Justin, you're not kind, not kind," she whispered. Her low voice cracked on the words.

Resting on his elbows, he slowly dried the trails of tears on her face as he studied the fresh pain in her luminous, widened eyes. "No." His voice had a certain gentle timbre. "Sometimes it's not possible to be kind. No one can always be so."

She turned her head away from him looking into the fire. A tear rolled quickly from the bridge of her nose to be absorbed into the cream-velvet bed cover. "You make me unhappy."

Melbrooke swung his legs gracefully to the edge of the bed, sat up, and turned to her, smoothing her hair with his hand. "It's not my wish to." He pulled her chin around carefully, trying to look into her face.

She closed her eyes against him, heard him sigh, and felt him gather her into his arms and pull her to him. The soft touch of his lips was in her hair as he massaged her back soothingly. "What am I to do with you, Lynden?"

After a moment he laid her gently back upon the bed and kissed her on the forehead. The mattress gave a bounce as he left her. She heard the door to his room click shut.

He was gone. Lynden stared at the ceiling, a devastating loneliness growing within her. She had won; she had gotten rid of him. Why was victory so bitter?

CHAPTER FOURTEEN

The days that followed held Fern Court in an abstracted tension. Lorraine, missing Kyler, settled into a state of calm melancholia. A new and even more impenetrable formality characterized Lord Melbrooke's behavior. Lynden owned a superficial composure that had a tendency to slip into belligerence over trivial irritations. She had devised ingenious strategems for avoiding her husband and was both relieved and hurt when they succeeded. They met only at dinner, where Lynden cunningly led involved discussions on the best political direction for the Whig party, the stability of the pound relative to the franc, and the economic benefits of the West Indies trade, thus rendering mealtime an impressively high-minded, if rather dull, experience. There always came a time, however, at that delicate interval between the removal of the entremets and the arrival of dessert, when Lynden ran out of probing political questions to her husband's deft answers and there was nothing further to say. Lynden would sit, staring into her plate, hideously conscious of the silence and her husband's nearness, though Melbrooke never let the silence continue to unbearable lengths before asking her, perhaps, if Mr. Coniston could procure her anything on his trip into Penrith on Wednesday, or whether or not the baying of the foxhounds on the fellside had waked her that morning.

Lorraine and Lynden spent the days near Fern Court, leaning over rough stone walls to watch the farmers muck their fields. Often the twins were invited to enter the cottage kitchens through low, slate thresholds to snack on goat cheese, oak cakes, and home-brewed ale. On days of inclement weather they laid claim to the music room, and while Lorraine coaxed haunting melodies from the pianoforte, Lynden thumbed diligently through complete works and anthologies, tirelessly selecting and then discarding countless verses mentioning spring flowers from Chaucer, Donne, Milton, Pope, and Burns.

She was not alone with Melbrooke until the night of Lady Silvia's ball. At eight that evening Lynden sat before her gold-trimmed mirror, splendidly dressed in a high-waisted gown of lake-red shot silk, with a low-sloping décolletage trimmed in a narrow frilling of white lace. Her maid, having finished dressing Lynden's hair in clean falling curls, had gone to Lorraine's room to assist her. Lynden had shyly slipped onto her finger the ruby-and-diamond engagement ring when Melbrooke himself knocked on her door.

Tonight, in his dark-blue jacket, waistcoat of white-on-white embroidered satin, and tasseled Hessians, he was a picture to make a maiden's heart flutter—and Lynden was no more immune than the next maiden. She inadvertently drew her knuckle to her lips, then nervously extended her hand to him.

"Good evening, My Lord. You look very elegant tonight, I think."

He dropped a cool kiss on her fingers, released them, and smiled, the gray eyes remaining distant. "Next to you, My Lady, I am a poor patch of seed grass near to a rose bush in full blossom."

"You are gallant, My Lord," observed Lynden, fighting an unseemly and rather girlish urge to cover her plunging bodice. "But—is it time to leave already? I thought we were to go on the quarter hour."

"We are. But I wanted to give you this before we left." He handed her a small box trimmed in black velveteen and engraved in gold leaf with the name of a well-known Bond Street jeweler. "They complete a set with your ring."

She looked at him, eyes widened in surprise, setting the box carefully in her lap. Then she slipped off the tiny clasp and opened it. Against the black-velvet interior of the little box, lying in a shimmering network of light, were a bright, crescent-shaped gem hairpiece and dainty twin earrings which matched a dancing river of rubies and brilliant diamonds set in a necklace of delicate white gold filigree. She looked at Melbrooke, her mouth open slightly in amazement.

"You shouldn't buy me things like this," she said, a rush of emotion bringing a prickle of tears to her eyelids.

"Nonsense, my dear," he said with slight amusement. "I shall often buy you things like this. How else should I spend my royalties?" He picked the necklace from its plush ebony bed; she bowed her head and felt the deliberate movements as he clasped it at the back of her neck. When he was finished, he rested his palms on her shoulders and they looked at the reflection of the necklace in the mirror until Lynden noticed he had shifted his gaze to her face. She blushed and looked down again.

"Lynden, I . . ." began Melbrooke. His conversation was interrupted by Lorraine's perfunctory knock and entrance into the room. She wore a summer-sky-blue gown and her grandmother's pearl set. "I'm ready, Lynden," she called, "and several minutes early, so . . ." She broke off with dismay when she saw Melbrooke in the room. "Oh dear! I'll return later!"

Melbrooke sanctioned her presence with an admonishing wave. "No need. Ladies, shall we go?"

The great banqueting hall in the sollar of Crant Castle had been transformed into a ballroom. A false floor of oak planking had been laid across the uneven stone to accommodate the dancers; a modern orchestra in formal evening wear sent stately harmonious chords wavering through the throng; the walls were hung, no doubt at Lady Silvia's orders, in yards of gold sateen; and Lord Crant's bizarre collection of footed chairs had been removed to the nether regions of the house to be replaced by up-to-date sofas, ottomans, benches, and single chairs.

Lady Silvia was receiving guests in a clinging gown of silk gauze of a color politely called Cupid's pink, but more accurately termed flesh, which made her seem in certain postures and turns of lights to be wearing nothing at all. She greeted Lorraine and Lynden with condescending smiles and Melbrooke with a delicious heavy-lidded gaze.

"Lady Melbrooke!" she purred. "How delightful you look. Our young men will be quite smitten, I vow. I hope you have come prepared to dance every set."

"I *was* prepared, but after climbing your steps, I feel I will collapse after the first measure." Lynden's tone was sadly lacking in cordiality.

Lord Crant stood at Silvia's side. In response to his sister's words, he said, "Wit and beauty in one small frame. It is what one finds so particularly . . . taking in you, Lady Melbrooke."

Lynden arched her brows in what she hoped might be a fair imitation of Lady Silvia's style and proceeded to embark upon flirtation with Lord Crant calculated to show Lord Melbrooke (not that he seemed to entertain any doubts on the matter, she thought wrathfully) that she was as likely as he to pursue and be pursued by the opposite sex. Lord Crant, in a spirit of appreciative mischief, soon proved himself an able, if rather frighteningly unreliable, ally in this object. He obliged Lynden with an exchange of dalliance strong enough, surely, to raise Lord Melbrooke's ire—finally discomforting her completely with a remark that succeeded in reminding Lynden that Crant was both a scoundrel and a blockhead. Crant, out of nowhere, said that he was considering adding to the family collection some examples from the Flemish school of interpretative architectural representation. Surely, being such an expert, she could advise him? Lynden was sure it would have aroused more of Lord Melbrooke's ire than she was willing to deal with if he learned about the visit Lorraine and she had made to Crant Castle—and heaven knows what sort of difficult suspicions!

For a moment Lynden was thrown off balance, torn between her desire to keep Melbrooke in the dark about the incident and her need to maintain her precarious imposture as an amateur archeologist in Lord Crant's vision. She waved her hand distractedly in the air before her as though magically erasing Crant's words, and said forcefully, if rather obscurely, "What a joke-smith you are, My Lord! Indeed, I'll not reply in kind —'tis too, too unfitting to talk of such at a ball! But we noticed on our way in that you've lighting on the castle walls. At once you must escort me to your oriel windows so that I can admire the prospect from this height!"

Lord Crant showed himself all compliance, but as he led her across the crowded floor on his arm, he bent toward her, regarding her with those strange eyes that on him seemed so unnatural and on Kyler so attractive. "So," he said, raising one quizzical eyebrow, "Justin doesn't know that you've been playing under my castle walls. I thought not. It's very prudent of you not to tell him, my delight. I think he might not like it."

"What an imagination you have!" said Lynden, now in better command of herself. "Lorraine and I were only painting outside the castle walls. Why should that disturb anyone?"

Crant scanned her with a cool smile. "It shouldn't, of course—so long as you were *only* painting."

"But naturally. What else?" said Lynden, all the time aware that wedged between the stays of her light damask whalebone corset was the skeleton key she had received from Kyler.

Lorraine and Lynden had planned to slip away from the ballroom at some auspicious moment to explore the locked tower in the east wall that Crant had pointed out to them in their first visit. It was Lynden's vaguely optimistic hope that Crant's having ordered the tower locked meant that there might be something in it that he wished to hide. But even the anticipation of this risky operation had no positive effect on Lynden's enjoyment of the ball.

It was a large affair, at least by Lynden's standard, with more than one hundred couples. The guest book glittered with the distinguished names from the highest ranks of nobility and celebrity that Lady Silvia could either find sojourning through winter in the immediate county or import from surrounding counties. The aristocracy, present in great numbers, found themselves in the company of an important playwright, four of the nation's leading poets, a lady novelist lately receiving recognition from the Prince Regent himself, a major portrait painter, and a scattering of up-and-coming Whig politicians. It was a level of society Lynden had never dreamed of entering, and yet she saw that even the most august of these persons greeted her husband with deference and warm affection. They talked intimately of his family—his mother, father, seven brothers and sisters, and many cousins—all of whom were unknown to Lynden; they also discussed his writing, of which Lynden knew little. Each of these illustrious personages seemed to know him more intimately than she, his wife, and it was clear that this company would have thronged Fern Court had it not been Melbrooke's season to seclude himself with his work.

Of course, it was not that Lynden was ignored. In fact, she received a great deal of attention. Lord Melbrooke's marriage was news to no one, for it had been the occasion for much lively speculative interest. His acquaintances met Lynden with a flattering mixture of friendliness and curiosity, but clearly their kindness was for Melbrooke's sake. Lynden was aware that they were wondering why, after remaining a bachelor until twenty-eight, Melbrooke had suddenly committed himself in marriage to this rustic teenager of squirearchy birth and with no talent, no fortune, and little seasoning. And more galling, there was a caution in their efforts to be nice to her, as though it was tacitly assumed that her tender age and country upbringing had left her unprepared to fathom sophisticated conversation.

It was eleven and three-quarters before Lynden was able to steal away, meeting Lorraine in an upstairs ladies' cloakroom.

"What took you so long?" demanded Lynden. She had sent the young maidservant to fetch their cloaks after purchasing her discretion with an extravagant tip.

"I couldn't help it," answered Lorraine. "It was Ottmar Wishke. He cornered me to talk about his pedometer."

"His what?"

"His new pedometer watch. Besides telling the time, it records the distance walked if one carries it on one's person when taking a constitutional—which he has been doing daily, and he heartily recommends its benefits to me."

"Foppery!" said Lynden severely. "I'm surprised you would sit and listen to such stuff when there's work to be done! Ah, here are the coats. Grab yours and follow me."

They threaded their way down the stairs, unnoticed in the commotion created by scurrying waiters, resting musicians, maidservants, and trysting couples. They stopped at a landing to pick up the filled and burning oil lamp the bribed housemaid had left for them. "I think she believes we were going to meet some gentlemen," said Lynden, giggling. Then it was out into the chill night air, past the Elizabethan garden, past the apex of the triangular courtyard to the locked tower near the east wall.

They left the walk after a quick survey of the area, and Lorraine held the lamp, shielding its light with her body, while Lynden reached under her bodice, remov-

ing the nettling key with a gasp of relief. In the courtyard there were a few strolling refugees from the activity inside the house, but the twins were shielded by
the looming shadow of the tower, alone with the flat
odor of cold stone and the pungent reek of the stables.
Sounds of laughter, and a few discordant notes played
by the musicians as they tuned their instruments for another set, drifted out to them from the Great Tower
rising at their backs like a giant kiln, spangled with
light. An indistinct babble of servants' talk emanated
from the kitchens, mingling with the lovely scent of
baking pastry. Lynden fussed with the key in the rusty
lock for a few moments before it clicked open; at the
same instant a party from the tower drew dangerously
near, so near that certain phrases of conversation
could be heard, as well as the scrape of footsteps on
the walk.

"Someone's coming!" said Lynden. She pushed Lorraine and the lantern into the dark interior of the tower,
and followed her, closing the door behind them as
quickly and quietly as she could. They stood in silence
as Lorraine lifted the lantern high, causing a wide circle
of dim yellow light to spread about the place. Dusty,
dark cobwebs laden liberally with fly carcasses hung in
the corners like a petrified mist, and a bat, barely
seen, fluttered across the top reaches of the light. A
staircase spiraled up and around the wall—a staircase
made impassable by the gaping cavities and broken
boards appearing at too frequent intervals. There had
been a second story to the place, as evidenced by a
skeletal framework of cross-beams over the girls'
heads; but what had been the floor of that story was lying in a musty, spiky jumble of planks and fallen
masonry. A star winked far above through the slit of a
window, and the wind whistled tunelessly through a
crack in the far wall, a crack that reached from the
ground up into oblivion and appeared large enough to
put one's hand through.

Lynden picked up her skirts and walked gingerly forward into the mess, lost her footing on a broken board, and put her hand out to catch her balance on an old gray upright beam, which promptly gave way under her meager weight and fell with a grinding, hollow crash into the rubble. A shower of grime and small stones fell from the darkness above them, accompanied by a large chunk of masonry.

"What a miserable, rubbishing place!" exclaimed Lynden, coughing and shaking the dust from her cloak. "Trust Crant to have something like this on his property." She gave a disgusted sigh. "One thing, anyway: We can depend upon it that Lady Irmingarde never hid anything in here, or she'd have been toppled by falling masonry."

"Of course she didn't," responded her sister with resignation. "I tried to tell you, Lynden, but you'll never listen to anyone. What could this ruined tower have to do with a poem about spring flowers? And as I've told you about thirty times, it can't be the 'roofless tower' in the Robert Burns poem because you can see clearly that it has a roof. Furthermore, Crant couldn't have ordered this tower locked if he suspected that Lady Irmingarde might have hidden Kyler's documents here, because Lord Crant knows nothing about Lady Irmingarde's clue. If he did, he wouldn't have left it in the mausoleum box for us to find. And you can see for yourself, Lynden, the mess in here hasn't been cleared for centuries. If Lord Crant suspected any material dangerous to him was here, he would have had the place cleared and searched."

"I hope you're not turning into one of those horrid people who are forever telling one 'I told you so,' Rainey. Besides, as I told _you_, if one is going to solve a mystery, one has to explore _all_ the possibilities, no matter how unlikely."

"Very well, but we've explored this one enough," said Lorraine, reaching for the door handle. "Let's return before we're missed." She rattled the handle and pushed against the door. "Lynden, get out your skeleton key—I think the door has locked behind us . . . Lynnie, what's the matter?"

"Nothing, Lorraine. Just push harder on the door. It will open. Here, let me try." Lynden had no better success, and after a bit leaned her back on the door, muscles sore from pushing, panting slightly from the effort.

Lorraine stared at her sister. "Lynden, what have you done with the skeleton key?"

"I haven't done anything with it. I must have dropped it outside when you rushed us in here so quickly."

"*I* rushed us in here so quickly?"

"Oh, very well, then, I rushed us in here," said Lynden. "Recriminations won't help matters any. Isn't that what you're always saying?"

"I might have said so," agreed Lorraine tartly, "but that was before I was locked in a batty belfry by my sister. How do you propose to get us out?"

"What a question—as though there were a hundred ways," said Lynden. "We are going to bang on the door until someone comes and unlocks it for us." She hammered her fists on the door, then pressed her ear to its oaken thickness and listened for a reply. She repeated this procedure three more times before she finally heard female voices outside, voices thick with North Country accents.

"Help, let us out!" she cried, banging forcefully against the door. A second passed; the outside voices became shrill, and there was the sound of running feet.

"What did they say?" asked Lorraine.

"They said," replied Lynden, " 'Lord save us, 'tis ghoulies and bogies in the Old Tower!' "

Moments went by before heavier footsteps and deeper voices came, muffled but audible even to Lorraine, though not one directly approached the door. The jumble of noise seemed to hover indistinctly outside, until a particularly weighty bass overwhelmed the general grumbling current.

"Ought to fetch the parson," boomed the voice authoritatively. "Happen it could be a demon in 'ere."

"Stupid, ignorant . . ." muttered Lynden. She raised her voice and called loudly, "You out there! Fetch the key and open this door!"

An excited gasp flickered through the crowd outside. "It spoke, it spoke!" came a cracked, adolescent pipe.

"It speaks with a woman's tongue," blurted another voice.

"A witch!"

" 'Tis the Witch Woman of Wetherian!"

"Get back from the door! It may try to get out!"

"You superstitious boobies! Of course we're trying to get out!" screamed Lynden, banging on the door with a piece of broken masonry. "And I'm not the Witch Woman of Whatever. I'm the Witch Woman of Fern Court . . . no, I mean, Lady Melbrooke!"

There was more exclamatory murmuring outside.

Lynden groaned. "What a to-do, Raine. The stables and cookhouse must have emptied out there."

From outside came another voice. "Someone fetch Lord Crant! *Fetch Lord Crant!*"

"No," screamed Lorraine and Lynden together. "Don't fetch Lord Crant!"

Lynden pressed her ear to the door and then leaned against it, rolling her eyes in exasperation. "It's too late—I can hear someone going." Lynden sat down on a bristling split plank, disregarding her beautiful satin evening cloak, and put her face in her hands.

Someone, doubtless a brave soul, was standing very near the door and muttering a sporadic, quavering incantation: "Bogie woogle, leave our lives, go to where the devil thrives."

"Idiots," said Lynden through clenched teeth.

The external murmuring rose again. "Lord Crant's

coming—with Lady Silvia," came a voice. "And Lord Melbrooke himself is with 'em."

"That's it. I'm finished," stated Lynden flatly through her palms. Lorraine patted her on the head.

Lord Crant's cultured tones responded to a thickly accented male voice. "Yes, yes, Rob, I know. Take those pitchforks back into the stables. And the rest of you, go back about your business. Do you think I pay you to stand around exchanging ghost stories?"

There was a protest, a wheedling explanation.

"I won't be needing any help at all," replied Crant. "There's nothing supernatural behind this door." There was a tramp of receding footsteps.

A key turned in the lock; the door opened, revealing Lynden, head buried dejectedly under her arms, and Lorraine, eyes blinking into the bright light of the lantern carried by Lord Crant, who stood in the doorway behind Melbrooke. After three heartbeats of silence, Lynden looked up directly into the cold gray eyes of her husband.

The long metallic shape of the skeleton key dully caught the light, as it lay in the dust at Crant's feet. He bent to pick it up, and flipped it in his lantern-free hand, then held it still and examined it with great interest.

"This must be yours, Lady Melbrooke," he said softly, handing her the key. He then turned to Melbrooke, and drawled, "One regards with awe, my dear Justin, the myriad accomplishments of your young bride."

It was a silent coach ride back to Fern Court. Lord Melbrooke preserved a grim, if courteous, demeanor. As they were pulling into the carriageway, he turned to Lynden and, in a conversational tone, requested a moment with her in his study. Lynden and Lorraine exchanged apprehensive glances. Lorraine worriedly bit her lip, but Lynden shrugged her shoulders nervously, kissed Lorraine good night, and followed her husband into the study, her nose defiantly in the air.

Melbrooke closed the door behind her, but did not offer her a seat.

Lynden spoke first. "I suppose you want an explanation of why Lorraine and I were in that tower."

"What I want and what I expect are two different things. You had no explanation for Lord Crant. Why should I think you would have one now? Unless you've thought on the way home of some weak fabrication you'd like to offer," he said, a definite restraint in his voice.

"I had," Lynden admitted candidly. "But there's no point in saying it now because you're obviously not disposed to believe it."

"You may be a rogue, my dear, but at least you're an honest one," said Melbrooke wearily. "But you can't expect me to play Friar Tuck to your Robin Hood without telling me who you've cast as the Sheriff of Nottingham. If it's Lord Crant, as I suspect, Lynden, it won't do. I've told you that before. You have quite a propensity to cheerfully ignore my most reasonably offered advice. What amazes me, though, is that just when I think you've gone as far as you possibly can, you initiate still more ill-conceived escapades in the furtherance of some scheme you are unable to confide. Tonight, though, was the last."

"The last?" said Lynden with trepidation. "Justin, you wouldn't do anything horrid, would you?"

"It's not a question of doing anything horrid, Lynden. It's a question of exercising my responsibility for you. You *are* only seventeen, and whatever you're up to, if it involves Crant, it can't continue. Don't be deceived that because Crant is an acquaintance of mine— an acquaintanceship formed before I had any idea of marrying—I think he is a safe subject for your petty intrigue, whatever it is. Sometimes I find him an interesting companion, but there is nothing admirable about his principles. Without sullying your ears with any details, let me assure you that he can behave in ways regardless of the normal sensibilities. I won't ask you again to confide in me. If you had intended to, you would have done so by now." Melbrooke turned and walked to the window, gazing out to the stables where the grooms were walking the steaming horses, the burning rush lights glistening off the sweating equine musculature. He spoke, still looking out the window. "Lynden, I am ordering Mrs. Coniston to begin packing tomorrow morning, and the day after we will leave for Melbrooke Court in Buckinghamshire."

CHAPTER FIFTEEN

"If only there was some way to get a message to Kyler," said Lynden, for the fifth time that day. The twins were sitting on the piano bench in the music room, Lynden with her back to the piano, Lorraine facing the piano with her arms crossed on the closed cover. It was twilight, the day after Lady Silvia's ball, and the day before their precipitously scheduled trip to Buckinghamshire. The candelabra sent soft, dusky flickers of peach glimmer in an indistinct oval around the girls, causing the fabric of their dresses to flow and shine. The bodice of Lynden's soft pink gown was embroidered with roses; Lorraine's dress was an attractive creation in blue-bell blue, matching the ribbon that tied back her hair.

"There's no way to send one," answered Lorraine with gentle desolation in her soft, brown eyes. "And Lord Melbrooke told you that we are forbidden to leave the house unaccompanied."

Lynden nodded glumly. "I know—and I blanch to think what Melbrooke would do if either of us tried to sneak out, because after he made me give my word that I wouldn't try it, he said, 'let us hope you mean to honor that'—and in the coldest way, too! He positively loathes me now."

"Don't say that!" said Lorraine, dropping her hands to her lap and clasping them in distress. "Oh, don't! How could anyone loathe you, Lynnie?"

"Aunt Eleanor and Uncle Monroe did," Lynden pointed out inexorably. "*They* didn't find it too hard,

212

and Melbrooke finds me just as troublesome as they did! What's more, he has less reason to feel obliged to like me—he's not even a relation."

"Not related? You're married!"

"That," said Lynden, darkly, "he could have annulled."

Lorraine paled. "Lynden—he hasn't said anything on that head, has he?"

"No, but heaven knows what he's thinking—*I* don't! I never suspected that he would do anything so drastic as drag us south to keep us out of Lord Crant's vicinity. What a fool I was last night to drop that skeleton key. Raine, your happiness hangs in the balance. There's nothing for it. We must act!"

Lorraine sighed and opened the lid of the piano, her fingers trilling the keys. "I hope that doesn't mean that you are again going to suggest that I flee to the smuggler's cabin and elope with Kyler while you distract the household by feigning a spasm of the heart. No matter how desperate the circumstances, I couldn't bend my principles to participate in an elopement . . ." She paused to perform a thoughtful arpeggio. "Unless—oh, unless Kyler asked me first. Besides, it would never work. No one would believe you could fall to a spasm of the heart at your age."

Lynden was about to argue that she could pretend a weakness of the heart, arising from an early bout of measles, when Lord Melbrooke pushed the door open. The candlelight shimmered in his amber locks, but it was a glint made cold by his distant demeanor, like the sun reflecting on the top of a mountain that is otherwise shrouded in mist. He bade the twins good evening, and said, "I wanted to inform you our departure is set for nine o'clock tomorrow morning. The roads are dry and if the weather tomorrow is as mild as it has been, travel should be pleasant."

"That," said Lynden, "depends on where you're going."

He gazed at her coldly. "So, you are still angry about

my decision to leave. Don't say any more on that score; last night you said quite enough. I know your feelings, but that doesn't alter my determination. I won't be moved, Lynden."

"Like a hound over a fresh-buried legbone," muttered Lynden ungraciously. "I ought to tell you this about your travel plans: I doubt I'll feel able to leave in the morning."

"Oh?" He raised his eyebrows in ironic solicitousness. "Do you predict you'll be feeling too delicate?"

"Yes, I do!" said Lynden defiantly, angered by his skeptical tone. "I have a heart flutter from childhood measles, it may surprise you to learn."

"The only thing that surprises me is that you've had all day to plot and you haven't thought of anything better than a heart flutter," Melbrooke observed.

Lynden stared furiously at him. "If I died, you'd be sorry you said that, wouldn't you?"

Only the most optimistic of observers, upon reading Melbrooke's expression, could have ascertained that His Lordship might greet his young wife's demise with anything other than the most profound relief.

"Sometimes, Lynden," he began, "I have a strong urge to . . ." But before Melbrooke could complete his sentence, Lynden had decided that she preferred to remain in ignorance of the nature of his urge, and stood up, stamped her foot, announced she was having a spasm, and collapsed gracefully in Lord Melbrooke's direction, having carefully calculated that he was near enough to catch her.

"Lynnie, what have you done?" cried Lorraine, jumping to her feet.

Supporting Lynden's limp body in his arms, Melbrooke could not bring himself to regret a circumstance that prescribed his pretty bride throwing herself into his arms, no matter how unflattering might be her motive. His hand touched the healthy, glowing skin of her cheek, and her eyes fluttered open and looked up at him with suspicious limpidity. There was a noise in the doorway, but Melbrooke assumed it to be one of the servants and didn't turn his head. Lynden's view, however, included the doorway and she looked toward the sound. What she saw changed her from an inanimate and sickly caricature to a vibrant young lady in a soft pink evening gown, who in the space of three seconds had pulled herself from her husband's embrace, shrieked, and then stood gaping at the doorway.

Lorraine clasped one hand to her bosom and rushed forward, exclaiming, "Oh, you've come! You shouldn't have! Oh, Kyler, you're here!"

The disreputable gentleman referred to was leaning against the door frame, legs casually crossed. When Lorraine reached him, he gave her a quick, one-armed hug.

"Aye, I'm here . . . Dash it all, though, you oughtn't to charge like that—could knock a man full over." He grinned lovingly at Lorraine, the wide, sensitive mouth curving. His chapeau-bras was shifted back over his dark curls, and his long leather cape and shiny, black leather riding boots were splashed with mud. A large flintlock pistol was hanging backward at his hip; and the black patch over his left eye completed his raffish and piratical appearance. "I was worried when you two rascals didn't come to our rendezvous today. I thought maybe Lord Melbrooke had discovered you'd been sneaking out at owl-time and so I'd better come down and help you explain away the mess. Mind you, here I find the hornet thump into her husband's arms, amorous as you please, so I may have been wasting my time."

"Kyler, sometimes you're so stupid," said Lynden indignantly. "We weren't making love—I was having a heart spasm."

"Maybe *you* were having a heart spasm," retorted Kyler, "but I think His Lordship there was having a different kind of sp— Ow! Blast it, hornet! Good thing I've got my high boots on. You almost kicked my leg off! Between you and your sister, a body could be bruised black from head to toe. What are you glaring at me for—that *is* your husband, ain't it?"

"Of course he's my husband!"

"I'd better make myself known to him, then." Kyler doffed his hat and made His Lordship a graceful bow, a charming light dancing in his eyes. "Behold me, My Lord, Kyler Miller at your service."

Lord Melbrooke beheld this rather astonishing young man for the space of a full minute. Kyler, quite unabashed by the survey, smiled at Lorraine, gave Lynden's curls a playful tug, and sauntered into the room, slapping his hat on his thigh.

"Indeed." There was a spark of interest in Melbrooke's smoky eyes. "I have no obsession for ponderous formalities, Mr. Miller, but I couldn't help observing that you weren't announced by a servant. Did you, perhaps, not enter the house by the front door?"

"I snapped the latch and crawled in through the parlor window," Kyler disclosed casually. "But I could have gotten in a dozen ways. Devilish easy house to enter. No need to bother about it, My Lord, cracksman ain't my lay."

"I'm delighted to be so informed," said Melbrooke dryly. "Could it be, then, that your—lay—is . . . What was it? A tinsmith?"

"Tinker," corrected Lorraine in a small, scared voice.

Kyler laughed. "Oh, I do tinker in this and that. But I know naught of the trade. That's just a tale the princess here thought up so she wouldn't have to 'fess that she met me on the High Toby. In short, sir, we met when I held up milady's coach."

"A congenial circumstance," observed Melbrooke.

"You wouldn't think so if you'd ever held up a coach," Kyler informed him knowledgeably. "The princess fainted dead away in my arms and the little one attacked me like a weasel at a trout. I decided right then that a snaffler's life was not for me! To tell you the truth, My Lord, I'd like to go honest, but if

216

you don't believe that and have a case of the distrusts, I'll let you train my snapper on me while we talk."

He turned out his pistol and handed it, butt-end, to Lord Melbrooke, who received it, gave it a short, expert examination for weight and balance, and then returned it to Kyler. "A pretty weapon," said Melbrooke, "but I'm afraid I'd feel a little silly pointing it at you, since I can't help remarking that it's not loaded."

"Of course it ain't. I didn't want to take the chance of you getting mad and blowing it off at me, which Lord knows, you might do once you hear the full story of what these twins and I have been about." He reholstered the pistol.

Lorraine slipped her hand through Kyler's gloved hand and spoke. "Are we to tell all, then? How glad I am! Kyler, your decision does you great honor!" She turned to Lord Melbrooke and said earnestly, "My Lord, you cannot know the depth with which I have regretted those dictates of conscience which have kept Lynnie and me from sharing Kyler's story with you. But how could we have spoken without his sanction, or even, in honor, have asked him to give his sanction when this regards a matter so painful, so private, and so fraught with danger?"

Melbrooke took this dramatic announcement with what was in Lynden's eyes a disappointing degree of calm. He merely remarked that they had better waste no time in relating to him so weighty a narrative, and motioned his wife, sister-in-law, and dashing young guest to be seated. Kyler added a festive note to the occasion by drawing a bottle of duty-free brandy from a capacious pocket in his cloak and offering to share it with his companions. Lynden hurried to bring from a wine table a set of glasses embossed with the Melbrooke coat-of-arms.

Kyler took a fortifying gulp of the brandy, modestly pronounced it very tolerable stuff, and, after a somewhat lengthy introductory comment, handed to Lord Melbrooke the letter containing his stepmother's deathbed revelations. The three younger members of the party waited in suspense while Melbrooke read the letter and then reread it. When Lynden could bear it no longer, she left her padded armchair and, with a sigh of pink skirts, sat on the Chinese floral carpet at Melbrooke's feet.

"Well?" she demanded, looking up at him.

He carefully folded the paper and gazed at the company, new comprehension dawning in his eyes. His hand stroked Lynden. "It appears, little one, that my judgments were too quick. Almost, I begin to see the light. This letter is remarkable—I should say, incredible."

"You don't believe it?" said Lorraine, clenching a fist, knuckles white with anxiety. Lynden sat alert at her husband's knee, challenge bright in her eyes.

Kyler leaned back against the sofa cushion, resting his ankle on one knee, looking soberly at Melbrooke. "Can't blame him if he doesn't," he said frankly. "Don't know whether or not to believe it myself. At least I didn't until the girls discovered that sundial."

"Sundial?" inquired Melbrooke reflectively. "Could you be referring to the sundial in the castle courtyard at Crant?"

"Yes, that one," said Lynden from her place at his feet. "You'll be mad as mare's meat, though, once you've heard what Raine and I have been about."

"Will I? Then somehow I shall strive to moderate my temper within the bounds of civilized usage. No doubt your two comrades here will be able to protect you from the more violent exigencies of my wrath."

"Not me," disclaimed Kyler ignobly. "I think she should be beat! Never know what she'll do next, but it's likely to turn me into an old man wondering about it. I was foolish enough to give her a skeleton key and spent the whole time I was down in Broughton worrying what she would do with it. Don't know what possessed me to give it to her in the first place."

"Neither do I," said Lynden crossly. "Because all it did was get us in a parcel of trouble without producing the least reward." She gave a sideways, underlashed glance at her husband. "I suppose you want to hear it from the beginning, My Lord? Very well. Things began with Lady Irmingarde's sundial . . ."

In a discourse much amplified by Lorraine and amended by Kyler, Lynden related the story of the initial trip to Crant Castle and the evidence of the sundial rubbing; with some embarrassment and defiance, she told how the three had broken into the Crant mausoleum on the night Melbrooke had been waiting for her; and faltered to an end with an exposition of their (weak) motives for exploring the locked tower on the Crant property.

"What a trouble merchant you are, child," said Kyler with disapproval. "It's plain as friar's smocking *that* horse wouldn't run." The disapproval left his face at her indignant expression, to be replaced, strangely, by chagrin. "There now, don't needle up on me. I don't know why I was talking about poor schemes, hornet, when this morning I went to Crant Castle and belled out a dozen times worse than you."

"To Crant?" questioned Lorraine worriedly.

"Without us?" said Lynden, not at all pleased.

"Aye, missy, without you, and it was a good thing, too, from the way things turned out. I made it back from Broughton last night and recollected that Crant was throwing a gala ball, so I decided that this morning early would be a good time to poke around the castle. I thought since the place was bound to be teeming with guests and their servants, no one would be too suspicious when they saw another stranger floating about."

"Excellent plan," said Lynden sarcastically. "Gentlemen floating about in leather capes, eyepatches, and riding boots were bound to be three pennies a dozen."

"Of course I wasn't going to go like this. I, um, borrowed a livery from one of the Countess Chepstow's outriders. But the fellow didn't appreciate it when he came into the tower storeroom to see me halfway into his coat and set up a squawk like a damn rooster—loud enough to wake half the place up. I made a fast exit down the hallway and ran smack into Lord Crant himself as I was turning the corner. My Lord Crant looked at me as if I was the walking dead, and then gave me a smile that would chill your soul. 'Now who could you be?' he said. 'Unfinished business, eh?' " Kyler's face darkened. "Damned if that man doesn't have a lot to answer for. Anyway, this other fellow sneaks up behind me. Turns out to be some gone-to-seed Prussian henchman of Crant's called Otto."

"Ottmar!" corrected the twins in unison.

"That's it, Ottmar. He was planning to hit me over the head with a chair. I ducked out the side door and ran up the staircase on the inside of the castle wall, with Crant urging Ottmar after me. There was a murder-hole in the walkway that my own ancestors used to drop stones on invaders trying to climb the castle walls. I dropped through it into the putrid, freezing moat. That was a long fall, let me tell you! And I'll wager they were surprised to see me go that way. But I had my horse tethered nearby and got away." Kyler paused. "There's something I'm worried about now. He saw me, and it concerns me that he'll connect my reappearance in his life with the twin's snooping."

Melbrooke had been listening intently to Lynden's narrative, then to Kyler's. For the most part his face remained impassive, but occasionally a smile would touch his lips. All the while, his fingers played gently in Lynden's dark curls. He gave no sign that any of the story surprised him, nor did he appear angry; and beyond remarking at one point that once the mystery had reached Lynden's hearing he supposed the rest was inevitable, Melbrooke had ventured no other comment. Now he leaned forward, his face serious.

"I think you may be right. Lord Crant came to see me this afternoon."

His words produced surprise. "He must have been here while Lorraine and I were in the bake shack eating fresh finger cakes!" said Lynden.

"Possibly," agreed Melbrooke. "Crant didn't stay long. He was on his way south, escorting his sister to Leeds. He came, it seems, to tell me he had been attacked this morning, and the villain—a prodigal illegitimate son, to whom it seems Crant had already behaved with great generosity. Crant told me that this young man had become more and more demanding, and this morning visited him requesting payment for an ill-considered gambling debt. After being refused, the boy became violent—Crant's story went—and fled after threatening Crant's life."

"A wicked, wicked lie," said Lorraine, her soft voice trembling with anger.

"Aye, but it's a clever blackguard," said Kyler. "No doubt he thought if the girls came to you about me, you'd already be convinced I was his ne'er-do-well by-blow." He looked at Melbrooke, tension in the dark young face. "Now who do you believe, Crant or me?"

Melbrooke smiled. "I've known Crant for fifteen years, so naturally I believe you."

"Huzzah!" cried Lynden, grabbing Melbrooke's hand and kissing it fervently. "Oh, Justin, I knew you were a right one!"

Lorraine's eyes misted, and she favored Melbrooke with a warm smile. "Indeed he is!"

"Then you approve of what we've been doing?" said Lynden.

Melbrooke pinched her chin lightly. "Now *that* I didn't say. You ought to have told me, my dear."

"Perhaps I ought, but I'm not in the habit of confiding in you, and, besides, it wasn't my secret. Anyway, I've got a dandy idea now. You see, I've figured out why Crant's taking his sister south. Probably she doesn't know anything about Kyler's birth or Crant's treachery, so Crant would like to have her out of the way should things get lively. And with Crant himself out of the way tomorrow, it would be a prime opportunity for all of us to go to the castle and begin a thorough search . . ."

Melbrooke shook his head. "No, Lynden. From now on you and Lorraine will have no more active part in the matter. I'll do what I can to help your friend here, but only on the condition that you refrain from any involvement. Is that agreed?"

"It is if I have anything to say in the matter," assented Kyler. "There's nothing I'd like better than to see the girls safely out of this, and I don't mind telling you, My Lord, I'm devilish grateful to have your help because I was sharp-staked out to know what move to make next."

"I doubt if this will appeal to Lynden's appetite for attack," said Melbrooke, touching his wife's little nose. "But I think first we ought to put what evidence we have into the hands of a lawyer. I'm not sure how much is needed to support a claim against Crant's title, but I think we should waste no time finding out the legalities. Perhaps what you have already might be enough to initiate an investigation. I have a lawyer in Penrith, a man of excellent reputation, integrity, and discretion. With your permission we could ride there tomorrow and interview him."

CHAPTER SIXTEEN

The dawn was a wildly spreading red and orange fire-
storm as Lord Melbrooke and Kyler left Fern Court,
riding over the hill northward to Penrith. Before leaving, they had issued a strongly worded injunction forbidding Lorraine and Lynden from leaving the house.
In fact, so strongly worded was the injunction that it
took nearly until noon for Lynden to persuade Lorraine to accompany her on another unauthorized trip
to Crant Castle. At first Lorraine turned a deaf ear to
Lynden's arguments, listening unmoved to assurances
that it was quite safe to visit Crant Castle today with
Lord Crant headed south, and her proclamations that
Lord Melbrooke and Kyler were unnecessarily cautious
and stuffy in their notions where the twins were concerned. Lynden went on to point out that they had
handled the affair quite well so far with a minimum of
masculine assistance and there was no reason for them
to step down just because Lord Melbrooke had decided
to interest himself in the matter.

Even this ploy had no effect on Lorraine, but Lynden
craftily changed her argument to a glorious word picture of the happiness that would greet Kyler and, con-
sequently, Lorraine, on the proof of his aristocratic
birth. Of course it was true that searching the locked
tower in the castle wall had led to nothing; Lynden
graciously acknowledged that fact. But had not every
other avenue they had explored borne fruit? Lynden
perceived signs of weakening in her sister, and quickly
made good her advantage with a stirring speech that

might have led one to believe that the only ladies who ever listen to male prohibitions were whiny, weak-spirited, mewling creatures beneath the contempt of a female of resolution and resource. She ended with a generous concession that they would not actually go inside Crant Castle, but only to the slope at its back.

"The slope in back? What's the use of going there?" protested Lorraine.

"Every use in the world. We're looking for something to do with spring flowers, right? On the hill behind the castle are a king's ransom of them. We'll go there and dig for another hidden box."

"Dig?" said Lorraine. "Lynden, you've got spring fever. I remember distinctly that you told me Lord Crant said that Lady Irmingarde had planted *acres* of March-blooming flowers there. It would take an army to dig that up. And speaking of armies, what about Ottmar Wishke?"

"Wishke-swishke. If Crant didn't take him along, then he'll probably be in his bedroom oiling his pedometer and shining his dress sword. I refuse to be put off by anyone who can't take two steps without clicking his heels together. And as for the acres of flowers, we'll go to the spot on the wall that would be directly in line with the sundial and march out one step for every syllable in the sundial poem. You see, like clapping out the meter of a poem."

"Of all the ridiculous, obscure ideas, Lynden—this has got to be your masterwork. How could you possibly put that interpretation on Lady Irmingarde's clue? It makes no sense at all."

"My dear, doubting sister, Lady Irmingarde was an eccentric, and when you're dealing with an eccentric, you can't be forever expecting everything to make sense. Intuition, Lorraine. That's what's needed here. And I was right about the tomb, wasn't I?" said Lynden triumphantly.

"You were also wrong about the locked tower."

"So I was wrong. I am capable of error—I'm not God, you know."

Thus Lorraine found herself being whisked out the door and on her way to Crant Castle before she had even begun to guess what Lynden's not being God had to do with her present predicament.

It was a fine, warm day, the first great day of this year's spring. The morning was graced with a crown of fine, cream-velvet clouds eddying gently through a bright blue sky; a warm breeze drew pungent, spicy scents from the thawing ground and made heavy winter coats unnecessary. The sun was brilliant white, its rays gifted with an unmistakable spring slant which angled in to turn to a light mist all the hidden, secretly die-hard winter ice. The girls stopped at the gardener's cottage where they found Mrs. Robins hanging out a fresh wash while her baby twins slept nearby, their pine cradles hung from an oak branch where a quiet nurserymaid wind rocked their slumbers. Lynden borrowed two shovels on the pretext of needing them to dig fishing worms, and as they walked along the path in the direction of Crant Castle, they heard Mrs. Robins sing a lullaby:

I've placed my cradle on yon oak top
And aye, as the wind blew, my babies did rock.

Discretion counseled the twins to approach Crant Castle from the side, following the rocky spine of the hill behind instead of attacking the broad open space in front of the fortress. From the brow of the hill to the rear, the castle looked like a fairy-tale dollhouse, slumbering in the spring sun, done in perfect detail. The girls could make out the tiny, precisely formed figure of the sundial in the garden. Instead of the portcullis and giant, impressive drawbridge, there were two posterns, small gateways set low in the walls toward each corner, fronted by the plank bridges spanning the moat. On the gentle slope at the foot of the hill lay the exquisitely colored garden of spring flowers: the thick, white and pink carpet of the wood anemone punctuated beautifully by the golden yellow, heart-shaped lesser celandine, sweet violets, and the lonely, brilliant white snowdrops—a deep, velvet floor reaching to the moat.

The wild garden covered more area than was immediately suggested from the hilltop, as the twins discovered when, hem-deep in vegetation, they stood in the middle of "spring's floral harbingers." Lynden had paced off an area consistent with her theory of where the documents might be buried, but she could not help confessing to herself now that this excavation might be another exercise in futility. Yet her determination to beat Lord Melbrooke and Kyler to the punch was strong, so she began to chop at the hard earth with the blade of her shovel. Lorraine joined her and soon they had dug the beginnings of a narrow trench.

At the beginning, Lorraine sent nervous, sporadic glances at the castle wall looming above them, but her efforts to keep up with her sister soon required all her concentration. After what seemed like hours of digging, but what she knew to be a quarter hour at the most, her hands were red and raw, a fair blister rose under her soft, leather gloves, and her shoulders ached as though she had been stretched upon the rack. She finally jammed her shovel upright in the ground and reached up to rearrange her hair where it had escaped its heavy brass hairpin during the course of her labors. She gazed wonderingly at Lynden, who was still working the ground with a will.

"It's hopeless. We'll never find it this way," Lorraine said.

Her reply came from behind. A male voice spoke. "I'm inclined to agree. But I can't be sure unless you tell me what you're looking for."

Lorraine whirled to face the tall, dark figure; her skirt caught on the shovel blade and she fell to her knees, crushing a small sprig of sweet violets.

"Lord Crant!" said Lynden with miserable dismay. "I thought you were taking your sister into Leeds."

"I was. But as luck would have it, yesterday when we stopped at an inn for dinner, there was a fond acquaintance of Silvia's there who agreed to escort her the remaining distance, thus relieving me of the duty. How fortunate I have returned to receive such fair visitors. But I must ask you again: What are you looking for?"

Lynden stared at him, her eyes wide. "W—worms. That is, we're looking for worms."

"Ah," said Crant, lifting one dark eyebrow and clasping his hands behind his back. He was not smiling. "And no doubt you intend to use them for fishing in the lake. A pleasant recreation for such a pretty day. But I see you don't have a pail in which to carry them. Come inside with me. I'm sure we could find you something suitable."

There was danger in every inch of Crant's bearing. Lorraine struggled to her feet and backed away several paces. But Lynden stood her ground.

"No, thank you, My Lord," she said in a voice remarkably steady for the circumstances. "We'll put them on a lump of earth and carry it on a shovel blade."

A smile lit the murky depths of his pitiless eyes. "I'm afraid I couldn't allow that, because, you see, then they might . . . escape."

Lynden felt her throat grow dry. "Then we'll fish another day."

"One ought to do these things when one is in the mood," said Crant, moving a step closer to them.

Lynden took a step backward. "I think I'm getting out of the mood for fishing."

"That's unfortunate, my dear. Because I am not." He started to close the distance. Lynden dropped her shovel and turned to flee, Lorraine two steps ahead of her. But Lynden had an insufficient start on him, and almost immediately felt a strong hand clamp mercilessly upon her wrist. She struggled against him, but it was useless—she was caught. Lorraine had not looked back, and was halfway through the bank of flowers.

"Damn Ottmar!" Crant hissed. "Where is he when he is needed? Oh well, I'm sorry, Lady Melbrooke. You're going to take a little nap."

Lynden saw his fist poised in the air above her, and then it descended, causing the spring flowers at her feet to flash and grow, filling her vision with dizzying pinwheels of colors—pinwheels that faded into nothing like a watercolor under a rain.

Crant swung the little, unconscious body in his arms and strode rapidly toward the moat, calling over his shoulder to Lorraine. Lorraine stopped her flight and turned to see Lord Crant holding her sister over the water in his outstretched arms; Lynden's thick dark curls fell lushly over his bent elbow.

"Come back, Miss Downpatrick. Now. Or shall we see if your sister can swim while she's asleep?"

Lynden awoke to find herself in a dark, cold room, the air permeated with damp. An oil lantern hovered somewhere nearby; its pale light shone on the fuzzy outline of her sister's face above her. She felt the hard cold of brick floor under her body and the softness of Lorraine's lap supporting her head. Her sister's voice penetrated the high-pitched keening in Lynden's head.

"Lynnie! You're all right! I was afraid . . ." Lorraine very gently rubbed Lynden's tender temples.

"Were you?" replied Lynden vaguely. "Where are we?" The light shifted, drawing her attention to the doorway where Crant stood, holding a lantern which cast a long shadow into the indefinite space behind him. His cheekbones were etched and prominent in the light; his eyes, two dark unreadable hollows.

"You're in the castle," he said, his voice reverberating and sounding unnaturally close in the damp air. "I have a place to put bad little girls. Do you like it?"

Lynden struggled to her elbows, giving an involuntary moan as she lifted her head. "A dungeon! Trust *you* to have one, Lord Crant. But perhaps it's a good thing you do, because it will be a wonderful place to hide when Melbrooke finds out what you've been about with us."

"Indeed?" he inquired politely. "But you haven't considered properly, Lady Melbrooke. Will Melbrooke find out?"

"Yes, because we'll tell him," snapped Lynden, her temper shortened by her headache. "Unless you intend to murder us. Do you think you have a better chance with us than you did with a newborn baby?"

"How knowledgeable you are, my dear. And such dangerous knowledge. I'm flattered that you take such a keen interest in my chances of success. They're better than you think. But then, you haven't seen my well. Ottmar!"

Ottmar Wishke materialized out of the gloom behind Lord Crant, carrying a brace of pistols—two dull-gray barrels bracketing his round belly.

"Watch them, Ottmar. Would you two fine young ladies mind stepping to the door, please? But no further, or Ottmar may get nervous. I would like to demonstrate something for you."

Lorraine helped the aching Lynden to her feet; together they crossed the cell. Ottmar stayed behind them, standing close, and Crant walked into the space beyond, lifting the lantern to reveal a larger, high-vaulted chamber. He hung the light from a hook on the wall.

Lynden gave Ottmar a darkening look over her shoulder. "You ought to be ashamed to participate in this, *Major* Wishke. You, a military man."

"I would not mind it if you did not talk so much," growled Ottmar. The pistol barrels did not waver.

"Put your pistols away and let us go—I guarantee you'll never hear my voice again," she said.

Crant gave a short, sharp laugh. "I don't want to be deprived of your company so soon." A round wooden plate, about three feet in diameter, was lying on the floor beside where he stood in the middle of the outer room. He lifted it with the toe of his boot and kicked it aside; it clattered and spun into the corner, revealing a dark, mossy, brick-lined hole from which a pungent, dank aroma rose and wafted through the room.

Crant looked back at the twins. "Have you ever wondered how the inhabitants of castles supplied themselves with water during a siege? They have their own wells. And what better place for it than down here, where it could be easily protected from treasonous rogues attempting to poison it? Naturally, this one hasn't been used in years, but I never had it stopped because I felt it could be used to dispose of . . . unwanted clutter. How deep do you think it could be? I don't really know, but listen." Crant turned toward the wall and pried loose a broken half brick with his fingertips. Holding the brick gingerly between thumb and forefinger, he walked to the well, stretched his hand over the dark maw, and released it.

"One . . . two . . . three . . . four . . . five." From far, far below there came a faint hard slap as the surface of a mucky pool was broken—the sound resembling less a splash than a pair of loose, watery jaws clapping shut, devouring the broken brick. "Ah, there it is," said Crant. "They say the well is connected with an underground river that eventually washes into the Irish Sea. Once something is thrown into it, it's gone forever." Crant's eyes glittered in the lantern light. "At first I couldn't guess why the pair of you were so fond of spending your leisure hours at Crant Castle, especially since you seemed to foster no very fond feeling toward me; and certainly had none toward Silvia. For a time I even considered the possibility that you might be trying to hatch some girlish plot against Silvia to improve your odds with Justin. But that wouldn't be quite in your style, would it, my dear?" He addressed this to Lynden. "Naturally, all became clear yesterday morning when I received a visit from that charming young man—my nephew, I believe." He kicked the cover back over the well. "A chapter in my life I had thought was long finished. The affair was botched. But I was young then, and now . . ." He shrugged. "It appears that I must finish this old business." He looked straight at the twins. "There are certain papers—documents that I must have. It has been a generation since they were stolen from me . . ."

"*You* were the one who stole them," interrupted Lynden. "They belong to Kyler!"

"Kyler? Is that what they decided to name the brat? A suitable name for a peasant boy. To continue: I suppose it will remain a mystery to me how he met you and what kind of hold he has over you to make you come here and do the job of discovering his secrets for him. A brave, young fellow."

"He is!" cried Lorraine. "You'll see that when he comes to rescue us."

"Is he coming then? Good. We have a special reception planned for him. A pity that I will enjoy it much more than he. In the meantime, you have some secrets to confide in me. Somehow you've managed to learn something about the whereabouts of those marriage documents. If it was my crazy Aunt Irmingarde who took them, as I suspect, did she somehow manage to give Tom Miller a clue to their hiding place? How like her that would have been, the crazy old woman. She couldn't have given Miller the real documents, of course, or our eye-patched young friend would have come with his lawyers. But to give a clue to Tom Miller?" Crant made a dismissive gesture and laughed. "It would cause me no worry; the man was a dullard. But perhaps in your fertile little minds, who knows? You haven't found the documents yet. That's obvious, or you wouldn't still be looking. So tell me, why you were digging in the garden? Did Irmingarde bury the papers there?"

Lynden put her hands on her hips and lifted her chin. "We won't tell you. Not in a thousand years."

Undisturbed, Crant took a step toward her. "I don't have a thousand years. I doubt if my patience will last out the afternoon. I'll leave you two to think about it. When I return, you must tell me or . . ." He indicated the well.

Ottmar waved his pistols, and the twins edged backward into the cell. "You ought to separate them. They will break faster that way," said Ottmar, pushing the door closed with one foot. Crant dropped the short oak plank into the iron brackets on either side of the door. The light from the lamp shining through the small lattice window made a stark grillwork on the opposite wall of the cell, a chessboard pattern which grew rapidly less distinct with the retreating footsteps of Crant and Ottmar Wishke as they began to climb the stone steps on the other side of the well room.

Lynden stood on tiptoe and peered through the grill. "Melbrooke will make you sorry for this!" she shouted.

The steps paused. "Melbrooke again," Crant replied wearily, his voice echoing back to them. "Your faith in him is rather touching, but, I'm afraid, a little misplaced. That he knows nothing of this affair, I'm sure. If his wits were behind this, I'm afraid Kyler would be in the castle and I in the dungeon instead of you. I make no doubt he'd suspect your disappearance was somehow linked with me, but then suspicion and proof are two different matters, aren't they?"

He walked back to the grill and put his finger through to stroke Lynden's nose. She jerked her head away. "Better that you tell me what I want to know, my precious creature. I could let you go if I had the documents in my hand."

"Fiddle!" said Lynden rudely.

"But I would," said Crant. "Because without written evidence, Kyler is what I say he is—my illegitimate son. Anything you say to the contrary, my child, I could swiftly discredit. At seventeen one has so little credibility. Think on it."

Crant set the lantern at the top of the stairs; the faintest of gray glows lit the cell. The sisters were silent for a long time before Lynden spoke.

"I've just had a funny thought."

If Lorraine felt this to be a strange moment for funny thoughts, she didn't say so but only asked in a tired voice, "What?"

"Even if we wanted to tell him where the papers were, we couldn't, because we don't know where they are ourselves."

"Why not tell him a convincing lie so he would let us go?"

"We could stall him with that, but it won't get us out of here because he can check and find out that we were lying before he lets us go."

"What about calling for help?" said Lorraine. "Everyone in the castle can't know he's imprisoned us. He couldn't let a secret like that become general knowledge."

"No, but you can be sure he's arranged things so no one will be within hearing distance while we're here. We'd exhaust ourselves by yelling. Instead, we'll put our energy into escape."

Lorraine gave a wan smile, barely visible in the dim light. "Not another heart spasm, Lynnie."

"No, but I shall have a real one if he tosses me down that well. Let's not talk. We must concentrate."

The twins sat down on the hard brick, backs to the wall, and thought. Their concentration was long and not immediately fruitful. Lynden, feeling the dampness uncomfortably on her hair, took off her bonnet and, holding its strings, swung it forlornly between her knees. Lorraine removed hers as well but placed it sedately upon her lap. The stony silence was relieved only by the plink of dripping water and a quick scuffling in a far-off corner.

"They need a cat down here," said Lorraine nervously.

Time elapsed; seemed to fade into . . . an hour? Three hours? At last Lynden spoke.

"It'll be too difficult to trick Crant. The best thing to do is to escape before he returns."

"That's sterling, Lyn. But the question of the moment is: how?"

"I don't know yet. We must explore the possibilities. You examine the room in detail and I'll take the door."

"Fine. I'll examine the room." Lorraine stood in the center of the room. "There are no windows. The walls are solid brick, as is the floor."

"Then the only way out is the way we came in—through the door," stated Lynden. She stared at the door, then rattled it; it gave only slightly. The bars of the grill were immovable and placed too closely to allow her hand to pass through. She stood on tiptoe and looked out to where the lantern flickered in the stairway. At the foot of the stairs to the right, a broad puddle, fed by the drip from above, broke into circles with clock-like regularity, causing the light caught from the lantern to dance and shiver. Lynden stared at it, hypnotized. There seemed to be something tangible reflected in the pool—something in the well room that she could not see from her narrow vantage point, its reflection nearly steadying and then breaking again with the next drop. As she stared, her vision blurred to a point which compensated for the unsteadiness of the reflection until suddenly she realized what she was seeing in the watery mirror: a portion of the door that imprisoned them! She could make out the broad plank stretched across the door between the brackets on either side.

"He has underestimated us indeed," she said aloud. "If only there was some way . . ." Lynden thoughtfully bounced her bonnet up and down on its long strings, and then turned to Lorraine.

"Mmm?" said Lorraine, who was opening a hairpin with her teeth prior to placing it back in her hair.

Lynden dimpled in a broad smile and snatched the hairpin from her sister's hand, holding it up with her bonnet. "Rainey, we're going fishing after all!"

Lorraine watched, fascinated, as Lynden yanked the long velvet strings from her bonnet and tied them together, pulled apart the heavy brass prongs of Lorraine's hairpin, and tied the string to one end, speaking as she bore down on the knot.

"Kyler said you can open almost any door!"

"Yes, but with a skeleton key, which we don't have."

"And we don't need, not for this door. What we need is something to lift a plank, and I have it right here." She held up her jerry-built but serviceable looking fishing line.

Lorraine slowly drew a finger along the vee of the hooked hairpin as if casting a spell of good luck upon it. "Will it work? If the plank is heavy, won't the knot slip off?"

Lynden turned with a swish of skirts and went back to the grate, where she stood again on tiptoe and dropped the hook and line through the bars.

"Do you remember Robert Style?" she said, letting the line slip through her hand. "The groom at Fern Court who used to be a sailor? He taught me this knot, and everyone knows that knots of British sailors are the best in the world. Why do you think Sir Francis Drake beat back the Spanish Armada?"

"*Not* because the Spanish didn't have their ropes knotted together properly," said Lorraine firmly.

"All right. So pray." Lynden bit her lip and looked out through the grate into the puddle. She could see the bright yellow hairpin swinging down past the plank, and felt the tick of the metal against wood vibrating through the string as it gently hit the door. It twisted wildly, wrong side to the plank, and she let it down again. This time it caught, one side of the vee slipping firmly behind the plank.

"Huzzah!" she said softly. Carefully, she inched the string up, letting it dangle down on her side of the door as she pulled. There came a scrape of wood, and, miraculously, the plank fell with a loud clatter, and only Lynden's small forceful push was required to swing the door open.

The falling of the plank had sounded like a thunderclap to the girls, and they stood frozen, expecting the entire household to arrive on the spot; a minute passed and no such thing occurred. The twins exhaled simultaneously. Lynden took Lorraine's hand and they ran up the stone steps. At the top was a solid door. Lynden placed her ear to it and listened intently; hearing nothing, she slowly pushed it open and peeked around. Beyond was a brickwork corridor stopped at one end by a narrow spiral staircase and at the other end by a high door, this one with a grillwork opening similar to the one in the door of their cell. Through it could be seen a few circling pigeons, a patch of dark blue sky, and the top of the shadowed Great Tower.

The grill was set too high in the door for Lynden, so Lorraine put her fingers on the bottom edge of the opening and looked out. It seemed they were within the castle wall, because outside lay the inner courtyard, the long shadows of evening spreading a gray shroud over the Great Tower. At its base the wide double doors to the kitchens were open. A fire was burning in a great hearth where a lamb roasted on the spit. A white-capped scullery maid stood nearby, basting it constantly. The stables were to the right; several grooms sat in front sharing ale and gossip with male servants from the household; a stableboy had one of the riding horses tethered nearby and was grooming it carefully. Tomorrow's bread was baking in the old-fashioned cookshack, and at the threshold Ottmar Wishke stood leaning against the door frame. He was talking to a comely dairymaid with a yoke on her shoulders. A milk pail hung from each side of the yoke, swinging gently back and forth in the cool evening breeze.

"We can't go out this way. Ottmar's there."

Lynden nodded. "Then it will have to be the stairs."

The girls climbed the spiral staircase to emerge, winded and dusty, into the fresh, strong breeze at the top of the wall. They were even with the pigeons now, and could see the setting sun, a deep-red semicircle lying across the darkening hills. Below them lay the busy courtyard. The crenellation rose to one side, and on the other, courtyard side, was a low wall.

"Get down," said Lynden, falling to her hands and knees. Lorraine did the same. "We don't want them to see us below. Listen. This walkway must go the full length around to the drawbridge in front. Stay down and follow me. Let's see if we can find the murder-hole that Kyler said he dropped through to escape."

They crawled low to the walkway, passing through the alternating square patches of red sunlight and black shadow created by the sun streaming through the crenellation. The walkway at last widened into a large stone balcony which projected over the moat and open drawbridge. The machicolation, stonework slats punctuated by four rectangular murder-holes, took up the front part of the balcony floor. Lynden crawled to the nearest murder-hole and looked down to where the thick, black water of the moat lay forty feet below.

"Rainey, this has to be the last resort," she said. "I'd almost as soon jump into the dungeon well."

"We can't get out through the courtyard; it's too risky."

"I agree, but . . ." Lynden crawled to the end of the balcony, entering a small stone tower. It was a housing for the massive spool pulley which raised and lowered the drawbridge. The pulley had not been used for many years; this was obvious from the corroded state of the iron bar which served as a brake upon the heavy chain—it had nearly rusted into its holding-link. The thick chain wound around the pulley through a large open window and angled to its attachment at the left corner of the drawbridge.

Lynden pulled at the chain with one hand. It was steadfast. "We'll climb down the chain," she said with satisfaction.

Lorraine closed her eyes. "This is better than dropping through the murder-hole?"

Lynden smiled and hugged her twin, and then went to the window. Holding on to the chain, she fearlessly swung her feet out over the moat. "At least we won't get wet. Thank God we've got on leather gloves." Lynden crossed her legs over the chain and moved slowly down, hand-over-hand, while Lorraine watched from the window. "We can do it," called Lynden to her sister. "It's like climbing trees."

"I've always hated climbing trees," answered Lorraine. "I only ever did it because you made me."

Lynden answered, panting with exertion: "Good thing, too, because now you know how to climb down these chains. Have a care, though, they are slippery."

Lorraine followed her sister, hands trembling. She inched slowly down the chain. The pink and purple sky floated above her. The chains bit cruelly into her hands, tearing her clothing and covering it with streaks of red rust. She hung on to her sister's words of encouragement as if to a lifeline, until she felt Lynden's hands upon her waist.

"Drop your feet down, Lorraine. You'll be standing on the drawbridge." Lorraine did as she was told, and stood up, catching her breath, her aching arms folded in front of her. Lynden pulled her forward. Lorraine stumbled blindly after her sister. Her side began to ache.

"Lynnie, not this way . . . to the road back to Fern Court."

Lynden grabbed her arm with a new vigor—they were going up the slope of the fellside toward the back of Crant Castle, past the fateful spring flowers. "No, Lorraine; the mountains are our only chance. We've got to take the footpath. If we make for the road, Crant can chase us down on horseback before we're halfway to the first cottage. On the footpath we've got an even chance, because they have to go on foot in the mountains, too. Hurry! Someone might already have seen us!"

The soft grass of the slope ended suddenly in the rocks, and they took to the footpath. Behind they heard the unmistakable yammering and yelping of a pack of hounds. Lynden turned to see a pair of lanterns moving across the greening slope, bobbing like fireflies in the dusk.

"They've got the dogs after us!" cried Lorraine.

"Then we shall have a taste of what it feels like to be a fox," answered Lynden. They reached the crest of the hill; Lorraine, gasping, rested for a moment on a large rock while Lynden looked down at their pursuers. The sun left them as the girls stumbled down the other side of the hill. The sky was taking a deep-purple tint in preparation for night, and a pale large moon floated low on the horizon. The thick twilight made it difficult to move with speed.

"It will be better once the moon rises," said Lynden. They fled on over the next hill which rolled like an ocean wave before them. A low, wide stone wall coursed down the other side of the hill. There was a ripple and bustle in the underbrush to one side, and the flash of a long brush tail. A dark shape fleeted across the path before them, and the animal leaped to the top of the stone wall. They caught a glimpse of a pearly white throat underneath a sinuous, weasel-like face, and a nasty set of bared fangs which glistened in the moonlight.

Lorraine put her hand in front of Lynden. "Stand still. It's the sweet-mart! The guidebook tells about it. It's a fierce killer. It jumps on the backs of ewes, digs its claws into the fleece, and begins to bite, half eating the poor ewes before they are dead."

They stood for a tense moment as the yowling of the pack of hounds behind came closer and the sweet-mart looked them over. Finally it flashed its fangs again and disappeared. The girls hurried on. At the crest of the next hill they could see white, crawling mist forming in the valleys about, creeping as if to entrap them in tendrils of curling dead-white sinews. Fear of capture spurred the twins on; they stumbled often in the dark. Lynden's hands became a mass of cuts and bruises; Lorraine could feel the blood trickling down her leg from a gash in her knee. A cold chill rose out of the night ground, causing them to shiver. The moon, against a background of silver stars, high and bright now, was no comfort at all, but seemed rather to be leering at them ahead and above, as elusive and tantalizing as safety. They passed a waterfall which roared down the fellside away from them, obliterating the keening of the hounds; when they were far enough beyond it, they stopped to rest and listened again. The yowling of the pack had taken on a deep, self-assured baying quality, and grew in intensity as they listened.

The girls were standing on an outcropping shelf of rock overlooking a broad, black valley. Directly below them, some fifty yards straight down, they observed three torches moving in single file. A rough hand was visible on the shaft of each torch, and three capped heads below them. As the sisters watched, the torches were swung and thrown, making three fiery arcs in the inky blackness, and suddenly the darkness was dispelled by an erupting volcano of fire which roared and leaped, sending sparks high into the night sky and illuminating, with daylight clarity, the grizzled faces of three farmers who stood behind a shallow fire trench, about ten yards in front of a tumbled-down shepherd's shack. A small herd of Herdwick rams huddled at the cliff base away from the fire, which spread quickly to cover half the floor of the valley, creating a swirl of red smoke that blotted out the stars and darkened the moon. The farmers watched for a few moments before going back up the path.

"They're burning off last year's heather," said Lorraine. "Spring will make a tender new growth for the sheep."

"Whatever they're doing it for, look what's it's doing for us!" Lynden pointed. The bright gleam of the heath fire lit the footpath at the point where it ran down the hillside to the fire trench and then turned, coursing along the edge of a deep gully and disappearing over the ridge of the next hill between two giant boulders. "We can double back down the fellside away from them on this path." The twins started down the rugged trail, but before they were halfway to the fire trench, Lorraine stumbled and cried out in pain; she fell to her knees and looked up at Lynden with tears in her eyes.

"Do you think your ankle's broken?" asked Lynden.

"No, it's only turned, but, oh, Lynnie, what are we to do?"

"Carry on like the allies at the Battle of Waterloo! 'Stand until the last man falls.'" Lynden bent and helped her sister up. "Lean on me, Raine, as heavily as you need." She put her arm around her hobbling sister and together they continued down the path, the heat from the monstrous fire warming them as they neared it. The roar and crackle were deafening; smoke filled their lungs, causing them to choke for breath. Lynden pulled her silk neck scarf over her mouth and did the same for Lorraine.

They reached the bottom, where the path was intersected by the shallow fire trench. The smoke puffed over them in thick, black billows as they made their way blindly across the trench. Growing weaker, Lorraine foundered for her footing while Lynden tried desperately to support her. The fire was close, licking around them now in lashing tongues of flame. Lynden lost her direction. The girls were coughing from the fumes, huge spasmodic, lung-wrenching coughs, and tears streamed from their eyes.

"We have to . . . to turn back, Lorraine. It's no good . . . I can't see . . ." Lorraine, who had been leaning heavily on Lynden's shoulder, suddenly cried out; then her weight lessened and was gone.

"Lorraine! Where are you?" Lynden was frantic. A pair of arms grasped her own waist, strong male arms. She struggled and kicked desperately as she was lifted through the air and then set down on a higher level. She drew back her fist, still blinded, trying to strike at the shape before her, when with a mixture of joy and bewilderment she recognized the voice of the Bard of the Lakeland.

"Lynden. Easy, my love. You're all right now," said her husband. With a sob of relief, she leaned forward into his arms.

"Melbrooke!" she said in a cracking voice. "Oh, Melbrooke. We've gotten into such trouble!"

His reply was indistinct but sympathetic. She looked up as her eyes cleared, and saw that he had placed her on the ground near the shepherd's shack. Kyler was near, bending over Lorraine, a concerned look on his lean, soot-blackened face. He shouted something to Melbrooke, who shouted back. Their words were lost in the boom of the fire.

Melbrooke wiped his wife's face with a handkerchief as she coughed weakly. "I must look . . . like a coal miner," she said. "Oh, Melbrooke. Crant's coming with Ottmar and . . . and his dogs. They've been chasing us. But how did you know we were here?"

He pulled her close into his arms. "Kyler and I returned to Fern Court and found you'd been gone all afternoon, and knowing you as I have come to . . ." He stroked her hair. ". . . it didn't take long to figure out where you might have disappeared to. At the Castle we found a servant willing to tell us, for a small fee, that Crant and Ottmar had set out not five minutes before with a pack of trail hounds. It seemed only too likely that you and Lorraine were their quarry, so we've been following the trail behind their lanterns."

One of the hounds appeared out of the smoke, nosing an aimless pattern around the huddled group, growling querulously, then whining as it sighted them.

"Oh, Justin, it's him! They're coming!" said Lynden.

"Good," said Melbrooke, his face hard. "I have something to say to him." There was a heartening confidence in his voice, and Lynden found herself rather childishly clutching at his hand.

"At least you're angry with someone other than me," she said with a tired measure of her usual impishness.

Two more sniffling hounds appeared out of the smoke and suddenly Crant and Ottmar were coming toward them, with the fire at their backs, like demons emerging from the mouth of hell. Melbrooke stood, facing Crant; Kyler crouched near Lorraine like a panther ready to spring. Crant and Wishke were armed with pistols, which they trained on the group.

"Percy, you've been tramping around the mountains since sunset," Melbrooke said calmly. "You think you can intimidate us with pistols full of damp powder? They'll never fire."

"The accuracy of your perceptions is a never-ending source of delight to your friends, my dear Justin." Crant lowered his pistol and shrugged. "So the match is even."

"Bah!" exclaimed Ottmar. "This is good expensive powder and I have kept the pistols in my official Prussian army holster. We'll see about damp powder." He stretched his arm, taking aim straight at Kyler, and pulled the trigger. It clicked worthlessly. "Damn no-good British powder."

"Blame it on the British weather," said Crant. "But, Justin, it seems you've made the acquaintance of my illegitimate son."

"Your legitimate nephew," replied Melbrooke. "As you know, Percy, I've no taste for melodramatics, but I find myself in the position to tell you that, after years of thinking you were merely a common cynic, I find you are, in fact, a blackguard. We have found the proof needed for this young gentleman"——he indicated Kyler ——"to assume his rightful place as holder of the Crant title and lands."

"So. You have been busy, haven't you?" said Crant. His eyes narrowed into dark slits as he rocked back slightly on his heels, dropping his pistol to the ground. "Documents? Marriage lines? Is that what you have?"

He turned his dark gaze on Kyler. "But perhaps I can prove that they were forgeries, and that your poor sainted mother was no better than a whore."

Fury transformed Kyler. He uncoiled from his crouch and stalked across the turf separating him from Crant, his face a mask of rage. "You jackal's whelp! I'll make you eat those words . . ." Crant's sardonic smile froze as Kyler's hands closed on his throat, and the two men grappled. The hounds barked and the sheep scattered.

Lord Melbrooke's gently bred young bride, her clothes torn and filthy, her hair in wild streaming ribbons about her face, struggled to her knees, waved both scraped fists excitedly in the air, and screamed, "Bravo, Kyler! Have at 'em!"

Ottmar Wishke moved toward the fray to be intercepted by Melbrooke who swung a fist straight and true into the military man's ample stomach, and took a crude but powerful blow from Wishke in return. The dogs were yapping and howling frenziedly now, tails straight, and the rams were bounding and kicking through the four combatants. Lynden managed to grab the collar of one hound and held it as it strained away. Crant and Kyler crashed through the wall of the sheep shack, knocking the flimsy structure flat, while Ottmar came back at Melbrooke, heaving a giant rock nearly as big as a man's head. Lynden screamed a warning, and Melbrooke ducked in time as the rock bounced heavily from his shoulder with a crunching sound, leaving a patch of blood oozing from his silk shirt. His wound did not seem to faze him as he gained ground on Ottmar, pounding him head and body with a merciless rain of punishing, lightning like blows. They were treading dangerously near the edge of the dark gully— black silhouettes against the red and bright yellow flames. Ottmar picked up a jagged branch and swung it at his adversary, breaking it on Melbrooke's upraised arm. At this moment an excited ram ran behind the two, brushing Wishke's legs; fatigued from the struggle, the Prussian lost his balance, and, as Lorraine shrieked and Melbrooke made a futile lunge to catch him, he pitched backward over the gully's edge into the fatal blackness. Any death cry or thud of his body hitting the rocks below was obliterated by the roar and crackle of the burning heath.

Lynden scrambled to her feet and ran into Melbrooke's arms. "I'm glad, so glad it wasn't you," she cried.

Crant and Kyler were still fighting amid the ruins of the shepherd's shack. Lynden picked up the branch Ottmar had swung at Melbrooke and ran back to the struggling pair; but Melbrooke restrained her from entering the fray.

"Crant is weakening," said Melbrooke, sliding an arm around his wife's shoulder. "Let Kyler have his fight." Indeed, it was true: The older man was reeling and gasping for breath under Kyler's furious onslaught. Crant, mustering an impressive surge of energy, picked up a wicked-looking, rusty awl from the shack's wreckage. Kyler dropped back; but not quickly enough to avoid receiving a long gash in the flesh over his collarbone. He lunged forward and pulled Crant off balance, then wrested the awl from him, holding it to Crant's throat. Crant's eyes were glazed with naked fear.

Kyler lowered the sharp point slowly, looking at Crant and speaking softly. "I'll give you until tomorrow morning to be out of the country. If you return, so help me God, I'll pursue you with the full force of the law."

The nephew and uncle gazed their last at each other, the sculpture of the lean dark faces so much alike, the souls so unutterably different. A minute passed before the former Lord Crant turned and disappeared into the smoky dark, followed by his dogs.

Kyler turned to look at Melbrooke; there was some uncertainty in his attractive young face. "D'you think I did the right thing?" he asked.

Melbrooke gripped Kyler's shoulder. "The right thing in every sense of the word."

"Thank you," said Kyler with sincerity.

Melbrooke smiled and glanced back toward Lorraine. "My contribution was a small one, and—I regard you already as one of the family."

"Thank you for that, as well," said Kyler, and started in Lorraine's direction. He halted no more than four feet from her, and turned suddenly toward the blazing heath, a dark slim figure against the flames. He pulled off his eyepatch, flinging it across the fire trench into the inferno. Lynden laughed with glee. Lorraine's eyes filled with happy tears as Kyler lifted her into his arms and pressed a fully reciprocated kiss onto her waiting lips.

Lynden watched with strong approval. "Rainey, after that, he'll *have* to ask you to marry him!"

Kyler turned to grin at her. "Lord, Hornet, won't you even let me do my own proposing?"

"Of course," conceded Lynden handsomely. "But first you must answer this: Justin told Lord Crant . . ." She paused. "Oh, dear. Now *you're* Lord Crant. What a muddle it will be until we're used to the name change! Anyway, Justin told your Uncle Percy that proof had been found naming you the rightful heir. Was that a bluff, or did you really find it?"

"Aye, that we did," said Kyler. "When we reached Justin's lawyer in Penrith, we took out what evidence we had to show the fellow. There was my stepmother's letter, of course, and the sundial rubbing, and the note we found in the mausoleum. You gave it to me last night to take along, remember? Justin had never seen it before, and no sooner did he set eyes on the blasted thing than he announced we had been reading it wrong the whole time. The note really said we were to look beneath the *dome* of spring's floral harbingers. What you read by lamplight as a *p* was actually a fancy, old-fashioned *d*. And you know where there turns out to be a flowery dome? Right there over the entrance hall of Crant Castle's Great Tower. It's a grand, flashy thing covered over with leaves and marsh marigolds and done in stained glass. What do you say to that?"

"Rats!" said Lynden.

"Just as I thought. You're mad as fire not to have figured the thing out yourself," said Kyler. "Anyway, when we arrived at the castle, Melbrooke marched straight into the tower, demanding to see Lord Crant, and, in the two minutes we were left waiting in the hall, he found the whole raft of documents—marriage lines, identification papers, love letters from my father to my mother, the whole business. I'll tell you, hornet, your husband's as smart as a whip. He lifts up the face visor of a moldering old suit of armor, puts in his hand, and pulls out the bundle. They were there in the helmet's jaw the whole time. Crant himself must have walked past them ten thousand times."

From her high, pale post in the black, crystal sky, the moon was spreading her light on the quiet fells of Westmorland. The twins had returned to their respective bedrooms at Fern Court, and Kyler Miller, soon-to-be the new Lord of Crant Castle, had been enthroned in one of Fern Court's charming guest suites. Lorraine had been asleep for more than an hour, having drifted happily off almost at once, after receiving Mrs. Coniston's soothing ministrations to her sore ankle.

Lynden had stayed awake, not only bathing, but scrubbing and rescrubbing her hair with a fine rosewater rinse to remove the last vestige of the acrid smoke smell. After Lynden's bath, Mrs. Coniston had laid out a familiar high-necked white flannel nightdress, but Lynden rejected it and self-consciously asked for a magnificent and rather shockingly transparent black lace negligee from her trousseau. She dabbed on a touch of French perfume, climbed into bed, and dismissed Mrs. Coniston for the night, graciously deigning not to notice the discreetly delighted smile on that lady's face.

Alone, bathed in the golden light of a single candle, Lynden picked up her lacquered hairbrush, her finger tracing her initial which was inlaid on the back in mother-of-pearl. She sat quietly on the bed, brushing her hair, until there came a knock from the door connecting her room with Melbrooke's. The knock was an unalarming, gentle one, and yet Lynden's pulse achieved its fastest pace of the whole eventful day.

"Come in . . . Oh, Melbrooke, it's you!"

He entered, his gray eyes shining. "How surprised you look. Were you expecting someone else?"

Lynden set the hairbrush down on a bedside table. "No, but, well—you ought to be chivalrous enough to let me pretend to be surprised. I see you're wearing your banian. Mrs. Coniston helped me into this negligee and left here looking smug, and there's no doubt your valet knows what you've been about. So I suppose we're the object of the most mortifying speculation in the servants' quarters! Tomorrow I shan't have the nerve to rise from my bed!"

"God knows what kind of speculation *that* would give rise to." He sat on the edge of the bed, giving her a caressing smile. "Never fear. We'll circumvent the gossips. I will arise betimes and muss my bedcovers. That will really confuse them."

Lynden's cheeks grew pink. "To think at first I thought you a most sober gentleman. Instead, My Lord, I find you are an accomplished flirt! You don't look angry, but I wonder—are you very much vexed with me for going to the castle today?"

"More with myself for having left you with the opportunity." He took her hands in his, kissing one and then the other scraped, bruised palm. "Your wounded hands reproach me for having underestimated your determination."

"They may reproach you, but they sting me! I'm sure if my Uncle Monroe were here, which I am very glad he is not, that he would say I came by my just deserts. I daresay when you found me in the fire trench, I looked like the Witch Woman of Wetherian!"

"Who?"

Lynden giggled. "Never mind. I'll tell you another

time. I'm just glad to know you're not horribly vexed with me. Besides, now you're probably England's only leading poet with the distinction of having a wife who's been tossed into a dungeon!" She crossed her hands in her lap and looked down, the dark curls falling forward over her shoulders. "I do have one more thing that I must confess. I—no, wait. I'll get it."

"More notes from Lady Irmingarde?" he asked.

"I wish it were," said Lynden, climbing from the bed and opening a drawer in her writing desk. She handed Melbrooke a folded slip of paper. "It's from Lady Silvia. A servant boy brought it from Crant and I ought to have given it into your hand without opening it, but I didn't."

Melbrooke opened the note and quickly skimmed the contents. He looked up at her. "Lynden, my poor child. When did you get this?"

"Weeks ago, on the day of the big rain."

"And you believe since then that I've been continuing to see Silvia?" He stood, placing his hands on her bare shoulders. "Is that why you held yourself back from me? Now I understand! Lynden, this note is a hoax. While it's true that Lady Silvia and I had a connection before I met you, on the first day after our arrival at Fern Court I rode to Crant Castle and told Silvia that it must end. No doubt she deliberately meant this note to come into your hands, merely to distress you."

"Well!" said Lynden, looking confounded. "Then I suppose I'm come by my just deserts this time, as well, for opening letters not addressed to me, because I was distressed. *Very* distressed. But I wonder. Was it very painful for you to break off with Lady Silvia? You must have liked her very much."

He had one hand on her cheek. At her last statement he bent over to kiss her lips softly. "In all the time I knew her, never enough to ask her to marry me. But in ten minutes of talking to you, Lynden, not only did I *not* regret that we were to marry, but, had your uncle and aunt not decreed our wedding, I would have returned to Downpatrick Hall, courted you until you gave in from sheer exhaustion, and married you with all the pomp my mother could desire. Have I shocked you, my love? Before, it always seemed too soon to tell you, but I think I must tell you now that I've cared deeply for you from the very beginning."

Lynden's brown eyes widened. "I don't believe you. Why, you're only saying that! How could it be true?"

He cupped her face in his hands. "Easily, so easily, my dear. It seems that falling in love with you is the most effortless thing I've ever done. I had this made to remind me of it." He took from his pocket a small jewelry case and handed it to her.

"Oh, Melbrooke, not more jewelry. Surely . . ." She opened the box, revealing a tiny, exquisitely detailed diamond and emerald kite blessed with a silver neck chain for a tail. Her eyes filled with tears.

"Do you like it?" he asked.

Her voice seemed to have deserted her; she nodded, and he took the beautiful little kite from its velvet nest and clasped it in place about her neck.

"You're trembling. It's too cold for you." He lifted back the bed covers and helped her into the bed. She moved over to make space and looked at him shyly.

"Are you coming into bed, too?" she asked.

The gray eyes sparkled tenderly. "I'm afraid that it's my most cherished ambition."

"Are you going to take off your banian?"

"It is the customary procedure," he admitted. "Do you object?"

"No, but you will notice I am closing my eyes." She could hear his light laughter.

"Very proper," said Melbrooke.

"Justin. You don't *really* think so!" She felt the bed give as he joined her, and heard his husky voice near.

"No, dear, I don't really think so. You can look now. I'm modestly covered with the blankets."

She opened her eyes to see Melbrooke smiling at

her, leaning on one elbow, his tawny hair glowing in the candlelight. He reached over and gently stroked an inky curl from her forehead.

"If you want to know the truth, Justin, I may have a reputation for being quite brazen, but at the moment I'm feeling shy."

He kissed her shoulder. "That's not unnatural."

"Perhaps not, but I wonder if you would mind—that is, could we talk a little first?"

He drew her to him and she felt the warmth and hardness of his body. One graceful hand was on her back, and the other softly brushed the strap of the nightgown away from her shoulder.

"Talk before, during, and after, if you like. Have we any more outstanding business?"

"There *is* the matter of Lorraine and Kyler's wedding. You know, at first I thought I wouldn't like to be a great lady, or at least, that I wouldn't be very good at it, but at Lady Silvia's ball I saw dozens of things that she might have done to make it a more exciting affair, if only she'd thought of them! I think I might find a fair amount of challenge in being an important society hostess. I should like to launch my career at it with Lorraine and Kyler's wedding. What do you think of this: instead of the usual humdrum organ processional, we could have the entrance hymn blown on trumpets? And at the ceremony's climax, two thousand white doves could be released in the air."

His lips touched the curve of her throat. "Two thousand birds inside the church?"

"No, not inside the church, of course. Only think of the mess." She cuddled closer into his arms. "Did you notice I put on perfume?"

"Yes."

"It seemed like the right thing to do, though it made Mrs. Coniston smirk! Justin? I wanted you to know that I'm sorry I had such mistaken ideas about poets. You're not in the least foppish and, besides, you're a splendid boxer, as I saw tonight. And so incredibly clever. It was one thing to figure out that we had to search beneath the flower *dome,* but how did you ever think to look inside the helmet on the suit of armor?"

"The helmet?" he said dreamily. "My dearest love, as much as I am enjoying your charming praise, I have to admit that it was no stroke of genius to look in the armor. You have been in the entrance hall of the Great Tower, haven't you? Frankly, child, there were very few places to look."

Her laugh was stopped by a long, sweet, searching kiss.

"I love you, Justin," she finally whispered breathlessly.

"I love you, too."

"Justin . . . ? After Lady Silvia's bosom, I hope mine isn't a disappointment."

She heard his chuckle, free and loving in her curls. "Lynden," he answered. "My lovely little friend, my joy, *nothing* about you could be a disappointment to me."

LAURA LONDON

Let her magical romances enchant you with their tenderness.

For glorious storytelling at its very best, get lost in these Regency romances.

____ A HEART TOO PROUD ... 13498-6 $2.95

____ THE BAD BARON'S
      DAUGHTER 10735-0   2.95

____ THE GYPSY HEIRESS 12960-5   2.95

____ LOVE'S A STAGE 15387-5   2.95

____ MOONLIGHT MIST 15464-4   2.95